ECHOES OF LOVE
HOPE CREEK BOOK 2

LAURA FARR

Copyright © 2022 by laura farr

All rights reserved.

No part of this book may be reproduced in any form or by any electronic or mechanical means, including information storage and retrieval systems, without written permission from the author, except for the use of brief quotations in a book review.

Website: laurafarrauthor.com

Edited by Karen Sanders at Karen Sanders Editing

Cover by Shower of Schmidt Designs

JOIN ME

I would love you to join me on my exclusive mailing list, where you'll be the first to hear about new releases, sales and bonus content. To sign up please visit: https//landing.mailerlite.com/webforms/landing/h3u7vs

Laura

xxxx

A HOPE CREEK NOVEL

Echoes of Love

LAURA FARR

PROLOGUE

Sophie
Age 18

"*I* wish you didn't have to go back. I'll miss you so much." I drop my head onto Cade's bare chest and he tightens his hold on me.

"I'll miss you too, baby. I wish there was a school closer to Hope Creek."

We're both silent as I lie in his arms. Cade's been at college in Tucson for two years. He's doing an undergraduate degree in biology before applying to med school. Tucson's around a four-hour drive from Hope Creek, and while he comes home whenever he can, school is full on and he doesn't get much downtime. We talk every day, but it's not the same.

"How long is it until summer break?" I ask, frowning as he tenses beneath me. He sighs, and an uneasy feeling settles in the pit of my stomach. "Cade?" I ask, lifting my head to look at him.

1

"I need to talk to you about summer break," he says, sitting up.

I sit up with him and pull the sheet around me. "Okay."

He takes my hand, his thumb rubbing circles over my skin. "I have the chance of an internship shadowing one of the best trauma physicians in the country—"

"That's amazing, Cade! I'm so proud of you," I say, cutting him off. I know his passion lies in emergency medicine, and his dream is to be an attending trauma physician. This is huge for him.

"It is, but if I take it, I won't be able to come home for summer break."

I can see the indecision on his face, and my heart drops. I blink away the tears that are stinging my eyes, desperately hoping they don't fall. I know if I ask him to come home, he will, but I don't want to ever put him in a position where he has to choose between his future and me.

"I haven't said yes yet. I wanted to talk to you." He pulls me back into his arms and drops a kiss on my head. "I know we had plans this summer. I don't know what to do."

I want to tell him to come home and do everything we've talked about. Camping by the lake and making love under the stars. Taking a road trip to Vegas and spending a night in the Bellagio. Just being together. Weekends never seem long enough, and I hate having to say goodbye. I know it isn't forever, but sometimes it feels like a lifetime.

"You have to do it, Cade. It's an incredible opportunity, and it will look amazing on your med school application." I swallow down the golf ball–sized lump in my throat.

"But what about all our plans?"

"There'll be plenty of time for us to do all of those things." I reach up and cup his stubbled jaw. "We've got the rest of our lives to be together. I want you to always follow your dreams."

"You're my dream, Sophie. You always have been."

I smile at him and brush my lips with his. "I'm not going anywhere, Cade."

"I love you."

"I love you too."

Six weeks later

I HUG THE TOILET BOWL AS I THROW UP FOR THE SECOND TIME IN less than ten minutes. I've had a stomach flu for the past week, and I really thought the worst was over, but when I woke up this morning, I'd had to run to the bathroom as nausea rolled through me.

"Honey, are you still getting sick?" my mom asks from the other side of the bathroom door.

"Yes," I manage to say, before dry heaving into the toilet.

"I'm going to call the doctor. A stomach flu doesn't last this long."

I don't argue. I haven't got the energy. Sitting back from the toilet, I lean against the bathtub and close my eyes. Silent tears run down my cheeks. I want Cade. I haven't told him I'm sick; he'll only worry. He's just started his summer internship and I know he'll want to come home if he thinks I'm unwell. I stand up on shaky legs and turn the shower on, brushing my teeth as I wait for the water to warm up. When the small bathroom fills with steam, I pull off my panties and tank top and climb under the hot spray.

I feel a little more human after my shower, and I dry off, pulling on some yoga pants and a t-shirt. I go downstairs, and my mom's in the kitchen making breakfast.

"Do you want some toast? It might settle your stomach," she says, looking over her shoulder at me.

"Yeah. I'll try some."

"You look wiped out, Sophie. I've called the medical center. You have an appointment at ten. I'll drive you."

"Thanks."

I sit down heavily at the kitchen table, dropping my head down onto the wood. I'm so tired, despite going to bed early last night. When my mom sits down next to me and takes my hand, I lift my head.

"Sophie, do you think you could be pregnant?" she asks softly, squeezing my hand.

My wide eyes meet her worried ones. "What?"

She sighs. "Honey, you're throwing up, you're exhausted, and it's unlikely a stomach flu would last this long. It's been over a week."

"But I'm on birth control," I say quietly.

"I know, sweetie, but it doesn't always work."

Fear washes over me and tears fill my eyes. I'm only eighteen. I love Cade and I know we're going to be together forever, but I can't have a baby now. He's halfway through an undergraduate degree, and I'm about to start law school.

"I can't be pregnant." The tears that were threatening to fall now streak freely down my cheeks. "I can't be," I whisper.

My mom wraps her arms around me and I sob against her chest. "I'll run out and get you a test and then we'll know for sure. It's going to be okay, Sophie." She drops a kiss on my head before heading out of the kitchen. If I am pregnant, it's not going to be okay. It's not going to be okay at all.

CHAPTER ONE

Cade
Present day

I groan as the shrill ring tone of my phone wakes me. Whatever this call is about, it better be good. I worked the night shift in the ER last night and it was after nine this morning when I crawled into bed. I snatch the phone off the nightstand and answer without even looking at who's calling.

"Hello."

"Shit, did I wake you?"

"Yes. What's up, Seb?"

"There's been a shooting at the bar."

I sit up, instantly wide awake. "What? When? Is everyone okay?"

"About half an hour ago. Everyone's okay except the shooter. He's dead. It was Paisley's ex."

"Fuck! Was she there?"

"Yeah. She and Sophie were having lunch."

Fear creeps up my spine on hearing Sophie was caught up in it. "Sophie was there? Is she okay?"

"That's why I'm calling. I know things aren't great with you two, but I'm guessing Paisley's with Nash, and she's on her own. She was a mess when she left here. Can you go and check on her? I'd go, but I can't leave the bar. The front window's been shot out."

I sigh loudly. "Okay. I'll go."

"Thanks, Cade."

"I'll stop by when I've checked on Sophie. Are you okay?"

"Yeah, I'm okay. See you later."

I end the call and drop backward onto the bed. The last thing I want to do is see Sophie, but I can't deny the fear I felt when Seb said she'd been there. It might have been fourteen years since we were together, but my feelings for her are still as strong as they were, as much as I wish they weren't. I want to hate her, and I guess a part of me does. She broke my heart when she left Hope Creek, and all these years later, I still have no idea what I did to make her leave. When she showed up in town eighteen months ago, she tried to explain, but it had taken me years to get over her and I didn't want to listen. At least, I thought I was over her. All it took was one look in her eyes and I was done for. I don't want to dredge up the past, though. What would be the point? It's not going to change anything. There was a time I thought Sophie Greene was my forever. Clearly, she didn't feel the same way.

Dragging myself out of bed, I pad across the room and into the bathroom, turning on the shower. I've had about four hours' sleep, but thankfully, I have the next couple of days off, so at least I can catch up on some rest. It's rare to get two days off, and I'm looking forward to doing nothing at all.

When I'm showered, I dry off and dress in shorts and a t-shirt. Grabbing my phone, I head for the entryway and pick up my car keys from the small table. I could walk. Sophie's place isn't that far, but I'm exhausted, and taking the car will be quicker. I'm apprehensive as I drive the short distance to her house. While I've seen her plenty of times since she moved back to Hope Creek, I haven't been completely alone with her. I haven't allowed myself to be. I'd messed up pretty badly a few weeks ago and ended up kissing her in Eden, Seb's bar. She'd looked so beautiful and I couldn't keep away from her. I can't make that mistake again.

After parking on the driveway, I climb out of the car and walk slowly up the porch steps. Taking a deep breath, I ring the doorbell. I frown when a minute or so passes and there's no answer. I look to the left of the door and the blinds at the living room window are closed.

"I wonder if she's in the backyard," I mutter as I head down the porch steps and around the side of the house.

There's a locked gate between me and the backyard, but this is the house Sophie grew up in, and I'd snuck into her bedroom more times than I can count. I know the latch is just in my grasp if I reach over the top of the gate. At six foot two, I'm easily tall enough, and my hand feels blindly for it. I groan as my fingers land on a padlock. Sophie must have increased the security when she took over.

I look around and find a large, empty ceramic flowerpot by the side of the house. Dragging it to the gate, I turn it upside down and use it to stand on. The extra height allows me to scramble over the gate. I hope the neighbors aren't going to call the cops after seeing me pretty much breaking into a women's shelter.

I'm met with an empty backyard, and I look through the windows at the back of the house. I guess there's a chance she's not home, but if she was as upset as Seb said, where would she have gone?

My eyes find her bedroom window, and I sigh. The trellis I used to climb years ago is still there, and I reach up, slowly scaling the back of the house. There's a small balcony off her bedroom, and I swing my leg over the railings, coming to stand right outside the door. I try not to think of all the memories standing here evokes. The door is open slightly, and my heart squeezes in my chest when I hear her crying. Opening the door, I step inside and find her lying on the bed, sobbing.

"Sophie," I say softly.

Her whole body jumps at the sound of my voice, and a small scream leaves her mouth. She sits up and scrambles back against the headboard.

"It's me," I add quickly, her frightened eyes meeting mine. Relief washes over her face before she promptly bursts into tears again. I've always hated seeing her cry and now is no different. I cross the room and sit on the edge of her bed. My hands itch to reach out and pull her into my arms, but I know that would be a bad idea.

"Seb told me what happened at Eden. Are you okay?" She's obviously not okay, but I don't know what else to say.

"I thought we were going to die," she sobs, tears tracking down her cheeks. "And then his body was on the sidewalk. There was so much blood. I can't stop thinking about it."

Her whole body is shaking, and I can't just sit here and watch. She's falling apart in front of me, and the need to hold her is overwhelming. I kick off my shoes and climb onto the bed. Reaching for her, I lie down and pull her onto my chest. I haven't held her like this in fourteen years and I'd forgotten just how perfectly she fits in my arms. She sobs harder now that I'm holding her, and I tangle my hand in her hair, pressing her against me. Her fingers fist the front of my t-shirt, and I drop a kiss on her head.

"It's okay," I say quietly. "You're safe now. It's over."

She's wearing the same perfume she always wore, and I inhale deeply, hundreds of memories flooding my mind.

God, I wish things were different between us. There's a physical ache in my chest that's been pretty much ever-present since she left me. Holding her now makes that ache even worse, but I don't let her go. I've waited what feels like forever to hold her again. I'll deal with my feelings later.

"All I could think about was you," she whispers. "I was so scared I'd never see you again."

She lifts her head, and her bloodshot eyes meet mine. Despite the tears and the red puffy eyes, she's still the most beautiful woman I've ever seen. I miss her so much.

Before I know what I'm doing, my lips are on hers and I'm kissing her. She moans into my mouth as I swipe against her bottom lip and she opens up to me, our tongues dueling.

My lips never leave hers as I roll her onto her back, my body pressing her down into the mattress. She winds her arms around my neck as my hand goes under her tank. I drag my fingers up her side and pull the material of her bra down when I reach her breast. I flick and roll her nipple between my fingers, and she gasps into my mouth, arching her back. My lips leave hers, and I pepper kisses along her jaw and down her neck. Sitting her up, I pull her tank over her head and toss it on the floor. My fingers undo her bra, and I slide the material from her body.

"God, you're so beautiful, Sophie."

She reaches for the bottom of my t-shirt and removes it, throwing it off the side of the bed. "So are you, Cade."

I inhale sharply as her small hands brush up my bare chest and over my shoulders. A voice at the back of my mind screams that this is a bad idea, but I ignore it. My body is crying out for her, and I can't stop myself. My mouth finds hers again, and I'm soon lost in her. Her fingers go to the button on my shorts and she undoes them, tugging them down my legs. Pulling out of the kiss, I stand up and kick them off. I'm not wearing any underwear, and my hard cock juts out in front of me. Going back to her, I make quick work of removing her yoga pants and panties. My cock jumps as my eyes take her in. She really is perfect. She was perfect at eighteen, but she's filled out more now, and I can't tear my eyes off her. Her nipples pebble as I continue to stare, and I drop my mouth, circling her bud with my tongue.

"Cade," she mumbles, her hands going into my hair.

Leaving her nipple, I kiss down her stomach and settle between her legs. She lets out a long moan as my tongue licks through her folds. She tastes as sweet as I remember, and I can't get enough of her. I lap at her clit and her legs trap my head in place. Her moans are getting louder and they're a direct line to my already aching cock.

When I push two fingers inside her, she cries out, and one of her hands leaves my hair to fist the comforter. I'm relentless with my tongue, and I can feel her walls fluttering around my fingers, telling me she's close.

Reaching my hand up, I pinch one of her nipples, and her whole body shudders as she comes, my name falling from her lips in a whisper. Her legs tighten like a vise around my head, and I continue working her over until her legs relax and her body sinks into the comforter.

"Fuck," I mutter, forgetting how her chest and neck flush pink when she comes. I reach my hand up and brush my fingers over her cheek. She leans into my touch, and I drop my head, kissing her again. She wraps her arms around my neck and holds me close.

"Please, Cade. I need you," she whispers against my lips.

Taking my length in my hand, I line up with her entrance and push gently inside her. She's so tight it feels like our first time all over again. Her tear-filled eyes hold mine, and she cries out as I push in all the way.

"Shit. Did I hurt you?"

She shakes her head. "I just need a minute. It's been a while."

I nod, barely holding it together. It's been a while for me too,

ECHOES OF LOVE

and she feels incredible. Her body is tense, and I kiss her, hoping she relaxes.

"How long has it been?" I ask against her lips. It'll be torture to know, but I can't stop myself from asking.

She bites down on her bottom lip and my eyes search hers.

"Fourteen years," she whispers, dropping her eyes from mine.

"What? Sophie, look at me." I wait until her eyes meet mine. "You haven't been with anyone since we were last together?"

She shakes her head. "There's never been anyone but you." A single tear falls from the corner of her eye, and I drop my head, kissing it away. "Please move, Cade." She rolls her hips, and I groan.

I can't comprehend what she's telling me when it feels so good to be inside her. Pulling out, I slam back into her and she moans, her fingers digging into my shoulders.

"Fuck," she gasps, her hips moving against mine as I relentlessly pound into her.

My lips find hers, and she pushes her tongue into my mouth. My orgasm is already building in the pit of my stomach, but I don't want this to be over. I want to stay buried inside her forever, even though I know that can never happen. Her hands wind into my hair and she tugs gently as I fill her. Knowing I'm close, I reach my hand between us and circle her clit with my finger.

"I'm going to come soon, Sophie. I want you with me."

"I'm close."

"Come for me, baby. I can feel you pulsing around my cock."

"Oh, God," she mumbles.

I increase the pressure on her clit along with my thrusts, and she comes, crying out as her body convulses underneath me. Her release triggers my own, and I groan, dropping my head into the crook of her neck.

Sex with Sophie had always been incredible, and fourteen

years later, nothing has changed. She set my body on fire then, and she still does now.

When we've both caught our breath, the reality of what we've done hits me like a smack in the face. We can't have any sort of future. It's too late for that. I've just blurred the lines even further between us and neither of us deserves that.

"Shit!" I exclaim as I pull out of her. In the haze of lust, I forgot the condom. "Are you on birth control?" My voice is harsh. I don't mean it to be, but I can't let her think this can happen again.

"Yes."

"I forgot the condom. I'm clean."

"Me too," she whispers.

I sigh and drag my hand through my hair. Standing up, I reach for my shorts and tug them on. "That shouldn't have happened," I tell her.

"Cade, please. We need to talk about what happened all those years ago."

"Why? It won't change anything. You broke me, Sophie, and there's no coming back from that. What just happened was a mistake."

She sits up and drags the comforter around her. "Please don't say that," she whispers. "I still love you, Cade. It's only ever been you."

I shake my head. "If you loved me, you would never have left." I pull my t-shirt over my head and slip on my shoes.

"It's because I loved you so much that I had to leave."

"That makes no sense at all. I can't do this. I need to go."

"Please, Cade."

"I didn't hear from you for years, Sophie. *Years!* You were my whole world, and then you were gone as if I meant nothing to you."

"You meant everything to me, Cade. Please let me explain. Please!"

I shake my head. She's begging me, but I can't give her what she wants. She wants to tell me what happened so *she* feels better. It's not about me. It's about her, and as much as I still love her, I want to hate her too. I don't want her to feel better. I want her to hurt like I have for the last fourteen years. It's not rational, but I can't help it.

I cross the room and open her bedroom door. Stopping in the doorway, I can't bring myself to turn around and look at her, terrified that if I do, I won't want to leave.

"Bye, Sophie."

I walk out and close the door behind me. Maybe that was the perfect way to say goodbye.

CHAPTER TWO

Sophie

My heart shatters as I watch Cade leave. It's been fractured for fourteen years, but being in his arms is the closest I've come to feeling whole again. I still love him, and despite knowing I don't deserve him, I've never wanted anything more in my life. I think in an attempt to guard my heart, I'd blocked out just how incredible it had been when we were together. What I did fourteen years ago, I did for him. Looking back now, I know leaving was the wrong thing to do, and then things happened which made it even harder to come back, but at eighteen, I thought I was making the right decision. I should have spoken to him. I made the biggest mistake of my life and I'd give *anything* to go back and change things. I can't, though, and unless I can try to make him understand, I think he's going to hate me for the rest of my life.

I cry myself to sleep after he leaves, and when I wake up, it's dark. I take a shower and pull on some clothes. Walking quietly along the hallway, I knock lightly on Paisley's door. I'm not expecting her to be home. She left earlier for Nash's place, and I'm hoping they've worked things out. When I'm met with silence, I make my way downstairs. I'll text her in a bit and make sure she's okay. We've grown close over the past few weeks, and knowing how I feel about what's happened today, I hope she's holding up. It must be so much worse for her knowing it was her ex who was killed. I'm glad she's found Nash. She deserves it after everything she's been through.

I frown as I reach the bottom step and see bags in the entry-way. I turn, hearing Lyra.

"Are you leaving?" I ask, looking from her to the bags.

She nods. "Trent's coming to pick me up."

"Are you sure, Lyra? What if he hurts you again?"

Trent is Lyra's abusive boyfriend. This is her third stay at the shelter in the past twelve months. I had hoped this time she wouldn't go back to him. She's found a job and we were looking at apartments for her. He must have persuaded her.

"I'm sure. He's promised me he's changed. I believe him."

I sigh inwardly. I can't make her stay. All I can do is be here if she needs me again in the future. I reach for her and pull her into a hug. "Take care of yourself. You know I'm always here if you need me."

"Thank you, Sophie." A horn blasts from outside, and she smiles. "That'll be him."

"Do you need any help?"

"No. I can manage."

"Stay safe, Lyra."

She smiles before picking her bags up and walking outside. I watch as she runs down the porch steps, climbing into Trent's car. I hope I'm wrong and Trent really has changed, but I doubt it. Men like that rarely do.

LAURA FARR

Closing the door, I realize I'm completely alone. Fear envelops me, even though I know it's irrational. Paisley's husband is dead. Still, I can't help feeling scared. Reaching for my phone, I send Paisley a message.

Me: Hi, did you sort things out with Nash?

I head into the kitchen and pour myself a glass of wine. At least if I have a drink, I stand a good chance of being able to sleep tonight. When my phone chimes with an incoming message, I expect it to be Paisley. I'm surprised when Seb's name pops up.

Seb: Hi, Sophie. Just checking you're okay after earlier.

I type out a reply to him.

Me: I'm okay. How are you? Did you manage to get the window fixed?

Seb: I'm okay. The window's fixed. We should be able to re-open tomorrow.

Me: That's good.

Seb: Are you sure you're okay?

Me: Not really. Wishing I had a big guard dog!

My phone rings in my hand, and I smile as Seb's name flashes on the screen. Cade's family had been a little distant with me after I'd come back to Hope Creek. I didn't blame them. I know I hurt Cade when I left, and I know they would have been the ones to pick up the pieces, but I'd worked hard to rebuild a relationship with his brothers and sister, despite not being able to do the same with Cade.

"Hi, Seb," I say as I answer, the phone pressed between my ear and my shoulder as I make myself a quick sandwich.

"Hey, Sophie. Are you on your own?"

"Yeah. Cade was here earlier, but he's gone."

"What about the woman you have staying with you? I'm guessing Paisley is with Nash?"

"Lyra just left. She's gone back to her boyfriend, and yeah, Paisley's with Nash."

"You shouldn't be on your own. Not after everything that's happened."

"I'm okay."

"Really?" I'm silent, and he sighs. "Do you want to come and stay in my spare room?"

My eyes widen in surprise. I'm tempted to say yes. The idea of being here alone fills me with dread.

"What? No. I'll be fine."

"I don't mind. Just for tonight. I could do with the company if I'm honest."

"I thought you said you were okay?"

"I lied. Like you did."

I chuckle. "All right, but only because you're not okay."

He laughs. "Pack a bag and I'll come and pick you up."

"On the bike?"

"Yes. I have a spare helmet."

"Okay. Thanks, Seb."

"See you soon."

He ends the call, and I take a mouthful of wine before making my way upstairs. I feel a little ridiculous spending the night at Seb's place. I don't believe for a minute he's not okay. He's just saying it to make me feel better. It just shows how incredible Cade's family is, especially after what I did. Not that they know the whole story. No one knows. The only people who did were my mom and aunt, and both of them are gone now. I try not to think about how completely alone I am. I had lots of friends before I left, but I lost touch with them all, and most had moved on by the time I came back.

Fifteen minutes later, I'm waiting on the porch for Seb. I've packed a small overnight bag, and I pick it up as I hear the roar of a motorcycle in the distance. When he rides into view, I raise my hand in a wave and jog down the porch steps. Without saying a word, he holds out the helmet to me. I slip it on and climb on the bike, my bag on my back. I wrap my arms around his waist, he pulls away, and I cling to him tightly.

It's a short ride to his apartment, and when we arrive, he parks in the underground garage and turns off the engine. I climb off the back and remove my helmet, standing awkwardly while I wait for him. I feel a little silly now that I'm here. I'm thirty-two; I shouldn't be scared to stay alone in my own house.

"You okay?" he asks as he takes off his helmet and swings his leg over the bike. He takes my helmet from my hands.

I nod. "I'm sorry for being so needy," I tell him, my cheeks heating.

He frowns. "Sophie, you aren't being needy. You've been through a hell of a lot today."

"Thank you for being so great."

He waves off my thanks and gestures for me to follow him to the elevator on the other side of the parking garage. We ride the car in silence, and when the doors open, he leads me along a hall-way, coming to a stop outside apartment twelve.

"This is me."

He opens the door and stands aside so I can enter first. I stop in the small entryway, my eyes going to a picture wall on the left that's full of images of his family. I smile as I see him and his brothers hanging out of the treehouse in their parents' backyard. Their knees are covered in mud, and all four of them have wide smiles on their faces. I love how close they are. When Cade and I were together, I was always made to feel a part of their family. I miss him so much.

The sound of Seb closing the door behind me pulls me from my thoughts, and I blink away the tears that sting my eyes. The last thing I need is to fall apart in front of Seb.

Dropping my bag on the floor, I walk farther into the apartment. There's a kitchen off to the right, and beyond that, an open-plan living room. A hallway sits off to the left that I'm guessing leads to the bedrooms and bathroom.

"Take a seat. Do you want a drink?" Seb asks as he puts the helmets down in the entryway.

"Sure. What do you have?"

"Bud, Diet Coke, or water."

"A Bud, please. I could do with a drink after today."

Taking a seat on the sofa, I watch as he opens the refrigerator and pulls out two bottles of beer. He hands me one and flops down next to me.

"Well, I've had better days. What about you?" Seb asks, clinking his bottle with mine before taking a pull.

"Yeah, you could say that." I take a mouthful of Bud and fold my legs underneath me. I can't help thinking that I've had worse days too, but I don't tell Seb that.

"So, Cade came over earlier?" he asks, and I nod. "How did that go?"

My cheeks heat again, and I drop my eyes from his, my fingers pulling at the label on my bottle.

I let out a long sigh. "You don't want to know."

"What happened with you two, Soph? I was only twelve when you left, but I remember how close you were."

I shake my head. "I made the biggest mistake of my life, and now I have to live with that."

He reaches across and takes my hand. "You can't work it out?"

"He won't talk to me, and even if he'd let me explain, once he knows why I left and didn't come back, he'll hate me even more than he does now. I don't know if I can deal with that." My voice breaks, and he squeezes my hand.

"He doesn't hate you, Sophie."

"I think he might. I should never have come back."

"Don't say that. I'm glad you came back. Cade's an idiot if he can't see how amazing you are."

I give him a sad smile. "Thanks, Seb. Enough about me. How are you? How's your love life? It has to be better than mine!"

He laughs. "My love life is non-existent. I spend every spare minute at the bar. I have no time for love."

"You should make time."

Before he can answer, a knock sounds on the door. He stands and jogs across the space, pulling the door open.

"Hey, man. Sorry I never made it to the bar earlier."

My stomach drops when I recognize Cade's voice.

"Hey, Cade. Come in."

He walks past Seb, his eyes landing on me. "What are you doing here?" he asks, his voice harsh.

"Cade!" Seb exclaims.

"I should go," I say quietly, standing up and placing my half-drunk bottle of Bud on the side table.

"No. You shouldn't. Cade, stop being an ass."

"Really, it's fine."

"I didn't see your car," Cade says as I walk past him and pick up my bag from the entryway floor.

"Seb picked me up. I can walk back. Thanks for the beer, Seb. I'll see you soon."

"Wait, don't go. I thought you were staying the night?" he asks, his hand going to my arm.

"Staying the night!" Cade shouts, his eyes dropping to Seb's hand. "Is something going on with you two?"

"What? No!" Seb cries. "I offered for Sophie to stay in my

spare room. She shouldn't be on her own after what happened today."

"She's not on her own! Paisley and Lyra are at her house."

"Paisley's with Nash and Lyra left," Seb explains, and I want to run and never look back. After what happened with Cade earlier, I can barely look him in the eye. It hurts too much.

"I was being stupid anyway. I'll be fine at the house. I'll see you later." I rush out of the apartment and down the emergency stairwell, not wanting to wait for the elevator. I can hear Seb calling my name, but I don't stop.

It's been the hardest eighteen months being back in Hope Creek. As much as I love the town and never wanted to leave, I didn't realize how painful it would be to be back in a place where every corner has a memory of Cade and me. I really believed I'd never come back, and I'm beginning to wonder if I made the right call taking on the shelter after my mom died. It was never something I'd planned on doing. Maybe I should have stayed away. Seems it would have been better for everyone.

CHAPTER THREE

Cade

I watch as Seb rushes out of the apartment after Sophie. I close my eyes and sigh.

"Wait. I'll go. I guess I owe her an apology," I call after him, and he stops, spinning on his heel.

"Yeah. You do! Make sure she comes back. She might not admit it to you, but she's scared."

I move past him and jog down the emergency stairs. When I get outside, Sophie's walking along the sidewalk and I catch up with her.

"Sophie, wait up." She spins around, her face etched with surprise. She clearly wasn't expecting me to follow her. "Look, I'm sorry. I just didn't expect to see you with Seb."

"I'm not *with* Seb."

I sigh. "I know. Come back inside."

"I'm just going to go home."

She goes to turn away from me, but I reach for her arm. As my fingers brush her skin, sparks of electricity shoot through my hand. She must feel it too as her eyes fly up to mine. "Seb's right. You shouldn't be on your own after what happened."

She pulls her arm away and my hand falls to my side. "I'm fine, Cade. You didn't care about leaving me alone earlier." She gives me a sad smile before turning away again.

"Sophie—"

"Tell Seb I said bye," she says, cutting me off.

I watch her walk away and know she isn't going to change her mind. She was always fiercely independent. The fact that she's here at all tells me she really is nervous to be alone. I feel like an asshole, and I know Seb is going to be mad when I go back without her. Pulling my keys from my pocket, I jump into my car that's parked by the sidewalk and follow her. Driving slowly alongside her, I roll down the passenger side window.

"Let me at least drive you home. It's late."

She stops and blows out a breath. "Okay. Thank you."

I unlock the door, and she climbs silently into the passenger seat.

"Are you sure I can't persuade you to go back to Seb's? He's going to kill me if I go back without you."

A smile pulls on her lips. "I didn't realize you were scared of him."

"Terrified." She laughs, and my heart flips in my chest. God, I wish things were different. "Is that a yes?"

"Okay," she whispers.

I breathe a sigh of relief and turn the car around.

I know I should probably say something about what happened earlier, but I have no idea what. I lost control. I was weak and gave in to something I've wanted for fourteen years. I always wondered what it would be like to be with her again. I didn't expect to feel like my heart was being ripped from my chest all over again.

It's only seconds before I'm stopping outside Seb's apartment building. She hadn't walked far when I talked her into getting into the car. When I don't turn the engine off, she looks across at me.

"Are you coming up?"

I shake my head, my eyes not meeting hers. "No. I'll catch up with Seb another time."

"Do you think we can ever be friends again?" I can hear the sadness in her voice, and I finally lift my eyes to hers, dragging my hand through my hair.

"I never wanted to be just your friend, Sophie."

"Neither did I," she whispers.

Silence fills the car, and I don't know what to say. How can I just be her friend when I'm still in love with her? If she hadn't left me, I know we'd still be together. I don't want to only be her friend, but how can we ever be anything more after fourteen years apart?

"Thanks for the ride. I guess I'll see you around," she says, climbing out of the car. "Bye, Cade."

She's closed the car door before I can say anything, and I watch her until she's safely inside Seb's apartment building. Sighing, I pull away from the sidewalk and drive aimlessly around Hope Creek. Eventually, I find myself parking on my parents' driveway. I haven't spoken to anyone about Sophie other than my mom in the eighteen months she's been back. I might be thirty-four, but sometimes I just need my mom's advice.

Making my way inside, I find my parents in the living room, watching TV. I don't normally just drop in on them, and I can see the concern on my mom's face as she looks up and sees me in the doorway.

"Cade, is everything okay?" she asks as she stands up and walks toward me, pulling me into a hug. It occurs to me they may not know about the shooting at Seb's place. I don't know if anyone's told them. I know Seb wouldn't have wanted to worry them.

"I'm fine. Everyone's fine," I say quickly, realizing if she hasn't mentioned it, they likely don't know.

She frowns. "What's happened?"

"Remember that everyone is fine." I take her hand and guide her back to the sofa. "There was a shooting at Eden—"

"Oh my God! When? Why didn't anyone tell me?"

"Earlier today. Paisley's ex showed up with a gun. Nash shot him."

Her eyes are wide and they go from me to my dad, who stands and comes to sit next to her. "Was Seb there?"

I nod. "Yes. Paisley and Sophie too."

"But they're okay?"

"They're fine. Paisley's with Nash."

"And Sophie?"

I sigh. "She's with Seb."

Her brow furrows. "With Seb? Why?"

"I guess she didn't want to be on her own."

"Have you seen her?"

"Yes. Seb asked me to go and check on her earlier. She was upset. I ended up… staying for a while."

She raises her eyebrows and squeezes my hand. "You're no closer to working things out, then?"

"No. She wants us to talk, but I don't know what good it would do. It's just going to drag everything back up, and that's something neither of us wants."

"Don't you want to know why she left? If only to draw a line under everything so you can move on? You haven't dated anyone in years, Cade. Maybe it's the closure you need."

"Maybe." I stand up and pace the living room. "She told me she still loves me today."

"And you still love her too?"

25

I blow out a breath. "Yeah, but it's a fine line between love and hate. How could she just walk away without a single word?"

"You need to talk to her, son," my dad says. "However hard it is to hear."

"And Carla definitely never said anything to you?"

Carla was Sophie's mom, and they used to be good friends. My mom met her when she came to Hope Creek needing a place to stay. Carla ran the shelter Sophie's now running and offered my mom a room while she found her feet. They become close, and when Sophie left, I know it put a strain on their friendship.

"No, Cade. I asked her. Lots of times, but she was protecting Sophie. As a mom, I can understand that. I would have done the same for you."

"What if I talk to her and she tells me something that makes me hate her even more than I already do?" I ask quietly.

"What if you talk to her and you find it's something you can get past? She was eighteen, Cade. Maybe it was a mistake she wishes she could take back. Don't you think it's worth finding out?"

"I don't know. I guess."

I'm torn. For years, I wanted answers. I was desperate to know what I'd done to make her walk away from me without a backward glance. For a long time, I thought it was my decision to take the summer internship, but she encouraged me to take it, so it couldn't be that. She wouldn't throw away our whole relationship over that. All I did know was that after that weekend, it was twelve years before I set eyes on her again.

CHAPTER FOUR

Sophie

It's been a few weeks since the shooting at Eden, and despite Paisley spending most of her time at Nash's place, I'm enjoying being in the house on my own now. It makes a change for me to have the place to myself for a while. As much as I miss having Paisley around, it's been months since I've had no houseguests.

I haven't seen Cade since he dropped me off at Seb's apartment on the night of the shooting. Although I'd pleaded with him to let me explain what happened all those years ago, part of me was relieved he didn't want to know. It was hard enough for me to have it in my head. I'm not sure I'd be able to get the words out to explain anyway.

My alarm sounds from the nightstand, and I groan as I roll over to silence it. I need to be up early to do some work this morning. As a sideline to running the shelter, I do some ad hoc accounting work for some of the businesses in Hope Creek, but I've been unwell for just over a week. I can't seem to keep anything down, and I feel awful. As I sit up, a wave of nausea rolls through me, and I throw my hand over my mouth and rush into the bathroom, throwing up in the toilet. My head is spinning, and as I stand up, black dots dance in my vision. I drop to my knees before I pass out.

"Fuck," I mutter when the dizziness has passed. I stand up more slowly and splash cold water on my face. Fear swirls in my stomach and my mind goes to a few weeks ago, when I slept with Cade. I've had nausea like this before. I know what it means, although I'm terrified to find out for sure. Initially, I thought it was just an upset stomach or something I'd eaten, but the longer it goes on, the more I'm convinced it's not. After what happened last time, I know I should be taking better care of myself, but I don't want to acknowledge what I'm almost positive is happening.

After brushing my teeth, I climb back into bed, exhausted. There's no way I can work this morning. The accounts will have to wait. I know I need to try to eat something, but I just don't have the energy to go downstairs and make anything.

I must have fallen asleep as I'm woken by a voice shouting my name.

"Sophie, are you home?" It's Paisley, and I sit up slowly. Standing on shaky legs, I make my way to the bedroom door. I have such a headache it's making my vision blurry, and I grab on to the dresser at the side of the door to stop myself from falling over. Opening the door, I make my way slowly to the top of the stairs.

"Are you okay?" Paisley asks, running up the stairs and taking my arm. I sway against her and my legs give out. "Whoa! Let's get you back to bed." Somehow, and I've no idea how, she manages to get me back into my bedroom and into bed. "You look really rough, Sophie. Have you seen a doctor?"

I shake my head.

"I'm going to be sick," I say, my hand going to my mouth. She passes me a bucket I keep at the side of the bed for when I'm too weak to make it to the bathroom, and I throw up, dry heaving into it. There's nothing to come up. I haven't eaten in days.

"I'm calling Cade," Paisley says. I shake my head, my eyes wide. "Yes. I'm calling him. Something's not right, and I'm worried about you. Your lips are dry, and you look like you've lost a ton of weight. When did you last eat?"

"I don't know," I admit, tears streaking down my face.

She sits on the edge of the bed and takes my hand. With her other hand, she pulls her phone from her pocket, and after searching her contacts, puts the phone to her ear. I'm sitting close to her, so I can hear when Cade answers.

"Hi, Paisley. Everything okay?"

"Are you at home?" she asks.

"Yeah, why?"

"Sophie's really sick and I don't know what to do. She can barely walk or I'd take her to the ER."

"I'll be right there."

"Thanks, Cade." She ends the call and squeezes my hand. "He's coming," she assures me, and nerves swirl in my stomach. Cade's a doctor. He's going to figure out what's going on.

"I think I'm pregnant," I confess.

"What? Have you done a test?"

I shake my head. "No, but I'm pretty sure I am."

"Who's the father?" I look at her and her eyes widen. "Cade?" I nod and burst into tears. "Hey, it'll be okay. Does he know?"

"No, but I guess he's going to. Please don't say anything. I might be wrong."

"Okay, but I think you need to tell him. When did you…?"

"The afternoon after the shooting. He came to check on me and one thing led to another."

I burst into tears again, and Paisley holds me while I sob. She doesn't say anything. What is there to say? It's a mess.

After a few minutes, I sit up. "Could you get me some water?" I have no idea if I can keep it down, but my mouth feels like I've eaten a ton of sand.

"Sure. I'll be right back."

She leaves me in bed and disappears downstairs. I curl up into the fetal position and close my eyes. I'm so tired. I feel like I could sleep for a week, and everything hurts from throwing up constantly.

I must fall asleep again, as I wake when I feel the bed dip. My eyes flutter open and Cade's sitting next to me, his worried eyes fixed on mine.

"How long have you been like this?" he asks, his palm going to my forehead.

I close my eyes as his hand touches my skin. "About a week, but it's getting worse."

"A week! When was the last time you drank anything?"

"I don't know. I can't keep anything down."

His hand goes from my forehead to my wrist. "Your pulse is racing, Sophie." He reaches for his bag at the side of him and pulls out a blood pressure machine. Fixing the cuff around my arm, he presses a button and the machine whirs to life. The cuff tightens around my arm for a minute or so and then relaxes. I see the numbers on the machine, but they mean nothing to me.

"Is it okay?" I ask, looking from the machine into his worried eyes.

"No. Your blood pressure is really low. You need fluids. I need to get you to the hospital."

"Should I call an ambulance?" Paisley asks from behind him.

"No. I'll take her in my car. Do you need to get to work?"

I only now notice Paisley's dressed for her shift at Eden. She bites down on her bottom lip and nods.

ECHOES OF LOVE

"I can let Seb know I can't come in."

"No, Paisley. Go to work. I'll be okay with Cade."

Her eyes find mine and she raises them in question. "Are you sure?"

"Yes. Go. I bet I've already made you late."

"Will you let me know how she is?" she asks Cade, who nods. She brushes a kiss on his cheek before coming and pulling me into a hug. "Talk to him," she whispers, and I give her a small smile as she stands up.

"Thanks for helping me, Paisley," I say softly.

"I'll call you later. I wish I could come with you."

"I'll make sure she's okay," Cade says as he packs the blood pressure machine away.

She smiles at him before raising her hand in a wave and rushing from the room. Slowly moving my legs to the side of the bed, I stand up, a wave of dizziness washing over me. I sway on my feet and Cade reaches his arm around my waist, steadying me.

"Okay. Why don't you stay on the bed until I've packed you an overnight bag?"

"An overnight bag?" I say, my voice wavering. "Do you think I'll have to stay in?"

"Yeah, I do." He frowns. "It feels like you've lost weight, Soph. I'm worried about you."

"I don't want to stay overnight," I mutter, tears tracking down my cheeks.

He reaches his hand up and wipes my tears. "Let's see what happens," he says gently. "You might feel better after some fluids, but I think we should take a bag, just in case."

"Okay," I whisper. "There's one in the closet."

He scoops me up and lowers me onto the bed. I watch as he crosses the room and grabs the bag from my closet. He goes to the bathroom and puts my electric toothbrush and toothpaste into the

31

bag, along with my hairbrush and some toiletries. When he comes back into the bedroom, his eyes find mine.

"Okay, point me in the direction of your pajamas."

"Second drawer down," I tell him, gesturing to the dresser on the wall opposite the bed. He opens the drawer and pulls out a couple of pairs, tossing them into the bag.

"Panties?" he asks quietly.

"Top drawer." He grabs a few pairs and adds them to the bag. "Thank you, Cade."

"I think that'll be enough for now. I'm sure Paisley can grab you anything else you might need. Let me put these bags in my car and I'll come back for you."

I nod as he grabs his medical bag along with my overnight bag and leaves the room. I know I should tell him why I think I'm sick, but I'm hoping I'm wrong. There's no point jumping to conclusions. I'll just wait and see what the doctor says in the ER. I'm sure he'll just drop me there and leave anyway. It's not like we're friends.

As saliva fills my mouth, I reach for the bucket and retch. My stomach hurts from all the straining I'm doing. There's nothing left inside me to come up, but it's like my body doesn't realize that and makes me retch anyway.

"Shit," Cade says as he comes back into the room. He goes into the bathroom and comes out with a wet washcloth in his hand. Passing it to me, he takes the bucket from my hand.

"What are you doing?" I ask, wiping my mouth with the cloth.

"Cleaning this up." He lifts the bucket, and my cheeks flush pink. "I'm a doctor, Sophie. I'm used to vomit."

"It's still embarrassing," I mutter.

"Do you need this in the car?" he shouts from the bathroom.

"We should go in my car. I don't want to throw up in yours!"

He walks out of the bathroom and shakes his head. "I don't care about my car, Sophie. Are you ready?"

ECHOES OF LOVE

"I think so."

He helps me put on my sneakers and takes my arm as I stand. My head is pounding and my heart is racing in my chest.

"I really don't feel good," I whisper, dropping my head on his shoulder. "I wish my mom was here."

"I'm not going to leave you, Sophie. I promise."

He slowly guides me downstairs and outside, closing the front door behind us. By the time I get into the passenger side of his car, I'm exhausted, and I drop my head back on the seat. He reaches around me and fixes my seat belt.

"Thank you," I whisper, my eyes closed. When I open them, he's parking outside the ER. "Did I fall asleep?"

"Yeah. Let's get you inside." He reaches into the back for my bag before climbing out of the car and coming around to the passenger side. Opening the door, he takes my hand and helps me out of the car. "I'm going to ask one of the other doctors to look you over. It's probably not appropriate for me to treat you."

"Okay."

When we reach the reception desk, I give over my details, and we're told to take a seat in the waiting room. Cade guides me to a seat but doesn't sit down himself.

"I'm just going to see who's working and if I can get you straight through. Will you be okay?"

I nod, and he turns and walks away, leaving me alone. I should be nervous that he's here, especially if I am pregnant, but I feel too unwell to care right now. He might hate me, but I love him and I'm glad he's here. I don't want to be on my own.

I've only been sitting for a few minutes when Cade returns and holds out his hand. "Come on. There's a bay free." I slip my hand into his and he gently pulls me up to stand.

"Thank you."

He drops my hand and takes my arm. I'm grateful for the physical support. I'm not sure I'd make it without someone to hold on to. When we reach the bay, Cade makes me lie on the bed, putting a plastic bowl next to me.

"How are you feeling?"

"Rough. My head is pounding and everything hurts."

Concern flashes across his face, but before he can say anything, the curtain is pulled back and a beautiful blonde woman enters the bay.

"Hi, Sophie. I'm Dr. Elise Wilcox. Cade tells me you're not feeling too good." She looks from me to him and drops a hand on his shoulder. I try to sit up, but I don't have the energy. Instead, my eyes go to where her hand rests before I look away.

"I can't keep anything down. Not even water."

"How long has this been going on for?" she asks, leaving Cade's side and coming to stand next to the bed I'm lying on. She picks up my hand, her fingers going over my pulse.

"About a week. Maybe a little longer."

"You look dehydrated. I want to run some tests and get some fluids in you. I'll be right back."

Cade smiles at her as she walks past him. A wave of nausea washes over me, and it's not because I'm feeling sick. Dropping my eyes, my fingers play with the edge of my tank.

"You don't have to stay, Cade. I'll be fine."

"I told you I'm not going to leave you, Sophie. I'm not going anywhere."

I sigh. "Okay. What tests will she do?" I ask, pushing away my wayward thoughts.

He stands up and moves to a chair nearer to the bed. "Blood work, most likely. Maybe a urine sample, but that might not be possible if you're dehydrated. You should start to feel better once you get some fluids on board."

"What about the nausea and vomiting? Can she give me something to stop it?"

"Yes, but we need to find out what's causing it first."

ECHOES OF LOVE

I drop my head back onto the pillow and close my eyes. I just want to sleep and to wake up without a headache. No one's mentioned me possibly being pregnant and I've no idea if it's crossed Cade's mind. I guess he knows I was on birth control when we slept together, so there's no reason to assume anything. I only have my suspicions because I've felt this way before. Maybe if he wasn't here, I might have said something to Dr. Wilcox, but I'll wait and see what the test results show and hope I'm wrong. I know if I am pregnant, I'm going to have to tell the doctor at least what happened last time.

A few minutes later, Dr. Wilcox returns with a rolling cart full of syringes and plastic containers to collect blood.

"I'm going to take some blood first. Do you think you can do a urine sample?"

"I'll try."

"Once we've done those, I'll get the drip set up and, hopefully, when the blood work comes back in an hour or so, we should know a little more."

I nod and look away as she gets everything ready to collect some blood. I'm not squeamish, but I still don't want to watch. After a couple of minutes, she's struggling.

"I've tried both arms but your veins are collapsing because of the dehydration. I'm going to have to try some less obvious places to draw blood. It might be a little more painful than normal."

"Okay," I whisper, my eyes finding Cade's worried ones.

After trying in various places, she finally gets blood from my foot, and I'm glad it's done. I feel like a pin cushion, and I know she has to somehow get a cannula in for the IV fluids. When she's labeled all the blood bottles, she passes me a urine sample bottle.

"The bathroom is just down the corridor," she says. "Do you need a nurse to help you?"

"I'll take her," Cade says, standing from the chair he's been sitting in. I notice the surprise on Dr. Wilcox's face.

"Oh. Okay. I'll just get these sent off and I'll be back to set up the IV."

She leaves the bay and I slowly sit up. "I'll be okay, Cade. Just point me in the right direction."

"Sophie, I practically had to carry you in here. I'm not going to let you go on your own so you can pass out in the bathroom. I'll take you."

"Okay. Thank you. I'm sure you have better things to do than look after me."

"No. Not really. Come on."

He takes my arm and helps me down from the bed. I hold on to him as we walk slowly to the bathroom. My head is spinning, and I'm glad he didn't let me go on my own. I'm not sure I'd have made it. When we get there, he opens the door for me and takes me to the toilet.

"Don't lock the door. I'll wait right outside."

"Okay."

He leaves me by the toilet and closes the door behind him. I don't need to pee, so I'm not sure if I'm going to be able to go, but I'll try. Turning the cold tap on, I sit down and hope for the best.

CHAPTER FIVE

Cade

I pace up and down the small corridor as I wait for Sophie to finish in the bathroom. Despite our strained relationship, I can't help but worry about her. It feels like something is really wrong, and my mind races with possible diagnoses. When the door to the bathroom opens, I go to her, slipping my arm around her waist.

"Did you manage to do anything?"

She nods and holds up the sample bottle that she's wrapped in toilet tissue. "There's not much. I hope it's enough."

I smile, looking at the wrapped-up sample bottle. "Why have you wrapped it in tissue?"

"I don't want you to see my pee," she exclaims, the slightest tinge of color covering her pale cheeks.

"Why not?" I ask incredulously.

"It's gross!"

LAURA FARR

"It's just urine."

"Well, I don't want you to see mine." She drops her head on my shoulder and I guide her back to the bay. It seems the trip to the bathroom has exhausted her, and she falls asleep as soon as I get her back on the bed.

Taking the sample from her hand, I leave her sleeping and go to find Elise. It's a little awkward that she's working today. After sleeping with Sophie a few weeks ago, I almost forced myself to move on. It's been fourteen years since we've been together, and although I still love her, I know we can never be together. I've always gotten along well with Elise, and I know she likes me, so I asked her out. We've been on a few dates, and although it's not serious yet, I've no idea how Elise sees things. We haven't even slept together, but I'm guessing she's going to be wondering who Sophie is to me. When I round the corner, she's at the nurses' station, completing some paperwork. She smiles when she sees me.

"Hey, how's she doing?"

"She's asleep," I tell her, handing over the sample. "What are you thinking?"

"Gastroenteritis maybe."

"Yeah, I was thinking the same. Or maybe some super bug, although I've no idea where she would have picked one up from."

"Let's see what the tests say. Fluids are the most important thing right now. I think I'm going to struggle with the cannula. Taking blood was hard enough."

"Let me try."

She frowns. "Who is this woman to you?"

"Just a friend. We used to be more, but it was years ago." She holds my gaze, and I wonder if she can tell I'm full of shit.

"Okay. If she's all right with it. I'll get everything ready."

"Thanks."

She brushes her hand over mine as she passes me and I make my way back to Sophie. She's still asleep, and I take a seat on the chair next to the bed. Despite the dark circles under her eyes and her pale skin, she's still beautiful. When Elise pulls the curtain back, she rolls a cart in with everything I need to put in the cannula. Knowing I need Sophie to be awake, I take her hand in mine and brush my thumb over the back of her hand.

"Sophie." Her eyes flutter open, the hand I'm not holding flying to her mouth.

"I'm going to be sick," she chokes out, and I grab the plastic bowl, holding it for her while she dry heaves into it. When her body stops, she flops back onto the bed, tears rolling down her cheeks. "I want it to stop, Cade," she whimpers, and I want to pull her into my arms and take all her pain away.

"I know, sweetheart. You'll feel better when the IV is up. Are you okay with me inserting the cannula?"

She nods and closes her eyes again. Dropping her hand, I stand and go to the small sink across the room to wash up. I try not to make eye contact with Elise. I can feel her staring at me. I'm guessing she has questions she wants to ask me. By the time I've got everything ready, I think Sophie's fallen asleep again. I hope I can get the IV in without hurting her too much. I look at her hands and choose the left one as the most viable.

"This shouldn't hurt too much, Sophie," I tell her.

"Mmmmm," she says, her eyes still closed.

I manage to get the cannula in after a couple of goes, and within a few minutes, the fluids are going in. Elise is still in the bay, and when I'm done, she moves to stand next to Sophie.

"Sophie," she says, placing her hand on her arm. "Can you hear me?"

She opens her eyes and nods. "Yes, sorry. I think I fell asleep again."

"That's okay. I've done some tests on your urine, one of which was a pregnancy test. It came back positive. Did you know you're pregnant?"

My eyes widen, and even though I heard what Elise said, the words don't make sense. Pregnant? She can't be. I didn't use a condom when we slept together, but she said she was on birth control. How the hell did I miss pregnancy as a reason for her being so sick? I'm a fucking doctor. I should have realized.

"No. I didn't know," she whispers, her frightened eyes meeting mine. "Are you sure?"

"The blood work will confirm it, but it's very unusual to get a false positive," Elise says. "I can see this is a shock. I'll give you some time to get your head around it. I'll call someone from obstetrics too. It could just be morning sickness, but it seems a little more than that to me."

I'm still staring at Sophie as I try to take in what she's just been told.

"Is this your first pregnancy, Sophie?" Elise asks, and more tears fall down her cheeks as she drops her eyes from mine.

"No," she whispers.

"No!" I exclaim, standing up so quickly the chair falls back, clattering onto the floor.

Sophie jumps, and Elise spins around to look at me, her eyes wide.

"When was that pregnancy?" she asks, turning back to Sophie.

Her fingers fiddle with the edge of her tank, and I know what she's going to say. Everything falls into place, and now I know exactly why she left me all those years ago.

"I was eighteen," she says quietly.

My heart thunders in my chest as she confirms what I already knew. I feel like I'm going to throw up. A million questions swarm in my mind, but I can't pull my thoughts together enough to ask anything.

"Did you experience morning sickness during that pregnancy?" Elise asks.

"Yes." Her voice breaks. "I can't go through that again. I can't lose another baby." She sobs and curls up into a fetal position on the bed.

She lost our baby? Why didn't she tell me? I feel like someone's punched me in the stomach. "Elise, can you give us a minute?" I ask, my voice shaky.

She looks between us and nods. "Of course. I'll get someone from obstetrics to come and see you." Her eyes stay on mine as she leaves the bay, and I know I need to talk to her. I need to talk to Sophie first, though.

When we're left alone, it's only Sophie's soft sobs that break the silence. Despite needing answers, I can't bear to see her so upset. Crossing the room, I sit on the edge of the bed and pull her into my arms. She feels so tiny in my embrace, and she clings to me as she cries. When her sobs finally subside, I lean back, my eyes searching hers.

"Why didn't you tell me?"

She closes her eyes and shakes her head. "You'd have given up school. I couldn't let you do that."

"But you had a miscarriage. Why didn't you tell me then? Where did you go for twelve years?"

"I didn't have a miscarriage," she says quietly, fresh tears running down her face.

I frown in confusion. "You just said you couldn't lose another baby."

"I had a termination. I was so sick, my organs started to fail. My morning sickness was even worse than now and nothing the doctors did helped."

"What?" I hear what she's telling me, but the words don't seem to penetrate my mind. "What do you mean?"

"They told me the baby wouldn't make it, and if I continued with the pregnancy, neither would I. I didn't want to abort our baby, Cade. I swear I didn't." Her hands claw at my t-shirt and her desperate eyes bore into mine.

"Shhhh, it's okay," I whisper, pulling her against me.

I don't know if it is okay, but my mind is racing after what she's just told me. I've spent fourteen years wondering why she left, but I never imagined what she's telling me now would be the reason. I can't even begin to imagine what she had to deal with on her own. I still have questions, but they can wait. I need to make sure she and our unborn child are going to be okay. They are all that matter right now.

"I'm going to be sick," she mumbles, pushing out of my arms and reaching for the bowl. Her body retches and more tears fall from her eyes. I hate seeing her like this, especially knowing how bad it must have been last time, and that I wasn't there for her then. We might not be in a relationship now, but I'm going to be there for her this time. She's carrying my child. I'm going to do everything I can to help her through this.

"I'm going to see if Elise can prescribe some anti-nausea meds," I tell her, climbing off the bed.

She reaches for my hand. "They wouldn't give me anti-nausea meds last time. They said they weren't safe."

"Things have changed in fourteen years. We can give them to pregnant women now."

"Okay. I trust you." She drops my hand and lies back down on the bed. "I'm sorry, Cade. I know I've hurt you."

"We'll talk when you're feeling better, okay?"

"Okay," she whispers, her eyes closing.

It takes seconds for her to fall asleep, and I step out of the bay, leaning heavily on the wall outside. It feels like everything I thought I knew about my relationship with Sophie was wrong. I guess I always thought she'd just met someone else and hadn't had the guts to face me. I spent years loving and hating her in equal measures, and now that I know the truth, I don't know how I should feel. If she hadn't needed the termination, would she ever have told me about the baby? Why didn't she tell me after the termination? Did she think I would blame her? These questions and more race through my mind, but I push them down. I know Sophie will tell me when she's well enough. If I'd just let her explain when she returned to Hope Creek eighteen months ago, maybe we wouldn't be in this position, but I didn't, and that's my fault.

"Are you okay?" Elise asks as she walks up to me. I nod and take her arm, moving her away from the bay. I know Sophie is asleep, but I don't want her to wake up and overhear us talking. Slipping into a side room, I sit down heavily on one of the sofas.

"The baby's yours, isn't it?" she asks quietly, and I nod. "And the baby when she was eighteen?"

"Mine too, although I didn't know. I was at college when she left me and I never knew why. I guess I do now."

"I'm sorry, Cade."

"I slept with her before we started dating. I had no idea she was pregnant. It was a one-time thing." My words tumble out in a rush. I don't want her to think I slept with Sophie after we started dating.

She sighs and sits down next to me, taking my hand. "I like you, Cade, I'm not going to lie. I don't know how this is going to work, but I want us to be together…" She trails off. "Maybe we need to talk when you've had time to get your head around everything."

"Yeah, we do." I lift my head, my eyes finding hers. I don't want to have the conversation with Elise right now, but I don't see how I can continue to date her. I like her, but Sophie needs me. "It's hyperemesis gravidarum, isn't it?"

"Yeah, I think so. I'm guessing when she was pregnant last time, it was hard to diagnose. It wasn't something doctors saw very often. They likely passed it off as just morning sickness, which is why things got as bad as they did." She squeezes my hand.

"There's nothing to say the same will happen again. Not with regular fluids and medication."

"I hope you're right."

"Does she have family to support her?"

"No, but she has me and my family. I'm going to take some time off and look after her."

"You are?" She sounds surprised, and I know this can't be easy for her.

I nod. "We might not be together anymore, but I wasn't there for her last time. I'm going to be there now."

"She's lucky to have you as a friend, Cade."

I'm not sure about that. Looking back, I wonder if I tried hard enough to find her when she left me. I'd begged her mom to tell me where she'd gone, and despite her not giving anything away, maybe I should have fought harder. Maybe we'd still be together if I had.

CHAPTER SIX

Sophie

I open my eyes when I feel a hand in mine and hear someone softly calling my name.

"Sophie, wake up," Cade says, his fingers stroking across the back of my hand. "The doctor from obstetrics is here."

My eyes land on Cade, who is sitting in a chair right next to my bed. I still can't believe after all these years, he finally knows what happened and he's still here. I thought for sure he'd hate me. Maybe he does and he's only here for his unborn child. I hope not, but I wouldn't blame him if that was the case.

My eyes go from Cade to an older-looking man, who smiles kindly.

"Hi, Sophie. I'm Dr. Black. Dr. Brookes, good to see you again." He shakes Cade's hand. I guess he knows him if he works here. It's not a large hospital. "Dr. Wilcox has filled me in on what's happening. How are you feeling?"

"A little better. My headache isn't as bad."

"That's good. The fluids will be helping. I need to ask you some questions. Do you feel up to talking?"

I nod. "Okay." I flick my eyes to Cade, who squeezes my hand reassuringly. It's then I realize he's still holding it.

"When was your last period?" Dr. Black asks, and I look from Cade to him.

"About two weeks ago, but it was very light."

"Are you on birth control?"

"Yes."

He nods and writes something down. "As you probably know, some morning sickness in pregnancy is normal, but when it's as bad as you're experiencing, it's called hyperemesis gravidarum, or HG for short. If it's left untreated, it can lead to complications like you experienced in your first pregnancy. Did anyone mention that term to you last time?"

I shake my head. "Could the same thing happen again?" I ask quietly.

"It could, but we're going to do everything we can, so that doesn't happen, Sophie." He smiles reassuringly at me, and I hope to God he's right. "Shall we take a look at your baby?"

I nod and glance at Cade, who looks like he's about to throw up.

"I'll get the portable ultrasound machine and be right back."

"Are you okay?" I ask Cade when Dr. Black has left the bay.

"It should be me asking you that." He stands up and paces the small space. I'm conscious he hasn't answered my question, and Dr. Black returns with the ultrasound machine before he's able to.

"Right, because we aren't sure how far along you are, we need to do an internal ultrasound. I'll pull the curtain around the bed while you get undressed."

When the curtain is closed, I try to remove my pajama pants, but I'm too exhausted, and the cannula in my hand doesn't help.

"Can you help me, Cade?" I call out, hoping he's still on the other side of the curtain.

He appears and gives me a small smile. "Sure."

I'm embarrassed to have him remove my pants and panties, but it's not like I have much choice. I can't do it myself, not with how awful I'm feeling. Even though he's seen it all before, he doesn't look and covers me with a sheet when he's done.

"Are you about ready?" Dr. Black asks, and I nod to Cade, who pulls the curtain back. I keep my eyes on Cade while the doctor sets up the machine. "This shouldn't hurt. It might just be a little uncomfortable. Ready?"

I nod again and Cade takes my hand. Dr. Black was right; it doesn't hurt. He's silent for longer than I'd like, though, and I squeeze Cade's hand. He smiles at me reassuringly.

"Is everything okay?" I ask when I can't take the silence anymore.

He smiles. "Everything looks fine. I was just checking there's only one baby. Sometimes multiples can cause severe morning sickness, but there's only one."

Relief crashes over me. If I'm doing this on my own, it's going to be hard enough with one, never mind multiples.

"You're measuring almost eight weeks." He turns the machine around and I gasp as a wriggling blob appears on the screen. "I'll just turn the sound on."

He presses a button on the machine, and a loud whooshing sound fills the bay. I turn my head to look at Cade, who has tears running down his cheeks.

"Cade," I whisper, and he discreetly wipes his eyes before standing up and pressing a kiss on my forehead.

"Does everything look okay?" he asks Dr. Black.

"Everything looks fine, Cade." He removes the internal ultrasound wand and passes me a couple of images he's printed. "I want to admit you for a couple of days, Sophie. Just to get your fluids under control and to try some medication, okay?"

"Okay," I whisper, my eyes fixed on the images he's just given me.

"I'll go and speak to Dr. Wilcox and arrange for you to be admitted to the obstetrics ward."

"Thank you." He smiles before leaving the bay, taking the portable ultrasound machine with him.

When it's just me and Cade, I bring my arm over my eyes and burst into tears.

"Hey," Cade says, dropping into the seat next to me and taking my hand in his. "The baby's okay. It's going to be okay this time."

I shake my head. "You don't know that. I couldn't keep our baby safe last time. What if I can't now?" My voice is a whisper, and I feel so useless. I'm a woman. My body should be able to carry a baby. Why can't it?

"Sophie, this isn't your fault, and it wasn't your fault before either."

"It is my fault. I should have kept her safe."

"Her?" he asks. "It was a girl?"

"I don't know. I was only twelve weeks when…" I trail off. "I always felt like it was a girl, though."

"I'm so sorry I wasn't there."

"I picked up the phone so many times. I wanted you so badly. If I could turn the clock back, I'd do everything differently, Cade."

He sighs and drops his head onto our joined hands. "We need to talk properly, but not until you're feeling better. Okay?" He lifts his head, his eyes finding mine.

"Okay."

"I'll help you get dressed."

He slips on my panties, followed by my pajama pants, and I'm exhausted again by the time I'm dressed. Even the smallest of tasks wear me out, but I am feeling a little better since the IV has been set up. I watch from the bed as Cade checks the bag of fluid.

"It's almost done. Why don't you try to sleep while we wait for you to be admitted?"

I nod, already closing my eyes. Other than when I got pregnant before, I've never felt exhaustion like this, and I can't keep my eyes open.

I don't know how much time has passed when I wake up, but I find myself alone in the small bay. I know Cade won't have gone far, but I can't help wondering where he is. Looking at the cannula in my hand, I notice I'm no longer connected to the IV. Someone must have been in while I was sleeping and removed the empty fluid bag.

Needing to use the bathroom, I sit up slowly and wait for the dizziness that's ever-present lately to pass. When it has, I slowly make my way out of the bay and along the corridor to the bathroom I used earlier. I keep close to the wall, using it for support. Passing a small room, I hear a voice and stop when I realize it's Cade. I glance inside and see he's on the phone with his back to the door. Standing to the side, I shamelessly listen to his side of the conversation.

"All I know is I need to be there for her… No. She's carrying my child. I've got an obligation… Does it matter what I want? I can't change what's happened as much as I wish I could."

He sighs loudly, and I peek around the doorframe. He's pacing the room, and I move back quickly before he sees me.

"Why is it as soon as I try to move on, this happens…? Yeah, well, it's pretty new." I glance around the doorframe again and he's sitting on the sofa, his head down. "Whatever it is, I don't know how I'm going to be able to continue seeing her… I'm having a baby with Sophie. How can I be in a relationship with someone else?" He sighs again. "Elise already knows about the baby. She's the fucking doctor treating Sophie. It's a mess…" He lets out a humorless laugh. "If that were true, we'd still be together now, and we're not... Yeah, well, I was thinking with my dick. It was a mistake."

With tears in my eyes, I've heard enough. I guess that teaches me to listen to other people's private conversations. There's always a chance you'll hear something you don't want to, and that conversation was full of things I didn't want to hear. After how Cade has been today, I couldn't stop my fractured heart from hoping that maybe I'd get a second chance with him, but he's dating Elise. I knew I'd seen something between them earlier, and if what I overheard is right, he's going to break up with her because of me. Another reason for him to hate me. The reasons are stacking up, and I'm surprised he's still here with me. Despite being pregnant with his child, it seems I'm still very much in his past, and that's all my fault. I did this to us and I have to live with that.

Slipping into the bathroom, I sit on the closed toilet seat and let the tears fall. After a few minutes, I wipe my eyes. I need to pull myself together. With everything that's happening to my body with this pregnancy, I can't afford to fall apart from a broken heart as well. It's been broken for fourteen years. I can get through another seven months. I use the toilet and wash my hands before slowly making my way back to the bay. When I get there, Cade is pacing the room.

"Sophie! Where did you go? Are you okay?" His voice is full of concern, and he reaches for my hand and helps me onto the bed.

"I'm okay. I needed to use the bathroom."

"You should have asked me to go with you."

"I didn't know where you were," I lie. "It's fine, Cade. I live alone. I'm going to have to get used to going to the bathroom on my own."

"I was hoping you'd come and stay with me."

I raise my eyebrows in surprise. "You were?" He nods. "Why?"

"So I can look after you."

"You don't want me in your space. I need to get used to doing things alone. I might as well start now." I heard what he said on the phone. He feels it's his obligation to look after me. I don't want that. I don't want to be anyone's obligation, and if he does decide to continue to see Elise, I definitely don't want to be in his space to watch that play out. He didn't ask for this. Neither of us did, but he's a good guy. I know he isn't just going to walk away from his responsibilities, but his responsibility is to the baby, not me.

"You're not going to be alone, Sophie," he says with a frown.

I let out a breath and lie down. "I know. I didn't mean you wouldn't be there for the baby—"

"I'm going to be there for the both of you," he says, cutting me off.

"Well, I guess we have seven months to figure it out…" I trail off. "If my body doesn't let me down."

"I'm going to do everything I can to make sure you get through this, Sophie. I promise."

He means it, I know he does, but before this happened, he didn't even want to be in the same room as me. If I let him take me back to his place and have him look after me, my heart is going to want things I can't have, even though my head knows he's moved on. Losing Cade Brookes was hard enough the first time around. I won't survive a second.

CHAPTER SEVEN

Cade

Stepping into the corridor, I silently close the door to Sophie's room behind me. She's been admitted to the obstetrics ward and they've just put up another bag of fluids. Visiting time is over, and while I could stay—no one is going to throw me out—I just need some time to process everything.

Before I head home, I make my way back to the ER and knock on the door to Harry Webster's office. He's my boss and the head of the trauma department.

"Come in," a voice shouts, and I push open the door and walk in.

"Cade. You're not working today, are you?" Harry asks.

"No. I'm here with a friend. She's been admitted."

"I'm sorry to hear that. I hope she's okay."

"I hope so too. That's actually why I'm here. I need to talk to you about taking some time off."

"Oh, sure. When and how long are you thinking?"

"Erm... now and about three months?"

He frowns. "Three months? Is everything okay? Take a seat." He gestures to the seat on the other side of his desk, and I sit down heavily, knowing I need to explain.

"The woman who's been admitted... she's pregnant with my baby and is suffering with hyperemesis gravidarum. She's already lost one baby. I can't let that happen again. I need to take care of them."

"Congratulations. I'm sorry she's having such a tough time." He takes a deep breath and drags his hand through his hair. "I'm not going to lie, Cade, I'm going to struggle to release you straight away for three months. I'm sorry. I can give you a few days. A week max."

"That's not enough, Harry. I can't leave her alone while I pull a fourteen-hour shift."

"Can't family help out?'

"She doesn't have anyone."

"I can give you a week, Cade."

I stand and pace the room. A week isn't long enough. HG could last until the baby is born, and while I can't have the whole pregnancy off work, I know she's going to need me in the next couple of months, even if she won't admit it.

"Then I quit. Sophie and this baby mean everything to me, and I *am* going to be there for them."

"Cade, you're going to have a baby to support. How are you going to do that without a job? Aside from the fact you've just made attending physician. I know that's something you've always wanted."

"I want this more. I've got money saved. I'll manage until I can find something else." I stop in front of the desk and hold out my hand. "It's been a pleasure working for you, sir."

"There's still your notice period. You can't just walk away, son."

"Then don't pay me. I know there's not much else you can do to stop me from going."

He sighs, knowing I'm right. "Good luck, Cade. With everything."

"Thanks."

When I get to my car, I sit for a few minutes, my hands gripping the steering wheel as the reality of what I've just done crashes over me. There's only one hospital in Hope Creek, and walking out like that pretty much secures the fact I'll never get another job there. There are other hospitals in neighboring towns I can try, though. Right now, I need to do this.

Needing to talk to someone, I find myself pulling up outside Nash's place. He's been asking for months for me to open up to him, but I just wasn't ready. I guess now I have no choice.

Knocking on the door, I smile when I hear Max barking. When the door swings open, Paisley's standing in the doorway, holding on to Max's collar.

"Cade! Come in." She steps to one side, and I slip past her into the house. When the door closes, Max goes mad, jumping up my legs. Bending down, I run my hands through his soft fur. "How's Sophie?" she asks.

I stand up and blow out a breath. "She's okay. They've admitted her for a few days. Do you think I could grab a beer?"

"Of course. Nash is in the kitchen cooking dinner. Why don't you join us? There's plenty."

"That would be great. Thanks, Paisley."

I follow her into the kitchen and she gestures for me to take a seat at the breakfast bar. Nash turns from the stove, his concerned eyes meeting mine.

"Hey, man. How's Sophie?"

"She's pregnant."

"Pregnant?" I nod. "It's yours?" I nod again.

"Fuck!"

"Yeah, that about sums it up."

"Is that what's making her so sick?" Paisley asks.

"Yeah. She's suffering from severe morning sickness. She's had two bags of IV fluids and they're looking at getting her on some medication. Once they've got that sorted, she should be allowed to come home. It's going to be a tough few months, though. I want her to come and stay with me. She shouldn't be on her own."

Paisley slides a bottle of Bud across the breakfast bar to me. "I'm going to give her a call and leave you two to talk. Does she have her phone?" she asks, and I nod. "Call me when dinner's ready, babe."

"Okay," Nash says. "Tell Sophie hi from me." She walks over to my brother and kisses him on the cheek.

When she's gone into the living room, Nash turns to me.

"How are you doing? It's a lot to take in."

"Honestly? I've no idea. I always thought when I had kids, it would be with the love of my life, and we'd be married and living in a house with a white picket fence. It couldn't be further from that."

He gives me a small smile. "You *are* having a baby with the love of your life, though, right?"

"She used to be."

"Do you think you'll be able to sort things out?"

"I don't know if either of us wants that. We've talked, but not properly."

"So you know why she left?"

I sigh. "Yeah, I know."

"Do you want to talk about it?"

"Not right now. I'm not sure I know everything myself. Not

yet." I take a pull of my beer, placing the bottle down on the countertop.

"Okay, well, I'm here when you're ready."

"Thanks, Nash."

"Does she know you want her to stay at your place?"

"I've mentioned it, but she didn't seem keen. She can't be on her own all day, though. She can barely make it to the bathroom."

"She's that sick?"

"Yeah. If she doesn't get fluids and food inside her, she and the baby are in real danger."

"Fuck. She's going to be okay, though?"

"I hope so. I need to look after them. I wasn't there last time. I *have* to be there this time."

"Last time?" He frowns before his eyes widen. "That's why she left?" I nod. "God, I'm sorry, Cade."

"Me too."

"What about work? Can you get some time off?"

"It seems not. I just quit."

"What? Does Sophie know?"

"No, and I don't want her to know. She feels guilty enough that her body is failing her. I don't want her to feel responsible for me quitting."

"It sounds to me like you still love her, Cade."

"Love was never the problem, but it's not always enough."

"No, but it's a good start."

I pick up my drink and swallow down a mouthful. "I've been dating a woman from work."

"You have?" he asks, his voice laced with surprise.

I nod. "Yeah. Sleeping with Sophie a few weeks ago made me realize I should try to move on. I've pretty much put my personal life on hold since she left. What happened between us showed me that."

"You like this woman?"

"I've always been so consumed with Sophie, no other relationship has ever worked. I've no idea if this one would have been any different. I need to talk to her, though."

Before Nash can say anything else, Paisley comes back into the kitchen with her phone in her hand.

"Did you talk to her?" I ask, noticing she hasn't been gone for long.

"Yeah, briefly. She kept throwing up."

"Fuck." I drag my hand through my hair and drop my head. "How was she other than that?"

"Teary. I think she's scared."

My heart squeezes in my chest, and I hate to think of her scared and alone at the hospital. I know technically she's not alone. She'll be surrounded by nursing staff, but it's not the same. "I should go back."

I stand from the breakfast bar and Paisley puts her hand on my arm. "At least have some food before you go. Have you eaten today?"

"Not since this morning."

"Then stay. You're no good to Sophie if you don't look after yourself."

"Okay. Thanks, Paisley."

"We're all here for you, Cade. You and Sophie. You just have to let us help you," she says.

"I know, and I'm grateful. I'm sure Soph will be too. I think she's going to need her friends."

After I've eaten, I head back to the hospital, stopping for flowers on the way. It's been years since I brought Sophie flowers, but I remember stargazer lilies are her favorite. When I get up to the floor she's on, I stop at the nurses' station and ask to see her chart. As my eyes flick over it, I breathe a sigh of relief that her blood work is back and it's good. All her organs are functioning within normal ranges. We just need to keep her hydrated. My heart sinks, though, when I see they've tried giving her some food and she brought it all back up. Fluids are important, but food is too. The baby will take what it needs from her and she's already lost so much weight. It kills me knowing I can't make her feel better. I'm a doctor; I should be helping her.

CHAPTER EIGHT

Sophie

It's dark when I open my eyes, and I'm surprised to see Cade fast asleep in the reclining chair next to my bed. I wasn't expecting him to come back tonight. After he'd left earlier, I'd been given some more fluids and I was beginning to feel a little more human. My headache had all but gone, and I'd even been brave enough to try some toast. That was when things started to go downhill again. I'd barely swallowed the last mouthful when I started throwing up, and I'd thrown up every few minutes for over an hour. There was nothing left in my stomach after the first three or four times, and after that, it was back to the dry heaving. I'd even started bringing up blood. I'd been so scared. Maybe the nurses called him and that's why he's here. Either way, I'm glad I'm not alone.

Turning on my side, I stare at him as he sleeps. I love him so much it almost hurts to have him here knowing he's not mine and never will be. As sick as I felt earlier, I noticed how beautiful Elise was. I don't want to hear the details about their relationship, but I guess we'll need to have a conversation if I end up staying at his place and they continue to see each other.

I drop my hand over my flat stomach. This baby is going to tie us together forever, but not in the way I imagined. Sleeping together had been a mistake, no matter how much I'd wanted him. Despite that, I don't regret it. How could I? Look what it's given me. A piece of him to keep forever.

"Please hang on, little one," I whisper to my stomach. "I don't think I'll survive losing you and your daddy."

"Sophie?" Cade says quietly.

My cheeks flush with heat at the thought he may have heard me. "Hey. I wasn't expecting to see you again today."

He sits up in the chair. "I wanted to make sure you're okay. How are you feeling?"

I shrug. "Not as bad as this morning. I tried some toast, but it didn't end well."

He smiles sympathetically. "Yeah, I saw on your chart. What about water?"

"I've managed to keep some down, I think. I'm not sure if the anti-nausea meds the doctor gave me are working a little or whether I threw them all up with the toast."

"You should be able to have some more in a few hours."

I look to the dresser behind him, seeing a vase of lilies that wasn't there earlier. "Did you buy me flowers?" I ask, my voice not hiding my surprise. He nods. "Lilies are my favorite."

"I know. I remember," he whispers. His eyes hold mine, and I can't look away.

Our connection is broken when one of the nurses walks in.

"Hi, Sophie. I just need to check your vitals."

"Okay," I say quietly, dragging my eyes off Cade.

I'm silent while she takes my blood pressure, temperature, and pulse, writing them down on the chart she's brought in with her. When she goes to leave, Cade stands.

"Could I take a look?"

"Of course, Dr. Brookes." She hands him the chart. "I'll leave it with you."

"Does everything look okay?" I ask when the nurse has left the room.

"Your blood pressure is still a little low, but that's to be expected. Everything else looks good. Did the doctor talk to you about the blood they took in the ER?"

"No. Were they okay?" My voice wobbles, and he sits on the edge of the bed.

"They were good. Everything is working as it should." My eyes sting with tears, and before I can stop myself, I'm crying. "Hey," he soothes. "It's good news."

"I know. I'm sorry. I just feel so drained and exhausted. I don't know how I'm going to get through the next few months. I'm going to have to close the shelter."

"Don't worry about that right now. Everyone, including me, is going to be there for you."

Despite his words, I can't stop the tears from falling. Before I can comprehend what's happening, he's climbing onto the bed and pulling me into his arms. My head comes to rest on his chest and his arms envelop me. I close my eyes and sink against him. Nothing feels as good as being in his arms, and after the day I've had, it's exactly what I need.

"Will you get into trouble for being on the bed?" I ask into his chest.

"No. The nurses love me." His voice is laced with humor, and I can't help but smile. I bet they do. He's gorgeous.

"Thank you for being here."

His chest rises and falls with a sigh, and I know this can't be easy for him. We desperately need to talk, but I just don't have the energy, and selfishly, I want to stay wrapped in his arms.

"When do you work next?"

"I'm not. I've taken some time off."

I tilt my head to look at him. "Why?"

"Because I meant what I said, Sophie. I'm not letting you do this on your own, and I can't look after you if I'm working fourteen-hour shifts."

"But your job—"

"Is just a job and will still be there when you're feeling better. Don't worry about it."

I drop my head back onto his chest and bite down on my bottom lip. I can't believe he's taken time off to look after me. The doctor I saw earlier told me the HG could last until, at best, sixteen weeks. I'm only eight weeks now. That's two months. I'm guessing Cade knows that. He's a doctor, after all, albeit in the ER and not obstetrics. He can't really be talking about taking two months off work, though, can he?

Despite my mind swirling with questions, a wave of exhaustion washes over me, and I close my eyes as I nestle against Cade's chest. I try not to think about how gross I feel not having showered for a couple of days, not to mention all the vomiting. I hope I don't smell.

OPENING MY EYES, IT TAKES ME A SECOND TO REALIZE I'M IN THE hospital and still lying in Cade's arms. It must be early morning, and sunlight streaks through the blinds of my hospital room. I've slept all night against his chest, and I tilt my head, seeing he's still asleep. I hope he's managed as good a night as I have. I lie still, not wanting to move and wake him. I want to make the most of being in his arms. Once I'm discharged, it's unlikely to happen again.

Even though I know anything I eat will likely come back up, my stomach hurts from the lack of food, and I don't know what's better. Not eating to ensure no vomiting, or trying to eat something to ease the pain. It's a no-win situation when the outcome is either pain, vomiting, or both.

"Morning," Cade says quietly, and I lift my head to look at him.

"Morning."

"How are you feeling?"

"Hungry."

He smiles. "That's good."

"I'm almost afraid to eat," I whisper.

"You have to try," he says gently.

I sigh. "I know. I hope I can have a shower this morning. I feel gross."

His jaw clenches and he swallows thickly. "I can help you."

"I'm sure I can ask one of the nurses."

"No. I'll help you."

"Okay. Thank you."

"Do you want to try some toast?" I nod. "I'll go and get you some."

I sit up, and he climbs off the bed. He stretches his arms, and I try not to stare at his toned stomach as his t-shirt rides up. Swinging my legs to the side of the bed, I sit for a second as the dizziness passes.

"Would you help me to the bathroom before you go?"

"Sure."

I use the toilet and brush my teeth while Cade waits on the other side of the door. When I'm done, his arm goes around my waist again and he leads me back to the bed.

"I'll go and get that toast. You should be due some anti-nausea medication too."

I drop my head back on the pillow, exhausted from just going to the bathroom. Despite being desperate for a shower, I have no idea how I'm going to get through one, not when brushing my teeth wears me out.

When Cade returns, he's carrying a slice of toast and a little plastic cup containing some anti-nausea medication. I really want the meds to work. I want to go home. I swallow down the tablets with a tiny sip of water, the liquid feeling good in my dry throat.

"Maybe you should shower before trying to eat. At least that way it'll give the meds a chance to get in your system. If the toast does make you sick, you won't be throwing them back up. What do you think? Do you have the energy for a shower?"

"Not really, but I'd like to try."

"Okay. I'll get you some fresh toast when we're done."

"Are you sure you don't mind helping me? I can ask a nurse."

"It'll be quicker if I help. It's fine."

He scoops me into his arms and carries me to the bathroom. "What are you doing?" I ask, my cheeks flushing with heat.

"Conserving your energy."

He sets me down on the closed toilet seat and reaches inside my bag for my toiletries. The bathroom is set up as a wet room, and a large open shower sits across from the toilet. He puts my shower gel and shampoo on a small shelf and turns the shower on to warm up. I try not to stare as he removes his shorts and t-shirt, but I'm not very successful, and he clears his throat as he holds out his hand.

"Stand up and I'll help you with your clothes."

"Okay, yes," I mumble as I'm pulled from my Cade haze. I lift my hands in the air and he pulls my pajama top over my head before pushing my sleep shorts down my legs and holding my hand as I step out of them. Now we're both in our underwear, and

ECHOES OF LOVE

I wish I didn't feel like shit so I could truly appreciate just how good he looks. He's filled out since we were kids, and he seems broader somehow. It's clear he works out, and I can't help my eyes dropping to his defined abs. His arms are still my favorite part of him, though, and I loved how it used to feel to have them wrapped around me. I drop my eyes and close them, praying the tears that are building don't fall.

"God, you've lost so much weight, Soph," he says, his voice low. I look up to see his eyes tracking over my body. Feeling self-conscious, I wrap my arms around myself and sit down on the closed toilet. "Shit. I'm sorry. I didn't mean that to sound…" He trails off and sighs. "You still look beautiful." He takes a step toward me and takes my hand, pulling me to stand. "Let's get you showered."

He reaches around my back and undoes my bra, slowly pulling the material from my body. I reach for the edge of my panties and drag them down my legs before kicking them off. His arm slips around me and we walk the short distance to the running shower. He puts his hand under the spray to check the temperature before guiding me underneath. I let out a little moan as the hot water cascades over my tired body. It feels so good, and I tilt my head back, letting the water fall over my face. With my eyes closed, I stand like that for a few minutes until Cade chuckles.

"Does that feel good?" he asks, his arm still around me.

"Mmmmm," I mutter. "You have no idea."

"Do you want me to wash your hair?"

I open my eyes and turn to him. "I think I'll be okay to do it." He nods, and I drop my head back under the spray, lifting my hands into my hair to make sure it's wet through. His arm falls from around me, and when I open my eyes, he's holding out the shampoo. I let him squeeze some into my hands. "Thanks," I whisper.

I do my best to lather the shampoo into my hair, but after only a few seconds, I feel exhausted and my legs begin to shake. Cade immediately slips his arm back around me.

"Will you let me do it?" he asks, and I nod.

He guides me to the pull-down chair and sits me down, both of his hands going into my hair. As he massages my scalp, I close my eyes, mainly because it feels so good, but also because my eyes are now level with his hardening cock that I can see the outline of through his wet boxer shorts.

"Can you stand?" he asks, his voice husky.

I open my eyes and nod as I reach for his outstretched hand. He gently pulls me up and guides me back under the spray.

"Put your arms around my waist so you don't fall and I'll rinse out the shampoo."

I do as he says, but it's a little awkward as I arch my back to get my hair under the spray while trying to hold on to him. It feels like I'm pushing my chest in his face and my hips against his. When my hips brush his erection, his hands still in my hair.

"I'm sorry," he whispers. "I know how inappropriate that is."

I squeeze his waist, not knowing what to say. I kind of love I'm having that effect on him, but I don't want to tell him that.

"I think maybe taking a bath will be easier than a shower next time," he says as his fingers continue to run through my hair.

Next time? What next time? There is no bath here.

"I'll quickly wash you and then we can dry off."

I lift my head and drop my arms from around him, quickly grabbing on to his hand as a wave of dizziness crashes over me. His arms slide around me, and he pulls me against him.

"You okay?" His voice is full of concern, and I drop my head onto his chest, waiting for the dizziness to pass. It doesn't pass, though, and black dots begin to dance in my vision.

"Cade," I whisper before everything fades to black.

CHAPTER NINE

Cade

I catch Sophie as she passes out and sit down on the shower floor with her in my arms. I hate that she's going through this and I can't do anything to help her. Thank God I didn't let her shower on her own. I reach down and brush a piece of her wet hair off her face. She looks so pale. Maybe the water was a little too warm, and that on top of everything else was just too much for her. Even though she's sick, she still sets me on fire, and I know she felt how my body reacted to her being naked in my arms. I'm an asshole. She's feeling like crap and I'm getting hard when I should be looking after her. She must think I'm a jerk.

Her eyes flicker open, and I see the panic in them as she lifts her head and looks around.

"Hey, I've got you. You're safe." She drops her head back on my chest and bursts into tears. "Please don't cry," I whisper, holding her closer.

"I just want it all to be over, Cade. I don't know if I can do this." Her voice is barely audible over the pounding of the water, but I hear her.

"You can. I'm right here with you."

"I want to go home."

I want to get her out of here too. There's nothing they're doing for her here that I can't do at my place. I can give her the meds and set up her IVs. I'll bring her back if things get worse.

"Let's get dry and we'll see about getting you out of here."

She looks up at me, her eyes wide. "Really?"

"Really."

I don't tell her she's coming back to my place, though. Not yet. I'll talk to her when she's settled back in bed. I know I mentioned it yesterday, but surely she realizes now that she can't be on her own.

I stand up with her in my arms, and she shivers when the hot water stops falling on her. I set her on the closed toilet and grab one of the towels, wrapping it around her. Her teeth chatter as I dry her, and her eyes stay fixed on me. After helping her into some clean panties and pajamas, I quickly dry myself, removing my wet boxer shorts and pulling my shorts and t-shirt back on. Scooping her into my arms, I carry her out of the bathroom and lay her on the bed.

"Let's try some more toast, and then I'll go and talk to one of the doctors." I pick up the plate of now-cold toast I brought in before the shower and head for the door.

"That toast will be fine," she says, gesturing to the plate.

I look down at it. "I can get you some fresh."

She smiles and places her hand over her flat stomach. "I like cold toast. Maybe this little one will too."

I smile back. "Okay." I cross the room and hand her the plate. "I'll be right back."

As I close her door behind me, I spot Dr. Black at the nurses' station. Making my way over, I wait until he's finished his conversation.

"Dr. Brookes," he says as he turns around. "How's Sophie doing?"

"She's just trying to eat something. Look, I want to take her home. I can give her the meds and set up her IVs there. Her blood work was all good, and if anything changes, I'll bring her straight back. What do you think?"

"Okay. If that's what Sophie wants. Everything we can give her here, you can do at home. I'll get the paperwork done and some fluids to send home with her."

I hold out my hand, and he shakes it. "Thank you."

I go back to Sophie, finding her asleep and the plate with the toast is empty. I hope she can keep it down. Her body desperately needs it. I pack up the few things she brought with her while she sleeps, stopping when my fingers land on the sonogram images Dr. Black gave us yesterday. I've done plenty of emergency ultra-sounds in the ER, and I've watched countless guys overcome with emotion when the sound of their baby's heartbeat fills the room. Yesterday, I was one of those guys. I didn't really appreciate what I was seeing before, but now I do, and I fell in love the second I saw our baby on the screen. It's hard to explain how something so small can grab on to your heart so quickly and never let go.

"Hey," Sophie says, her voice thick with sleep. "What are you looking at?"

"Just the sonogram pictures." I cross the room and sit on the side of her bed. "Dr. Black has agreed you can go home." Her face lights up, and I smile.

"He has?"

"Yep. He's just sorting the discharge papers and some fluids and cannulas to send home with you."

"Thank you."

"You know you have to come and stay at my place, don't you?"

She bites down on her bottom lip. "Are you sure that's what you want? Can't you just come to my house to change the IV?"

"It's not just the IV. What about when you're too weak to make it to the bathroom, or you need a shower and you pass out? Who's going to make sure you eat?"

She sighs. "I feel like such a burden."

"Sophie, you're carrying my child. You are not a burden. I want to do this."

She holds my gaze while her fingers pull at a loose piece of cotton on the sheet that's covering her. "Okay, if you're sure."

"I'm sure."

I look back down at the images in my hand. "Do you have any sonogram pictures from... before?" I ask awkwardly.

"Yes. Just one."

"I'd love to see it, if that's okay?"

"Of course it is."

We fall silent, and one of the nurses comes in to take her vitals for discharge. Her blood pressure is still low, but everything else looks good. When she's gone, Sophie slowly moves so she's sitting on the edge of the bed.

"Could you pass me my bag, please?"

"Sure." Reaching to where it sits on the floor, I scoop it up and put it on the bed next to her. She digs around inside, pulling out her hairbrush. I watch as she brushes her hair and braids it, securing it with a hair tie that was looped around the handle of her hairbrush.

"Should I get dressed? I'm not sure I can be bothered. It's such an effort."

"No, stay in your pajamas. You'll be going straight from this bed into mine."

"Your bed?" she whispers.

"My guest bed, Soph."

"Oh." Her cheeks flush pink and she nods. "Can we stop by my house so I can pick up some things?"

"Of course."

* * *

An hour and a half later, I pull into the underground parking garage of my apartment building. It's a fairly new development on the edge of Hope Creek, and I've been here about twelve months. The complex has a fully equipped gym, along with an indoor pool and sauna. It was the facilities that attracted me to the place. Working long hours at the hospital means I'm not home much, but having a gym and pool on site makes working out easier after a long shift.

"This is me," I tell Sophie, parking in my designated space and cutting the engine. Climbing out of the car, I go around to the passenger side and help her out. "Let me grab your bag."

We stopped at Sophie's place after leaving the hospital, and I helped her pack some of her stuff. Hopefully, she has everything she needs. If not, I can always go back for anything she's forgotten. I reach into the back and pluck out her bag, along with all the things the hospital gave me for her IV and meds. With my arm around Sophie, I guide her toward the elevator.

"How long have you lived here?" Sophie asks as we ride the car up to my floor.

"About a year. I'm not home much. It'll be nice to actually spend some time here."

The elevator doors open and we walk along the hallway, stopping when we reach my apartment. Opening the door, I slip my arm from around her and let her go in ahead of me.

"Wow, Cade. This is nice!"

I chuckle. "Thanks."

It is a nice apartment. There's a large entryway leading into a spacious open-plan kitchen and living room with double doors leading off the living room onto a balcony. The view isn't bad with the mountains and lake in the distance. A hallway to the left leads to two double bedrooms, both with their own bathroom. I know Sophie will be comfortable in the guest room.

"Come on, I'll show you where you'll be sleeping."

I gesture to the hallway and she goes ahead of me, stopping when she comes to two doors, one opposite the other.

"Which one is me?" she asks shyly.

"This one." I open the door to the left and she walks inside. I drop her bag on the bed and open the drapes to let in some light. "There's a walk-in closet where you can put your stuff. I can help you unpack, and this is the bathroom." I open the door and gesture inside.

"It's great, Cade. Thank you."

"How are you feeling?"

"A little nauseous, but I don't think I'm going to be sick. Do you mind if I lie on the sofa? I'm tired but fed up of being in bed."

"Sure. We can put a movie on. Do you want me to unpack your stuff?"

"Nah, leave it. I'll do it later. I will grab my phone, though." She reaches inside her bag and takes out her phone.

We make our way back into the living room and she flops down onto the sofa. "Do you want a drink?" I ask, heading into the kitchen.

"Just some water, please, and a bucket."

"Are you going to be sick?"

"No, but I'm not sure I'll make it to the bathroom if I need to be."

"Okay." I hope the anti-nausea meds keep working for her and she gets some rest from throwing up.

I reach into the refrigerator and pull out two bottles of water before looking under the sink for a bucket. On finding one, I go back to the living room. I hand over the water and place the bucket on the floor.

"Do you want a blanket or anything?"

She smiles. "I'm good."

I watch her struggling to open her water, and I reach over and take it from her. "Here, let me."

"Thanks," she says as I pass her back the open bottle. She takes the smallest of sips before replacing the lid. "I'm so scared I'm going to start vomiting again," she says quietly. "This is the longest I've gone without throwing up." She turns to me, her eyes wide. "What if the sickness has stopped because something is wrong with the baby?"

I reach over and take her hand. "There's nothing wrong with the baby, Sophie. It's just the medication working. Everything is fine. I promise."

She drops her head back onto the sofa. "God, I feel like I'm going crazy."

"It's normal to be apprehensive, especially after everything you've been through."

"Yeah, I guess."

I don't know if it's too soon to ask her to tell me what happened all those years ago. I have so many questions I need answers to. I don't want to upset her when she feels unwell, but I need to know.

CHAPTER TEN

Sophie

Sitting on Cade's sofa, I feel the best I've felt in days. I could sleep for a week, but there's only a slight headache now, and although I feel sick, I don't think I'm going to be. I've spent days wishing the vomiting would stop. As soon as it does, I'm questioning what that means. I hope Cade's right and it's stopped because the meds are working.

Despite feeling a little better, I can't help but feel awkward being in Cade's space. He's been so good to me over the past twenty-four hours, and after everything that's happened, I'm not sure I deserve it.

"Soph, what happened all those years ago?" he asks quietly, and nerves swirl in my stomach. It's a conversation that's long overdue, but I'm apprehensive to bare my soul to him. I know he has to know, though.

Sighing, I curl my legs underneath me and turn to face him. "I found out I was pregnant just as you started your summer internship. I thought I had a stomach flu, but when I was still vomiting a week later, my mom asked if there was a chance I could be pregnant. It hadn't even crossed my mind. I was on birth control."

"Why didn't you tell me?"

"I knew you'd have come home."

"Damn right I would have come home. You know I would have wanted to be with you."

"And that's why I didn't tell you. I knew you'd want to quit school to take care of us. I didn't want you to have to give up your dream."

"So, what, you were never going to tell me?" he asks exasperatedly. "Didn't you think I deserved to know?"

"Yes," I whisper. "Mom begged me to tell you. I wanted to prove to you we could manage first, and that you could continue with your education. I was always going to tell you. I thought I was doing the right thing. I didn't want you to give up everything you'd ever wanted."

"*You* were everything I ever wanted, Sophie," he whispers.

"You were everything I wanted too. I made the decision I did because I loved you. I know it doesn't make any sense now, but I thought it did at the time."

"What about after you had the termination? Why didn't you come and tell me then?"

"I was a mess. I blamed myself and hit rock bottom. I should have started law school, but I dropped out. I couldn't even drag myself out of bed, let alone concentrate enough to study. I wanted to call you so many times, but I convinced myself you'd hate me. It was my fault I couldn't keep our baby safe, and I couldn't bear to see the devastation in your eyes when you found out what I'd done." I drop my eyes from his and stare at my lap.

"Did you really think that little of me?" he asks, the hurt evident in his tone.

My eyes shoot up to his. "What?"

"I loved you, Sophie. With every part of me. I thought we'd be together forever. I never would have blamed you. You didn't choose to end the pregnancy." He drops his head in his hands and my stomach rolls. "Do you know how completely and utterly heartbroken I was to never see you again and to never know what I did to make you leave me?"

"You didn't do anything," I whisper, tears tracking down my face. "I was wrong, Cade. So wrong, and I regret my decision every minute of every day. If I could turn back the clock, I would do things so differently, but I can't, and because of that, I lost everything."

"So did I. I didn't just lose the woman I loved, I lost my best friend. My soul mate. I *never* got over you, Sophie. You don't get over a love like we had. I've just existed for the past fourteen years. My life pretty much ended when you left."

"Cade," I whisper, my heart breaking when I see tears running down his face.

He shakes his head. "Why didn't you come back sooner?"

"It took me months to accept what had happened, and the longer I stayed away, the harder it was to come back. I convinced myself you'd moved on and that coming back would only bring all the pain to the surface. I'd tried so hard to bury all of my feelings, and I couldn't deal with your feelings as well as mine. Not when I was only holding on by a thread."

"I never moved on. I tried a few times, but nothing felt right."

An image of him and Elise together pops into my mind, and I can't help but wonder if she's the woman he might move on with. "I'm so sorry, Cade. The last thing I ever wanted to do was hurt you."

He nods and stands up, sighing deeply. "I'll be in my room if you need me."

I watch him leave and curl up on the sofa as sobs wrack my

body. I know there's no chance we can ever come back from what I did. I broke him, and nothing I can say or do will change that. Despite being here with him now, I know after hearing him on the phone yesterday, I'm here out of some misguided obligation. He cares for me as the mother of his child, but I can never be anything more, and it feels like I'm losing him all over again, which is ridiculous when it's been years since he was mine. We're only in this position because of a moment of weakness. I might love him, and he might even love me, but I know now that's not enough. I ruined everything, and now I have to try and live with that.

CADE

LEAVING SOPHIE ON THE SOFA, I CLOSE MY BEDROOM DOOR BEHIND me and drop to the floor. I've waited fourteen years to hear the truth about what happened. I guess I always thought finding out would just give me more of a reason to hate her, but I can't fool myself anymore. I don't hate her. I never have. I really wanted to. I wanted to be able to push her from my head and heart and forget about her, but I never could.

As much as I don't want to admit it, what she said was right. If I had known about the baby, I would have left school. She was my world, and I'd have done anything for her. I couldn't have been four hours away while she stayed in Hope Creek and had our baby. I just wish she'd told me. I hate that she went through every-thing on her own.

As I replay over and over in my mind what she said, I realize for the first time that she was as devastated at leaving as I was that she'd left. It sounds like she really struggled for a long time after the termination, and her fear at what she thought she had a choice in kept her from me. The termination wasn't a choice. The baby wouldn't have survived and neither would she, but to make that decision alone... I can't comprehend what she went through. I would have given anything to have been there with her.

I stand up and strip out of my clothes. After sleeping at the hospital, I need a shower. Hopefully, standing under the hot spray will clear my head. I know we still have more to talk about, but I think we've shared enough for today. Everything else can wait.

I spend far too long under the water, and when I finally dry off and head back into the living room, Sophie isn't on the sofa where I left her. Sighing, I head into the kitchen and drop two slices of bread into the toaster. When it's done, I add some butter and pad silently down the hallway to her bedroom. I knock lightly on the door and wait.

"Come in," she says quietly.

My heart twists in my chest when I see her wipe her tearstained face. "I brought you some toast. Are you hungry?"

"A little."

I cross the room and put the plate on the nightstand. "Are you okay?"

She slowly sits up. "Are you?"

I drop down on the bed next to her. "As hard as it was to hear, I know it was harder for you to live it. We can't change the past. It's gone and that's all there is to it. I should have let you explain earlier. I know you tried. I just wasn't ready to listen."

"None of it is your fault, Cade. I should have come back sooner."

"I should have tried harder to find you."

"What?" she whispers.

"I begged your mom to tell me where you were, but she wouldn't. I should have tried harder to get her to tell me."

"I was with my aunt in River Falls," she says quietly.

My eyes widen in surprise. "You were in the next town over

the whole time?" I close my eyes and drag my hand through my hair. "Fuck. You were twenty minutes away."

"Not all the time. I was there for about a year and a half while I tried to pull myself together."

"Where did you go once you left your aunt's place?"

"Boston. I got a bachelor's in accounting and got a job there when I graduated."

"Accounting? What happened to law?"

She shrugs. "It just reminded me too much of everything I'd left behind. Studying law was part of the old me, and I wasn't that person anymore. I've always loved math, so accounting seemed a good fit."

I reach for the plate of toast and hand it to her. "Try and eat something."

"Okay."

She takes small mouthfuls, chewing slowly.

"I thought you'd fallen in love with someone else," I say softly.

She shakes her head. "Never."

I shrug. "I know how hard it was. We hardly saw each other." Being together while I was in school had been difficult. I tried to come back as much as possible. Sophie came to me a few times, but I was sharing a dorm room, and being together there was difficult. "I missed you so much."

"I missed you too."

"I shouldn't have taken that internship. I'd have been here with you when you found out if I hadn't."

She sighs. "You can't think like that. Trust me, I've spent years asking myself what would have happened if I'd done things differently. It eats you up inside."

She finishes eating and yawns.

"You must be exhausted," I say, standing. "I'll let you get some sleep. I'll be in the living room if you need me." She's brought in the bucket from the living room. I hope she won't need it.

"Do you still want to see the sonogram picture from before?" she asks quietly, just as I've made it to the bedroom door.

Turning around, my eyes find hers. "Did you bring it with you?"

She nods and slowly gets off the bed. Crossing the room, she goes to her bag on the floor and pulls out an envelope. My eyes drop to her hand and I take a deep breath as I sit back down on the bed. She comes and sits next to me.

"I only had one ultrasound, and the picture isn't as clear as the ones we've got for this little one." Her free hand goes to her flat stomach before she holds out the envelope. Taking a deep breath, I take it from her.

"How many weeks were you?" I ask, my eyes fixed on the envelope.

"Ten."

Opening the envelope, I pull out the picture, my eyes fixing on the grainy image in my hand. It might not be as clear as the images we got yesterday, but it still looks like a baby. Our baby. A million emotions crash over me, and I swing between heartbreak and anger. I don't want to be angry with her, and I'm only angry because she didn't give me the chance to be there for her. I know if I'd been there, the outcome would have been the same, but it was my baby too. I deserved to be there.

"I wish things could have been different," I tell her, brushing my thumb over the image.

"I wish that too."

"Thank you for showing me." I slip the image back into the envelope and pass it back to her. "You should get some sleep."

I stand up again and make for the door. "Cade, wait." I turn around, my eyes locking with hers. "I really am sorry. About everything."

I give her a small smile. "I know, Soph. Get some rest."

I head into the hallway, leaving her door slightly ajar. I want to be able to hear her if she needs me. I know how sorry she is. I can see it in her eyes when she looks at me, and I realize there's been an apology in her eyes every time I've seen her since she came back. I was destroyed when she left me, but there isn't just me to think about anymore. We're going to be parents. I have to leave behind how devastated I was and move forward. A part of me thinks we should see if what was between us before is still there, or if what we've weathered is just too much to come back from. For now, though, I just need to look after her and our baby. That's all that matters. Trying to repair my shattered heart will have to wait.

CHAPTER ELEVEN

Sophie

I watch as Cade leaves the room. He's been so incredible about everything, and part of me wonders if it's just because I'm so sick. If I wasn't, I'm sure he'd be angrier with me. Things have been tense between us ever since I came back to Hope Creek. Other than the night I got pregnant, and a pretty intense kiss in Eden one night, he's barely been able to look me in the eye.

Lying down, my eyes fall closed. I'm so tired. Paisley's sent me a message, but I don't have the energy to reply. Maybe I'll feel a little better after taking a nap. I'm just falling asleep when my stomach rolls. My eyes fly open and my hand comes over my mouth. There's no way I'm going to make it to the bathroom in time. Instead, I lean over the bed and grab the bucket, throwing up everything I've just eaten. Tears streak down my face and my heart sinks. I'm not naïve enough to think just because I kept some food down earlier, I'm never going to throw up again, but a small part of me hoped I might make it at least twenty-four hours.

Climbing off the bed, I slowly make it into the bathroom. I get there just in time to vomit again. I throw up a couple of times before Cade appears at the bathroom door.

"Shit, Soph," he says, coming in and sitting on the floor with me. He lifts my hair off my neck and holds it back as I'm throwing up again.

"I hoped it might have stopped for a bit," I choke out, sitting back against the bathtub. He stands up and wets a washcloth before gently wiping my mouth.

"I'd hoped that too. Do you feel like you're going to be sick again?"

Before I can answer, my head's back over the toilet and he's rubbing my back. I end up spending nearly an hour on the bathroom floor, and he stays with me the whole time. When I think it's finally stopped, I'm almost asleep against him.

"Let's get you back to bed," he whispers against my hair.

"I need to brush my teeth," I mumble. "My mouth feels gross."

"Wait there." He lays me on the bathroom mat and disappears into the bedroom. When he returns, he's holding my toothbrush and toothpaste. I'm barely conscious, but he sits me up and gently brushes my teeth. He picks me up and holds me by the sink as I spit out the toothpaste.

"Thank you," I mumble, my head on his shoulder. He climbs on the bed with me, and I reach for his arm as he lays me down. "Will you stay? Just until I fall asleep." I know it's unfair to ask, but I'm feeling emotional and I don't want to be on my own.

"Okay."

He lies next to me, and I turn on my side to face him. My eyelids are heavy and I can't fight the exhaustion. I inhale deeply, the familiar woodsy scent of his cologne invading my senses. The scent evokes memories from years ago, and I fall asleep, hoping my dreams take me back to being in his arms.

I OPEN MY EYES AND ROLL TO ONE SIDE, FINDING I'M ALONE. I didn't expect Cade to stay with me, even if a tiny part of me wishes he had. I roll onto my back and rub my temple with my fingers. My head is pounding again and I wonder how long I've been asleep. I reach for my phone from the nightstand. It's mid-afternoon. I never replied to Paisley's message from earlier, so I pull it up and re-read what she sent.

Paisley: Hey, Sophie. How are you feeling? Can I come and see you? Is there anything you need from home?

I'm guessing Cade hasn't told them I'm staying with him. I can't really tell her she can come and visit without asking him. Paisley might be his brother's girlfriend, but it's still not my apartment. I sit up and wait for a wave of dizziness to pass before climbing off the bed and slowly making my way to the living room. I come to a stop in the entryway when I hear Cade on the phone.

"No, she's asleep… I'm not sure when I can get away. I need to make sure she's okay before I leave her."

My heart twists in my chest, and I know it's Elise he's talking to. I feel like an intruder listening to his conversation, and I turn around to head back to my bedroom.

"Hey, I need to go. Can I call you back?" I look over my shoulder, my eyes meeting his. He ends the call and stands.

"You're awake," he says, crossing the room and taking my hand in his. "You should have called for me."

"Sorry if I interrupted your phone call."

ECHOES OF LOVE

"It's fine." He waves his free hand dismissively.

"If you need to go somewhere, I'll be fine here."

He sighs and drags his hand through his hair. "I do need to go out at some point, but not today."

"Okay," I whisper. Part of me wants to ask him about Elise, but I'm terrified to hear what he's going to say.

"How are you feeling?"

"My head hurts."

He guides me to the sofa and sits me down. "I need to check you over. I think you need more fluids. I'll get my bag."

I watch as he crosses the room and comes back with his bag. "Paisley messaged asking if she can come and see me," I tell him as he gets out the blood pressure machine and thermometer. "I think she might think I'm still at the hospital. Did you tell Nash I'm here?"

"No. I haven't spoken to him yet."

"Would it be okay if she came over?"

He stares at me, a surprised look on his face. "Of course she can. You're going to be here for a couple of months at least, Sophie. You can have your friends over. You don't have to ask."

"There's only really Paisley, but thank you."

"You're friends with Ashlyn, aren't you? And what about Bree Peters?"

"Yeah, I guess. I always feel a little weird around Bree. I know Nash is close to her and Leo, and when I came back, I didn't know how she'd be around me. I thought her allegiance would have been to you since you're Nash's brother."

He frowns. "Is that why you never really went out much before Paisley showed up? You cared about what people thought?"

"It's a small town, Cade. Everyone knows everyone, and I can only imagine the gossip when I left. Your family has always been at the center of Hope Creek and I knew everyone would hate me."

85

LAURA FARR

My voice has dropped to a whisper, and my fingers play with the edge of my tank.

He sighs. "No one that matters hates you, Sophie, especially not my family. I know my mom misses you."

I lift my head, my eyes finding his. "She does?"

He nods. "Yeah. You two were close."

"I miss her too," I whisper, biting on the inside of my cheek to stop the tears that are threatening to fall.

I was always close to my mom, but she was often busy with the shelter. When Cade and I got together, Tessa was like a second mom to me. I've only seen her a handful of times in the last eighteen months, and never to talk to. I'm ashamed to say I've almost avoided her. I have no idea what I'd say if we ever came face-to-face. I hurt her son, so I can only imagine what she thinks of me.

"She's going to be so excited about becoming a grams," he says, taking my hand and squeezing it gently.

"When are you going to tell them?"

"When you're well enough. We can either ask them to come here or go over and see them. Nash, Paisley, and Seb know already. I hope it's okay I told them."

"Of course it's okay. It's your baby too." I bite down nervously on my bottom lip. "You want me to be with you when you tell your parents?" I ask.

"Yes. Is that okay?"

I nod and continue to chew on my lip. Despite desperately wanting to reconnect with Cade's parents, I can't deny I'm nervous. I know I must have hurt everyone when I left, and I'm worried about how they'll be with me. I've managed to build a relationship back up with Nash, and Seb and Ashlyn were only kids when I left and have both been great, Seb especially.

"I can see your mind working overtime, Sophie. What are you thinking?"

ECHOES OF LOVE

"I hurt you. I'm worried what you parents are going to think, especially now that we're having a baby."

"They're going to be happy, I promise."

"I hope so." He sounds so sure, but I'm not.

He smiles reassuringly. "Let's get you checked over."

I watch him while he takes my vitals, my mind racing with our conversation. I try to push down my nerves, knowing I don't have to face them yet. Maybe Cade will decide to tell them on his own if I'm still feeling unwell in a couple of weeks. Especially if Nash and Seb know.

"You need some fluids, Soph. I'm going to grab the IV stuff the hospital gave you."

He walks toward my room where I know the bag is, and I sigh. I have a huge bruise on my hand from where the last cannula was. When he returns, he sets everything up on the side table next to the sofa. He picks up my hand and sees the bruise.

"Fuck. I didn't realize you had this. Is it sore?"

"Yeah, a little. Can the cannula go in my other hand?"

"Of course. I think I might leave this one in for a couple of days in case you need some more fluids after this." He reaches for one of the sofa cushions and puts it under my arm, resting my hand on top. He picks up the needle and squeezes my hand. "Are you ready?"

I nod and close my eyes. I wince when I feel the needle go in, but within seconds, the pain has gone. I open my eyes to see him putting an adhesive dressing over the cannula.

"You okay?"

"Yeah. It didn't hurt as much as the last time."

"You're dehydrated, but not as much as before, so your veins are still okay. I'm sorry I hurt you last time."

"It wasn't your fault."

"I just need to flush the cannula and then I can set up the fluids." He does what he needs to, and within minutes, the fluids are going in. "You should message Paisley and ask her to come over if you're feeling up to it."

"If you're sure you don't mind."

"I don't mind at all."

He clears away the stuff he's used, and I reach for my phone, deciding to call Paisley instead of messaging her. Finding her number, I put the phone to my ear.

"Sophie, hey. How are you?" Paisley asks when she answers.

"Hi, Paisley. I'm okay. Sorry I haven't replied to your message. I've been asleep."

"That's okay. Can I come and see you? Is Cade still there?"

"Yeah, he's here." I smile at him as he comes to sit next to me on the sofa.

"Do you want me to wait until he goes home?"

"Actually, I'm out of the hospital. I'm staying at Cade's place for a few weeks."

"That's great. Cade did mention you might be staying with him. How are you feeling about being there?" I slide my eyes to Cade, who's staring at me. He has to be able to hear what Paisley's saying with him sitting so close.

"Erm, yeah, it's fine," I say non-committally.

"Can he hear me?" she whispers, and I smile.

"Yep."

She laughs. "Okay, we'll talk later, then. Can we come over now? Do you need anything from the house?"

"Yeah, you can come now. Cade took me home before we came here, so I have everything, but thanks."

"Okay. See you soon. You too, Cade," she shouts before ending the call. I drop my phone onto the sofa next to me and turn to face him.

"Paisley and Nash are heading over."

He laughs. "Yeah, I heard. Do you need anything? Drink? Toast? A blanket?"

"I'm good, thanks."

He's been so attentive, and I know after everything I've done, I'm lucky he's taking care of me so well. I need to stop hoping this baby can bring us back together. We're speaking now, and friendly. That's more than I've had for the past fourteen years. It's not what I want, but I guess having him in my life like this is better than not at all. I just need to remember that when he's being incredible and making me feel like the most important person in his world. I'm far from that.

CHAPTER TWELVE

Cade

I try not to listen to Sophie's phone call with Paisley, even though it's almost impossible when I'm sitting right next to her. When I hear Paisley ask her how she feels about staying here, I can't help but wonder myself. I know how she feels about me; she told me the day we slept together. It can't be easy for her. I know it isn't easy for me, and I know I'm going to have to tell her about Elise at some point. Not today, though. I can't find the words.

When she gets off the phone with Paisley, she lies down and falls asleep. I cover her with a blanket, and after checking her IV, I head into the kitchen and grab a bottle of Bud. It's only late afternoon, but I need a drink. It's been a hell of a few days, and my whole world feels like it's tilted on its axis since Paisley called me and told me Sophie was unwell. I had no idea what to expect when I showed up at her house, but as soon as I saw her, I knew whatever was wrong, it was serious.

Taking a pull of my beer, I reach for my phone and fire off a message to Elise.

Me: Hey, sorry I had to cut our phone call short. Can we meet up to talk?

I slide my phone into my pocket and go back to the sofa. I sit down next to Sophie and pick up her legs, resting them over my lap. She's restless in her sleep, and I watch as she frowns, tears falling down her cheeks. Taking her hand in mine, I gently rub my thumb over her skin, conscious of the bruise on the back of her hand. I can't help but wonder what she's dreaming about. Whatever it is, it isn't anything good. After a few minutes, she wakes up with a start, her breathing a little labored.

"Bad dream?" I ask, her hand still encased in mine.

She lifts her other hand to her face and covers her eyes.

"Yeah."

"Do you want to talk about it?"

She shakes her head. "I really want this baby, Cade," she whispers, dropping her hand from her eyes. "I know our situation isn't perfect, but I'm already head over heels in love with him or her. I can't lose this one."

My heart stutters in my chest as I stare at her. I let go of her hand and place mine over her flat stomach. "I'm not going to let anything happen to you or this baby, okay? This is a second chance."

Her eyes widen, and she begins to say something but she's interrupted when the intercom sounds.

"That'll be Paisley and Nash," she says quietly.

I sigh and lift her legs. Standing, I lower them back down onto the sofa. "I'll let them in." As I cross the room to the intercom, I can't help but wonder if this baby could be a second chance for us too. I never thought I'd be able to forgive her for leaving all those years ago, but when I found out the reason she left, it changed everything. It wasn't like any of the hundreds of scenarios I'd thought about, and my conversation with my mom from a few weeks ago plays in my mind. Could it be something we can get past if I can open my heart to her again? I have no idea.

I lift the intercom phone and press the button to open the door downstairs. I swing open the apartment door and go back to Sophie, kneeling on the floor.

"How are you feeling? How's the headache?"

"A little better. Do you think I should try some more food? What if I'm starving the baby again?"

"You won't be starving the baby. We can try something else when Nash and Paisley go. Maybe some crackers this time?"

She nods. "Okay. I want to try. I have to."

She places a hand over her stomach, and I drop a kiss on her hair. "You're going to make the best mommy, Soph." She looks up at me, her eyes wide and her brows raised.

"Really?"

"Really."

"Knock knock," a voice calls from the entryway, and I drag my gaze off Sophie. Nash and Paisley are standing in the doorway. Paisley has a huge smile on her face as she watches us. I stand and wave.

"Come in, guys."

Nash is carrying a bouquet of flowers, and he follows Paisley across the apartment and into the living room.

"Sophie, how are you feeling?" Paisley asks as she leans over her on the sofa and pulls her into a hug.

"I've been better, but Cade is taking good care of me."

Her eyes find mine over Paisley's shoulder, and I give her a small smile.

"Congratulations, Sophie," Nash says, dropping a kiss on her

ECHOES OF LOVE

cheek as he balances the flowers in his arms. "Should I put these in the kitchen?" he asks, and she nods.

"Thank you. They're beautiful."

"They're in water," Paisley says. "I wasn't sure if Cade would have a vase."

"I have one, but it's in use," I say, gesturing to the stargazer lilies I'd brought Sophie. "Do you guys want a drink?"

"Just a soda for me, if you have one?" Paisley says as she takes a seat next to Sophie on the sofa.

"Sure. Nash?"

"I'll take a soda too, please."

He follows me into the kitchen and waits while I grab two cans from the refrigerator.

"How are you doing?" he asks quietly as he takes one of the cans from my hands.

"I'm okay. Worried about Soph."

"How are *you* doing, though?"

"Honestly? I don't think it's sunk in yet. I'm just focused on looking after her."

"Have you managed to talk to the woman you're dating?"

I sigh. "No. I've just messaged her asking if we can meet for a chat."

"What are you going to do?"

"End things. I can't focus on anyone else right now."

He reaches his hand up and squeezes my shoulder. "Do Mom and Dad know about the baby?"

I shake my head. "No. I want us to tell them together, so we need to wait until Sophie feels a little better. Seb knows, though. He called me while I was at the hospital."

"Well, I won't say anything until you've had a chance to talk to them, and I'm sure Seb won't either. Mom is going to be so excited, even though it wasn't exactly planned."

93

"I'm trying to convince Sophie they'll be pleased. She's not so sure."

"How are you two getting along? Have you managed to talk?"

"Yeah. It was a hard conversation for both of us, but it's in the past now and we have to move on."

"Together?" he asks, raising his eyebrows in question.

"I have no idea. I need to focus on getting her to a safe place in her pregnancy before I can even contemplate anything else."

He pulls me into a one-armed hug. "I'm here if you need anything."

"Thanks, man," I tell him, slapping his shoulder.

"Cade. I think the IV is finished," Paisley says as she stands from the sofa and looks at the bag of fluid.

"I'll come and have a look."

Crossing the room, I kneel in front of Sophie. "How you feeling?"

"A little better."

"Good."

The fluid bag is empty, and I disconnect the tube, leaving the cannula in her hand for next time.

"Have you managed to eat anything today?" Paisley asks.

"I tried some toast, but it didn't end well. We're going to try some crackers in a bit." She waves her hand. "Enough about me. Tell me something interesting."

Paisley laughs. "Like what?"

"I don't know. Anything."

"Okay. Well, Nash and I are planning a trip."

"Where to?"

"We're not sure yet. I'm trying to convince him to go to Vegas, but he's not too keen."

"You don't want to go to Vegas?" Sophie asks Nash, and he shrugs.

"I can think of more romantic places to visit."

ECHOES OF LOVE

"We can make it romantic," Paisley says with a wink, and Sophie laughs.

"You two are so cute. Stay at The Venetian. You can take a romantic gondola ride," Sophie says, and I smile as Paisley's eyes widen.

"A gondola ride! I love the sound of that!" she exclaims.

"We're going to end up in Vegas, aren't we?" Nash says.

"I think so," I say with a chuckle. "Just go with it."

"Have you been to Vegas?" Paisley asks Sophie, who looks up, her eyes meeting mine.

"No. It's somewhere I've always wanted to go, though."

Vegas had been something we'd planned to do in my summer break from school. With the internship and everything that happened that summer, we never got a chance to do anything we'd planned, and I know that's what Sophie's thinking about.

"You and Cade should come with us! You'll be feeling better in a couple of months, right? Maybe Seb and Ash could come too!" Paisley exclaims.

I try not to laugh as I see the look on Nash's face. I don't think he was planning on his romantic vacation including most of his family.

"You don't want us crashing your trip," Sophie says. "Plus, I have no idea how long I'm going to be sick for. I hope I'll be feeling better in a couple of months, but who knows?"

"We don't mind, do we, Nash? If you're feeling better, you should totally come."

"Why don't you two have your romantic trip and we can organize something as a group when Sophie's feeling better and before the baby comes?" I suggest, looking at Nash, who looks relieved. I turn my head to Sophie, whose eyes are wide as she stares at me.

"I love that idea!" Paisley exclaims. "We should save Vegas until we can all go. Maybe you and I could do that log cabin in the mountains like you suggested, Nash."

"Yes! We should do the log cabin," he says quickly, and I laugh. He's clearly relieved we're not all going to highjack his romantic vacation.

"That sounds perfect. You'll have a great time," Sophie says, a touch of wistfulness in her tone.

Paisley takes her hand and squeezes it. "We'll definitely take a trip when you're feeling up to it." She must have heard the same tone that I did.

My phone vibrates in my pocket, and I take it out. It's a message from Elise.

Elise: Sure. Lunch tomorrow?

I groan inwardly. I don't want this to seem like a date, especially when I'm going to be calling things off, but I know she deserves more than a two-minute conversation.

"You're tired. We should let you rest," Paisley says as Sophie lets out a yawn.

"I'm okay." She yawns again, and Paisley smiles.

"You should take a nap." She turns to me. "I'll come back in the next couple of days if it's okay with you, Cade?"

"Of course it is. You're welcome here anytime, Paisley."

"I can sit with Sophie if you ever need to go anywhere."

"I'll be okay on my own, you know," Sophie insists.

"If you're offering, are you free tomorrow? I need to… take care of something. I don't plan on leaving her again, but I have to run out tomorrow and I don't want to leave her on her own," I tell Paisley.

"I am right here. I'll be perfectly fine on my own," Sophie says again.

"I'd feel happier about leaving you if Paisley were here."

"What about when you need more food? You're going to have to leave me alone at some point."

I shrug. "I can order in."

"I'm free tomorrow. I'm happy to come and spend some time with you, Sophie."

"It's really not necessary."

"Is twelve thirty okay?" I ask Paisley, and she nods. I hold back a smile as Sophie rolls her eyes.

Nash laughs and stands up. "We're going to go and let you two argue this out." He leans down and brushes a kiss on Sophie's cheek. "I'd just give up now, Soph. I know how pigheaded my brother can be!"

I stand up and hit him on the shoulder. "Thanks for coming," I say sarcastically, and he laughs again.

"I'll see you tomorrow," Paisley says, pulling Sophie in for a hug. "If you need anything, just let me know."

"Thank you, and thanks for the flowers. They're beautiful."

I walk Nash and Paisley to the entryway, and after a round of goodbyes, I close the door behind them. When I get back to the living room, Sophie's already asleep. She must be exhausted.

I quickly reply to Elise, telling her I'll meet her at Eden tomorrow at one. Putting my phone on the side table, I lift Sophie's legs and sit down next to her, draping her legs across my lap. My heart flips in my chest as I look at her. As conflicted as I feel about what's happening with us, I want to pull her into my arms and never let go.

CHAPTER THIRTEEN

Sophie

I wake up the next morning, tired from a fitful night's sleep. Although Cade never said where he was going after arranging for Paisley to come and sit with me today, I know he's going to meet Elise. I hate that he is. Hot tears fill my eyes and my stomach churns as I think of them together.

I'm pulled from my thoughts by a soft knock on the door. I blink my tears away and take a deep breath. "Come in," I call out.

The door opens, and Cade walks in. My mouth waters as I stare at him. He's wearing a pair of sleep shorts, his chest bare. His hair is messy from sleep, and there's stubble on his jaw. He looks gorgeous.

"Morning. I didn't know if you'd be awake yet. I heard you moving around in the night. Couldn't you sleep?"

"No. Sorry. I didn't mean to keep you awake."

He shrugs. "It's fine, Soph. Do you want something to eat?"

ECHOES OF LOVE

I grimace and shake my head. "Just some water, please."

Before he can answer, there's a knock on the door.

He frowns. "Who can that be? It's only just after nine. I'll be right back."

He disappears, leaving my bedroom door open. I sit up and listen for any clues as to who is visiting this early. My eyes widen when I realize who's at the door.

"Elise. What's wrong? Come in," Cade says.

The door closes, and I strain to hear what's being said.

"I'm sorry to just show up. I know we're meeting for lunch, but I didn't know where else to go," Elise says, her voice breaking on a sob.

"Hey, don't cry," Cade says gently. "What's happened?"

"I've been suspended. I lost a patient yesterday, and the family has put in a complaint. They're saying I gave him a medication he was allergic to. It was in his notes, but I didn't check them. God, what have I done?"

I can hear her crying, although it's muffled now, and I think Cade must be holding her.

"Shhhh, it's going to be okay. You're a brilliant doctor, Lise."

"I have to go in this morning for a meeting with Harry and the medical director. Would you come with me? They've said I can bring someone. I hate to dump this on you when you have so much going on."

"Erm… I have to see if I can arrange for someone to come and sit with Sophie. What time is the meeting?"

She frowns. "Ten. What do you mean, sit with Sophie? Isn't she still in the hospital?"

"No. She's here. She's staying with me for a while until she's feeling better."

"Oh."

"Look, let me go and talk to her and we can talk more about it later. Everything's going to be okay."

99

"Thank you. I'm not sure what I'd do without you right now."

Neither says anything for a few seconds, and my heart hurts as I think of them kissing.

"Help yourself to a drink. You know where everything is. I'll be right back."

Of course she knows where everything is. She's obviously been here before. I can't help wondering if she knows her way to Cade's bedroom too. My stomach clenches at the thought.

Seconds later, Cade appears in my doorway. He walks in and closes the door behind him.

"Who was it?' I ask, not wanting him to know that I've been listening to their conversation.

He sighs and runs his hand through his hair. As hot as he looks, I wish he'd put a shirt on before he opened the door to her.

"You remember Elise who treated you in the ER?" I nod. As if I could forget. "Something's happened at work and she needs my help. I'm going to ask Paisley if she can come over earlier."

"No. You're not. I don't need someone to sit with me."

"What if you get sick?"

"I'll be fine. I don't need a babysitter."

He sits down on the edge of the bed. "I don't want to leave you on your own. I'd tell Elise no, but…" He trails off, and I wonder if he was going to say it's because they're dating.

I sigh. "I don't expect you to put your life on hold because I'm pregnant, Cade."

"I'm not putting my life on hold. I'm exactly where I want to be."

I only wish that were true. "When are you going?"

"In about half an hour. I just need to shower."

"Where's Elise now?"

"In the living room."

"I'll stay in here, then."

"You don't need to do that. I want the apartment to feel like your home while you're here."

"I don't think Elise wants to make small talk with me. I'm good in here." I roll over and pick up my phone, indicating that the conversation is over. I don't mean to be a bitch, but knowing he's with someone else hurts so much I can feel my heart splintering in my chest.

"I'll have my phone—"

"I'll call you if I need you," I lie, cutting him off.

He sighs loudly before leaving the room and closing the door behind him. I roll onto my back and stare at the ceiling. I knew staying with him was going to be hard. I don't think I realized just *how* hard, and it's only been one night.

About thirty minutes later, there's a quiet knock on my door. Instead of shouting for him to come in, I pretend to be asleep. I'm afraid if I see him right now, I might beg him to stay. When I don't answer, the door opens and I hear him cross the room. The bed dips as he sits next to me, and I'm surprised when he gently strokes his fingers over my cheek.

"I won't be long, I promise," he whispers, his lips brushing my forehead.

He sits next to me for a couple of minutes, and it takes everything in me to pretend to be asleep, especially when all I want to do is reach for him and kiss him. I can't do that, though, no matter how much I want to. His girlfriend is waiting in the next room. I keep my eyes closed until I hear the apartment door open and close.

Despite wanting to stay in bed all day, I need something to distract me, so I opt for the sofa and a movie. Anything is better than imagining Cade and Elise together. I've just settled under the blanket and turned the TV on when the apartment door opens. Swinging my head around, my eyes widen as Cade and Elise enter the apartment. I can't stand to see them together, and I quickly look away, swallowing down the golf ball–sized lump that's formed in my throat.

"You're awake," Cade says in surprise, and I turn back around to see Elise slipping her hand into Cade's. He quickly pulls his hand away. "Elise forgot her purse." He picks it up off the entryway table and holds it in the air.

"Hi, Sophie. How are you feeling?" Elise asks from the side of him.

I give her a small smile. "I'm okay." I'm lying. My heart is shattering at seeing them together, and I bite the inside of my cheek to stop from bursting into tears.

"Are you sure you'll be okay while I'm gone?" Cade asks, and I can hear the uncertainty in his voice.

I turn away from them and wave my hand in the air. "Yes. Go. I'll be fine." I try to sound upbeat, but I'm not sure I succeed. The silence from Cade tells me I haven't.

"We should go, babe. We're going to be late," Elise says quietly. It's not quiet enough for me not to hear, though, and I bite harder on the inside of my cheek, tasting blood in my mouth. I keep my head turned away from them, wishing they'd hurry up and leave.

"I'll be as quick as I can," Cade says, his voice strained.

I nod and raise my hand in a wave, not trusting myself to speak. When I hear the apartment door close, I let out a sob and clamp my hand over my mouth as silent tears track down my cheeks. I'm still crying twenty minutes later when the intercom sounds.

Pulling myself together, I wipe my eyes before standing and crossing the room on shaky legs. A wave of dizziness crashes over me, and I cling to the kitchen countertop as I wait for it to pass. Making it to the intercom, I lift the phone.

"Hello."

"Hey, Soph. It's me, Paisley."

"You're early," I say, glancing at the clock on the wall. "Cade called you, didn't he?"

"He might have. Don't be mad at him. He's just worried about you."

I sigh. "I'll buzz you in."

I press the button on the intercom that opens the door downstairs and replace the receiver. After opening the apartment door, I make my way back to the sofa. A few minutes later, Paisley walks in.

"Hey, Soph. How are you feeling?"

"Hey. I'm okay. Help yourself to a drink."

"Thanks. Do you want anything?"

"No, thanks."

She takes a soda from the refrigerator before coming to sit next to me on the sofa. She takes a mouthful of her drink and curls her legs underneath her.

"Have you been crying?" she asks, reaching to the side of her to put her drink on the table.

"Did you know Cade was seeing someone?" I ask quietly, and she stills, her back to me. When she turns around, the look on her face tells me she did.

"He mentioned to Nash when you were in the hospital that he was dating someone from work, but I don't know the details."

"She showed up here this morning. What did he say when he called you and asked you to come over?"

"Just that something had come up and he needed to go out earlier than planned. I'm sorry, Sophie."

"Me too. She was the doctor who treated me in the ER. I thought I saw something between them. She's beautiful. Beautiful and clever. The whole package."

My voice breaks. and she reaches across, taking her hand in mine. "You should talk to him, Sophie. You might have it all wrong."

"I don't think so. I heard him on the phone telling someone they were dating."

More tears fall down my cheeks, and she pulls me against her chest, holding me while I cry. I can't deny that a small part of me had hoped this baby might bring us closer together, and while we're closer than we've been in years, it still feels like we're light-years apart.

CHAPTER FOURTEEN

Cade

My head is pounding as I guide a shaking Elise through the trauma department and outside. The meeting with Harry and the medical director didn't go well.

"Shit, Cade. Why didn't I check the notes?" she asks, her voice breaking. I pull her into my side and press a kiss on her head. I don't know what to say to her. "It was right there in the notes, *allergic to penicillin*. Why didn't I see it?"

"I wish I could say something to make this better, Lise. All we can do now is wait for the autopsy results and ride it out. You're a good doctor."

She lets out a strangled laugh. "I *killed* a patient, Cade. That doesn't make me a good doctor."

"You made a mistake. What about the hundreds of people you've saved?"

"They mean nothing. All the good I've done is wiped out in an instant. This is going to be what defines me."

I pull her to a stop. "Hey. Look at me." I wait until her tear-filled eyes meet mine. "This is *not* going to define you."

"It is. They're going to strip me of my license to practice medicine. Being a doctor is what makes me me. If I lose that, I'll have nothing left."

"You don't know it will come to that."

She angrily wipes her tears away. "It should come to that. I'd want the same if it happened to a relative of mine."

"We need to wait and see what happens." I'm trying to reassure her, but I have no idea if they'll stop her from practicing medicine. Unfortunately, I've known people be let go for less.

As worried as I am about Elise, I can't stop thinking about Sophie. We've been in the meeting for over two hours, and I'm anxious about being away from her for this long. I know Paisley's with her. I'm so grateful she was able to come earlier. There's no way I'd have been happy leaving her on her own, despite Sophie saying she'd be fine. I want to get back to her, but I can't leave Elise like this. I had wanted to end things with her over lunch, but I don't know how I can do that now, not with her already so upset.

"Are we still heading to Eden? I could do with a drink. I'm okay to leave my car at your place, aren't I?" We'd taken my car to the hospital, leaving Elise's parked outside my apartment.

"Erm... okay."

I groan internally. If we go to Eden, it's going to be even longer before I can get back to Sophie, but I can't be the jackass who dumps the woman he's dating on the same day she finds out she might lose everything she's worked so hard for. I'm not that guy.

"I just need to make a phone call." I guide her to where I've parked my car and hold open the passenger door for her. When she's seated inside, I close the door and walk toward the trunk. I pull my phone out, find Sophie's number, and bring the phone to my ear. Nerves build in my stomach as her phone rings and rings before cutting to voicemail. Ending the call, I try Paisley. I let out a breath I didn't know I was holding when she answers almost immediately.

"Hi, Cade," she whispers.

"Is Sophie okay? She's not answering her phone. Why are you whispering?"

She laughs. "She's asleep."

"Oh. How's she been?"

"She's thrown up a few times. I think it's worn her out."

"Fuck!" I exclaim, dragging my free hand through my hair. "I should be there."

"She's okay, Cade."

I sigh. "I won't be long. Maybe another hour. Are you still okay to stay with her?"

"Of course."

"Thanks, Paisley."

I end the call and slip the phone back into my pocket. I want to go home and see for myself that she's okay, but I can't. I climb into the car, and Elise turns to me.

"Everything okay?"

"I just needed to check on Sophie." I start the engine and pull away from the hospital.

"How is she?"

"Not great. The vomiting is never-ending. She's lost so much weight."

"She's definitely keeping the baby, then?"

"What?" I ask, my head flying around to look at her.

Her cheeks flush pink. "It's just with you two not being together, I wondered if she'd want to do it on her own."

"She's not going to be on her own. I'm going to be there."

"Yeah, but not all the time. It's not like you're going to be living together once the baby comes. She's still going to be alone." She shakes her head. "I couldn't do it. That's all I'm saying."

"Did you forget that she already lost our baby once? There's no way she would *choose* a termination. She can't forgive herself for the termination she was forced to have years ago."

"But you have?"

"Excuse me?" My hands grip tightly on to the steering wheel, my knuckles turning white.

"You've forgiven her?"

"Forgiven her for choosing to live?" I bite out. "There's nothing to forgive, Elise. She. Had. No. Choice."

"She could have told you, though." She shrugs, and I flick my eyes to the road. I'm so angry I can hardly see straight.

"With all due respect, Elise, you don't know what happened."

She must see how angry I am and her hand comes to rest on my leg, her fingers rubbing circles on my thigh. My body recoils, and I want nothing more than to push her hand away.

How dare she say that to me? She doesn't know me, not really, and she definitely doesn't know Sophie.

"Of course I don't. I'm sorry. I didn't mean to upset you."

"Maybe we should change the subject," I tell her stiffly, grateful to be parking outside Eden so I can get her hands off me. Killing the engine, I open my door. "Ready to go inside?"

I don't wait for her to reply and climb out of the car, taking a deep breath to calm myself down. We're silent as we walk into Eden, and I'm grateful she hasn't reached for my hand.

"Grab a table and I'll get us a drink. What do you want?" I ask her.

I'm looking at the bar when she winds her arms around my neck. I turn my head, and she presses her lips to mine. "Thank you for today. I don't think you realize how much it meant to me to have you there."

I give her a tight smile, wanting to be anywhere but here with her arms around me. It's not that I don't like her, despite the conversation we've just had in the car, but I'm so confused over my feelings for Sophie. If there's a chance for us, then I want to explore that. It's always been Sophie, and deep down, I think it always will be. As soon as this shit at work blows up or blows over, I'm going to end things with Elise. Until then, I just have to keep things as much in the friend zone as I can. "How about that drink?" I ask, stepping away from her so her arms fall from around my neck.

She smiles, not noticing the distance I'm trying to put between us. "A red wine, please."

"Be right back."

I turn from her and make my way to the bar. Seb's there, and he's scowling at me.

"Who's that?" he asks, his eyes going past me to Elise.

"A friend from work."

"I don't kiss my *friends* on the mouth."

I sigh and lean heavily against the bar. "It's a long story and not one I want to get into now."

"Does Sophie know you're here with another woman?"

"Sophie and I aren't together, Seb."

"No, but surely you want to be now that you're having a baby? How can you not want to be with her?"

I frown and hold his gaze. "It's not that simple."

"It should be."

"Not that it's any of your business, but I came here to end things with Elise, but life threw me a curveball and now I can't."

"What? Why can't you end things? She's not pregnant as well, is she?"

"No!" I drag my hand through my hair. "She's been suspended from work. She could lose her whole career. How can I call things off with her the same day that happens? It's all fucked up."

"But you do want to be with Sophie?"

"Yes. No. Maybe." I drop my head in my hands. "Urgh, I have no idea."

"You can't string this woman along. Just rip off the Band-Aid."

I stare at him with wide eyes. "I'm trying not to be the asshole here. Her whole world just imploded."

"What about Sophie?" he snaps before blowing out a breath and shaking his head. "You know what, you're right. It is none of my business. What can I get you to drink?"

"Why are you so pissed about it all?" I ask.

"I'm not pissed. I'm fine. Now, what do you want to drink?" he asks again.

He clearly isn't fine, but I don't have the energy to try and figure out what's going on. "Red wine and a Coke, please."

He makes quick work of getting the drinks and slides them across the bar to me. "They're on me," he says before turning and serving someone else before I can even thank him.

I pick up the drinks and carry them back to the table where Elise is. I sit down in the booth and hand her the glass of red wine.

"Thanks," she says before taking a sip. She scoots closer toward me, her thigh pressing against mine. She's quiet, and I know she must be thinking about the meeting we've just come from. "I hate the not knowing," she says softly. "If I'm going to lose my license, I just want to know. I don't want to wait weeks to find out."

"I can't imagine how hard this is for you, Elise."

She sighs loudly. "I'm going to drive myself insane thinking about it. Let's talk about something else." She waves her hand. "How long do you think Sophie will be staying with you?"

"I don't know. Until she's over the worst of the HG, I guess."

"I'm sorry about what I said in the car. I know we haven't been together long, but I really like you, Cade, and I want this to work." She reaches for the hand that isn't holding my drink and laces her fingers with mine.

ECHOES OF LOVE

I take a mouthful of soda, giving myself an extra few seconds to think of what to say to her. Today hasn't gone at all how I'd planned, and I don't want to string her along. I also don't want to upset her.

"I'm not going to lie, Elise. Sophie's going to need me in the next few weeks, and I don't know how much free time I'm going to have while I'm looking after her."

"I can help. It's not like I'm going to be at work."

I groan inwardly. That's the last thing Sophie needs.

"That's kind of you, Elise, but I don't think she'd want anyone else there at the moment."

She frowns and wrinkles her nose. "Okay. I understand. How are you feeling about becoming a dad?"

"I don't think it's really sunk in yet, to be honest."

I discreetly look at my watch. I've been gone from the apartment for nearly three hours. "Look, I know I said we'd have lunch, but do you mind if we don't? I've got a friend sitting with Sophie, but I know she has plans this afternoon and I don't want Sophie on her own." I'm lying. Paisley doesn't need to be anywhere, but I want to get back.

"Oh, sure." She drinks down the rest of her wine and places the empty glass on the table. "Ready to go?"

I nod, forgetting for a second that her car is at my place. Swallowing down the last of my drink, I take the glasses back to the bar. Seb's nowhere to be seen, and Ryder looks busy as he mans the bar on his own.

"Tell Seb I said bye," I shout to Ryder, and he raises his hand in acknowledgment.

"Will do. Catch you later, Cade."

Meeting Elise by the exit, I walk her to my car and hold the passenger side door open for her. I drive quickly back home and park in the underground parking garage.

"Thanks again for today, Cade. I have to admit I was worried when I found out about Sophie, but now that we've talked, I'm not as worried. Of course, I wish it wasn't happening, but I guess you wish that too."

My eyes widen in surprise as I replay our earlier conversation in my head. We haven't really talked about Sophie and the baby, not in any great detail, anyway. Mainly because I've steered her away from the subject. Admittedly, I haven't been completely honest with her, but I'm trying to spare her feelings. I know I'm going to have to have that conversation with her, just not today when she's already dealing with so much.

She climbs out of the car, and I follow. I breathe a silent sigh of relief when my phone rings. I don't recognize the number, but it feels like I've been saved by the bell. I was expecting to have to dodge her goodbye kiss, and answering this call is the perfect out.

"I should get this."

She nods and walks to her car, raising her hand in a wave as she opens the driver's door. "I'll call you later." She's in the car and pulling away before I can answer her.

I send the call to voicemail and lock my car before heading to the elevator. A few minutes later, I open my apartment door and let myself in, finding Sophie and Paisley on the sofa where I left them.

"Hey. I'm back," I call from the entryway.

"Hey. You've been gone a while. Everything okay?" Sophie asks as she turns to look at me.

Kicking my shoes off, I cross the apartment and sit on the table in front of the sofa. When my gaze meets hers, I frown. Her eyes are red and puffy and it looks like she's been crying.

"Everything's fine. Are you okay? Have you been crying?"

Her cheeks flush pink, and she drops her eyes. "I'm okay. It's just the pregnancy hormones."

I don't believe her, but I don't push it. My eyes flick to Paisley,

ECHOES OF LOVE

who gives me a small smile. I'll message Paisley later and see if she'll tell me what's wrong. I hope it's not because of me and Elise.

"I should go," Paisley says as she leans over and hugs Sophie.

"Thanks for sitting with me."

"Anytime, Soph."

"Yeah, thanks, Paisley. I really appreciate it."

She waves her hand dismissively. "It was nothing."

"I'll walk you out," I say, standing.

"I'll call you later," Sophie says, and Paisley nods before heading to the entryway.

"Has she been okay?" I ask quietly when we're out of earshot.

"She hasn't thrown up again. She's just been a little teary."

"Thanks for being such a great friend."

"Always." She goes up on her tiptoes and kisses my cheek. "I'll see you soon."

"Bye, Paisley."

After closing the door behind her, I go back to Sophie and sit down on the sofa. As I do, she lets out a yawn, and I smile.

"You should take a nap. Do you want to go to bed?"

"Nah. I'll just nap here if that's okay with you."

"Of course it is."

She closes her eyes, and within seconds, her breathing has evened out and she's asleep. I can't drag my eyes off her as I watch her chest rise and fall. She's so beautiful, and seeing her like this just confirms to me that I don't want to be with Elise. I'm going to give her a few days to get over what's happened at work, and then I need to be honest with her.

Pulling my phone from my pocket, I send a message to Paisley.

Me: Thanks for sitting with Sophie. Why was she crying?

I stare at the screen as I wait for a reply. Three little dots appear under my message, telling me she's typing out a reply. I frown as the dots disappear and reappear a minute or so later. She's either typing out an essay, or she's changing her mind about what she's typing. When the phone vibrates in my hand, I look down.

Paisley: You two need to talk to each other.

Me: What does that mean?

Paisley: Just talk to her, Cade. Tell her how you feel. You still love her, right?

My fingers pause over the screen. Other than when I spoke to my mom, this will be the first time I acknowledge to anyone how I feel about her. I've hinted to Nash but never actually said the words.

Me: Yes.

Paisley: Then where have you been for the past three hours?

Me: It's complicated.

Paisley: Only if you make it complicated.

Me: What if we end up hurting each other again?

Paisley: What if you end up with everything you've ever wanted?

I sigh and stare at Sophie, who's still asleep. Despite everything going on with Elise, Sophie *is* everything I've ever wanted, but neither of us got what we wanted fourteen years ago. What if we don't get what we want now? Can I survive that again?

CHAPTER FIFTEEN

Cade

I'm in the living room watching a rerun of one of Wyatt's games while I wait for Sophie to get dressed. She's just taken a bath, her only pleasure after a week of nonstop vomiting. I glance at my watch, realizing it's been a while since I left her getting dressed. Making my way to her room, I knock gently on the door, not wanting to walk in on her, even though I've just seen her naked in the tub.

"Sophie," I call softly through the door. When I'm met with silence, I push on the door and walk in. Sighing, I cross the room and sit on the edge of her bed. She's fallen asleep with the wet towel over her. I guess she didn't get as far as getting dressed. Pulling the towel off her body, I cover her with the comforter and brush her wet hair off her face. I want to lie down and take her into my arms, but I know I can't for more reasons than one. Despite that, I lie next to her and watch her sleep. As much as I know she won't want to, if she doesn't start to pick up soon, I'm going to need to take her back to the hospital, if only to try some different anti-nausea meds.

After a few minutes, her eyes open and lock with mine. "Sorry. I didn't mean to fall asleep," she whispers, her voice thick with sleep.

"It's fine. Come and sit on the balcony. Some fresh air will be good for you."

She smiles. "Okay, Dr. Brookes."

"Cheeky." I tickle her side through the comforter. She laughs and pushes my hand away. It's so good to hear her laugh. With everything that's happened, it's been a while since I've heard it.

"It still seems surreal to call you *Dr. Brookes...*" She trails off. "I'm so proud of you, Cade. You did it. You're a doctor."

I sigh. "Not a great one at the moment. I can't make *you* feel better."

She reaches across and cups my jaw. "You're being amazing. I'm so glad you're here."

"I wish I could do more."

"Just being here is enough."

I tangle my fingers with hers. "I feel useless. I can't imagine how you must have felt before, doing this on your own."

"I wanted you so badly."

She bursts into tears, and I pull her gently against me and hold her while she cries. "I'm here now."

"I'm sorry I'm crying all the time," she sobs.

"You're allowed to cry." As much as it kills me to see her crying, I can't deny I love having her in my arms again. I can't tell her that, though. After a few minutes, she leans back and wipes her tearstained face.

"I don't think I can be bothered to get dressed."

"I'm not sure you can sit naked on my balcony, Soph."

Her cheeks flush pink. "I didn't mean I want to stay naked. Can I borrow one of your t-shirts?"

"Sure." I reach for the bottom of my shirt and pull it over my head. Her eyes drop to my chest and her cheeks color further. "I'll have to remember that taking my shirt off puts some color in your cheeks."

Her eyes widen and her hands come to her face. "I didn't mean that shirt."

I chuckle. "It's as good as any. Here, let me put it on." I lean over and slip my shirt over her head. "I'll run and get another one. Where are your panties?"

"Top drawer," she says, gesturing to the dresser on the wall opposite the bed. I climb off the bed and open the dresser drawer. Taking a pair out, I pass them to her and head to the door. I need her to have panties on under my shirt. I can't be around her knowing she's not wearing any.

"I'll be right back."

"Thank you," she says quietly.

Leaving her on the bed, I go to my room and pull on another t-shirt. When I go back to her, I pause in the doorway as I catch her holding the material of my shirt over her nose, her eyes closed.

"What are you doing?" I ask.

Her eyes fly open and she tugs the shirt down. "Nothing." She drops her eyes from mine and looks anywhere but at me.

"Does the shirt smell bad?" I ask, knowing it doesn't.

"No! It smells… good."

A smile pulls on my lips, and I cross the room to stand next to the edge of the bed. "Ready?" She nods, and I slip my arms under her legs, lifting her.

"Wait. Can I grab my hairbrush?" she asks just as I make it to the door.

"Sure." She points to the dresser and I carry her over, letting her pick it up. I've just gotten back to the door when she speaks again.

"Oh! I need a hair tie." She laughs, and I shake my head. I take her back to the dresser and she scoops up a hair tie.

I look down at her. "Is that everything? Or do you want to wait until I get to the door before you remember something else?" My voice is laced with humor, and she smiles.

"I think that's everything."

I carry her through the apartment and place her gently onto the sun lounger before heading back inside and filling a bowl with dry Cheerios. Grabbing two bottles of water, I go back out to her.

"I thought you could try some Cheerios." I hold out the bowl and she takes it from me.

"I don't want to be sick again."

I sigh. "I know, but you need to try and eat something. I'm worried about you."

Her wide eyes meet mine. "Do you think the baby's okay?"

"I'm sure the baby is fine. It's you I'm worried about. We need to try and find something you can keep down."

"Okay." She takes a few Cheerios from the bowl and eats them. "Do you think I'll be able to go to the obstetrician appointment tomorrow?"

"Yeah, if you're feeling okay in the morning. I'm going to suggest you try some different anti-nausea meds."

"I just want something to work."

"There are a few other meds we can try. I just hope you don't have to try several before we find ones that work."

"I hope so too." She closes her eyes and drops her head back onto the sun lounger. "It's so warm out here. I bet you can't wait to get outside, especially while the weather's so good."

"I'm okay. Maybe when we get your meds right, we could go for a walk. There's a pool in my building. We could go swimming too."

"Yeah, that sounds good. If you want to go to the pool or the gym, you can. I'm asleep most of the day. I'll be okay for an hour."

"Are you trying to get rid of me?"

"What?" she asks, her eyes flying open.

I smile. "You're always trying to get me to go out."

"I just feel bad you're having to babysit me."

"I'm not babysitting you. I'm looking after you."

She raises her eyebrows. "That's the same thing."

"No. It isn't." I drag my hand through my hair. "You know how bad you feel with me *babysitting* you?" She nods. "How do you think I feel knowing I've made you sick?"

She frowns and sits up. "You haven't made me sick."

"It's my fault you're pregnant, and you're sick because you're pregnant. I should have used a condom."

"I was there too, Cade. I didn't even think about a condom."

"You were upset. I came over to see if you were okay. We should never..."

She holds my gaze and shakes her head. "I know you regret sleeping with me, but we can't change what's happened. If we could, I'd have turned the clock back years ago."

"That's not what I meant, Soph…"

She lies down and closes her eyes. "It's fine, Cade," she says with the slightest shrug of her shoulder. "I guess it's not something either of us planned on, and definitely not with this outcome."

I can hear the hurt in her voice, despite her acting nonchalantly. I didn't mean to hurt her, and I didn't mean for her to think I regret what happened. As wrong as it might have been, it's brought us back to each other, and I can't ever regret that.

CHAPTER SIXTEEN

Sophie

It's been about half an hour since Cade pretty much said we should never have slept together. I know he's right, but it still hurt to hear. There's an awkward tension in the air, and I breathe a sigh of relief when the intercom sounds.

"Are you expecting someone?" I ask, wondering who it could be.

"No. Maybe it's Paisley or Ashlyn stopping by."

He walks inside and jogs across the apartment before picking up the phone.

"That's weird," he calls out. "There's no one there."

"Maybe they buzzed the wrong apartment or someone else let them in."

"Yeah, maybe."

He's just sat back down on the lounger when a knock sounds on the door.

ECHOES OF LOVE

He chuckles. "I guess you were right and someone buzzed them in."

He goes back inside, and I watch as he swings the door open. My stomach rolls when I see who's on the other side.

"Hey, what are you doing here?" Cade asks, moving slightly and blocking the doorway with his body.

"I brought you pizza. I figured we could spend an hour together while Sophie sleeps," Elise chirps.

He must have spoken to her while I was in the bath. I'm not sure why he'd tell her I was asleep, though.

"Erm… Sophie's not actually asleep. I'm not sure——"

"Oh, good. I can say hi, then," she exclaims, interrupting him.

She ducks under Cade's arm and walks in. When her eyes find mine on the balcony, she waves and walks across the apartment.

"Elise," Cade says, but she ignores him and continues to barrel toward me. I wish I could just get up and walk away, but I'm not sure after throwing up all day my legs will carry me. Even if I didn't feel like shit, there's still no way I'd want to make small talk with Cade's girlfriend.

"Hi, Sophie," she says as she stands in the balcony doorway. "It's good to see you again. How are you feeling?"

"Hi. Not great today."

I look up and find Cade's apologetic eyes as he comes to stand behind her.

"I'm sorry," he mouths silently, and I give a slight shrug.

"I should go inside and leave you two alone," I say as I gently swing my legs to the side of the lounger.

"No, stay, please," Elise says, coming onto the balcony and sitting on the lounger Cade just vacated. "It'll be good to get to know you. We're probably going to be seeing quite a bit of each other over the next few months. Even more once the baby comes."

My eyes widen as I look at Cade, who won't meet my eyes. It's clear Elise thinks their relationship is serious. Maybe Cade does too. Hell, maybe it is. I'm not sure how it can be when he slept with me a couple of months ago. It seems Elise thinks she's going to be involved in my baby's life. I guess if she stays with Cade, she will be. The realization hits me like a smack in the face, and suddenly I can't catch my breath.

"I didn't realize you and Cade were so serious," I say, trying to keep my voice from breaking.

"Sophie—" Cade starts.

"Would you excuse me while I go to the bathroom?" I interrupt, standing on shaky legs.

"Let me help you," Cade says, reaching for me.

I brush off his hand. "No. I'm fine."

Using the furniture in the living room to hold me up, I slowly make my way across the apartment and into my bedroom. When I close the door behind me, I slide down the wood and collapse into a heap on the floor. Tears streak down my face, and I clamp my hand over my mouth to silence the sobs that are threatening to escape. I have no idea how I'm going to get through watching him love someone else. I thought being apart from him for fourteen years hurt, but this hurts more, and my heart feels like it's breaking all over again.

Cade

"Did I say something wrong?" Elise asks as Sophie leaves.

I sigh and flop down on the vacant lounger. "I never actually told Sophie we're dating."

"What? Why?"

"It's complicated, Elise. We have a history. If she hadn't gotten pregnant at eighteen and left, I have no doubt we'd still be together."

"You still love her," she says quietly. It isn't a question, more of a statement. I don't want to hurt her, but by not being honest, I'm hurting Sophie, and right now, she's the most important person in my life.

"Yes. I'm sorry, Elise. I didn't want to hurt you, and especially not after everything you've been through the last week."

She nods. "Our lunch date at Eden. You were going to end things, weren't you? You didn't because of the suspension."

"I'm sorry," I say again.

"I guess that explains why it's always me contacting you. Are you two together?"

"No."

"But you want to be?"

"Like I said, it's complicated." I don't want to go into too much detail with her. I haven't even discussed my feelings with Sophie yet.

"There's nothing I can say to change your mind, is there?"

I sigh. "I'm sorry. No."

She stands. "I should go."

"You deserve to be loved wholeheartedly, Elise."

"Yeah. I do. Goodbye, Cade."

I close my eyes and press the palms of my hands into my eyes. I've hurt her and I never set out to do that, but when the apartment door closes, I can't help but feel relieved. I can stop pretending now and focus on Sophie.

I walk through the apartment and come to a stop outside Sophie's bedroom. I gently drop my head onto the door and steal a breath as I hear her soft sobs through the wood.

"Sophie. Can I come in?" I ask, my hand already on the handle.

I hear movement on the other side of the door, followed by sniffing. "No. I want to be on my own." Her voice catches, and I press my hand against the wood, willing her to let me in.

"Please," I beg. "I need to know you're okay. Elise is gone."

"I'm fine, Cade. I just need some space."

"I want to come in," I insist. I don't want her to have time to overthink everything. "I want to explain."

"God, you're infuriating," she snaps, swinging the bedroom door open. "Fine! Come in!" She gestures with her hand for me to come in, her eyes never meeting mine.

She leaves me standing in the doorway as she turns her back and crosses the small space to the bed. Climbing under the comforter, she keeps her back to me. Walking across the room, I sit on the edge of the bed.

"Can you look at me?"

"Why?" she asks.

"Because I don't want to talk to your back."

She blows out a breath before slowly rolling over. When she finally lifts her head, I find myself wishing I hadn't asked her to look at me. Guilt consumes me as I see her red, puffy, tearstained face.

"Fuck," I mutter as her eyes meet mine.

"What did you need to say, Cade?" she asks, her voice dejected.

"I'm sorry I didn't tell you about Elise."

She lifts one shoulder in a shrug. "It's nothing to do with me. I knew, though."

"You did?"

She nods. "I knew the minute she stepped into the room in the ER."

"How?" I shake my head. "Never mind. That doesn't matter."

She answers anyway. "The way she touched you. The way she looked at you. It wasn't hard to spot."

"It was Elise I was going to meet when I arranged for Paisley to come and sit with you last week. I was going to end things with

ECHOES OF LOVE

her, but then she showed up crying. Something happened at work and her whole career was suddenly in jeopardy."

"I knew that too. Well, at least the bit about her job."

I frown. "Why didn't you say anything?"

"Why would I? You never mentioned her, so I wasn't going to."

"I didn't know she was going to show up here today."

"She seems to have it all planned out. You and her playing happy families with our child. How long have you even been together?"

"Not long, and that won't be happening, Sophie."

She lets out a sarcastic laugh. "Does she know that?"

"She does now."

"What do you mean?"

"I've just ended things with her. Like I said, I wanted to do it last week, but I didn't want to be the asshole who dumps the woman he's dating the same day she loses her job."

Her confused eyes meet mine. "Why did you end things with her?"

"Because I don't want to be with her. It was never something that was going to go anywhere. Not for me, anyway." I pause and drag my hand down my face. "Look, I know we're not together, but I want to be able to focus on getting you through this pregnancy. You're carrying my child, and nothing else is important right now."

I don't know why I haven't told her the real reason for ending things with Elise. Maybe I'm just not ready to admit how I feel yet. My emotions are all over the place after finding out about the baby and what really made her leave me all those years ago. It's been so long since we were together, and maybe I need to know what I'm feeling is real and not just echoes of how it used to be. I think I know deep down they're as real as they've ever been, but I don't want to jump in blindly and do something that could push us apart forever. I barely survived losing her the first time. I know I won't survive a second.

CHAPTER SEVENTEEN

Sophie

It's been just over a week since Cade ended things with Elise, and while his reasons for doing so weren't the words I so desperately wanted to hear from him, I couldn't help but feel relieved he isn't seeing her anymore. I guess that makes me a horrible person, but I can't help how I feel. Cade is taking such good care of me, and it makes me hope for things I can never have. His kindness is bittersweet and reminds me of how good things could have been between us if I hadn't ruined everything.

It's not only Cade being amazing that's making me feel better. Thanks to a change in anti-nausea meds after seeing the obstetrician, I'm finally managing to eat a little. I'm still getting sick most days, but it's not as bad as it was, and with regular IV fluids, I can at least function and not sleep all day.

"Are you ready, Soph?" Cade calls through my bedroom door. I take a deep breath, taking one last look at my reflection. It's the first time in weeks that I'm wearing something other than yoga pants or pajamas, and it feels good to put a dress on. I've even managed to curl my hair and put some makeup on so I don't look deathly pale.

We're going to Cade's parents' place to tell them about the baby. If I said I wasn't nervous, I'd be lying. Cade's tried to assure me everything will be fine, but I'm not so sure. I didn't just hurt him when I left. I hurt everyone, and that's going to be hard to get past.

"Are you okay? Can I come in?" he asks when I don't reply, his voice tinged with concern.

"Sorry. Yes, come in."

I turn around as the door swings open, the breath rushing from my lungs as I take him in. He's wearing dark denim jeans, and a white button-down shirt is pulled tight over his chest. The sleeves of his shirt are rolled up, and my eyes are drawn to his tanned forearms. He looks gorgeous. His hair is styled messily, and he hasn't shaved for a while, a dark beard forming on his jaw. My hands itch to touch him, but I know I can't. Staring at him from afar will have to be enough. When my eyes reach his, I realize he's looking at me the same way I'm looking at him, and my cheeks flush with heat.

"You look beautiful, Sophie," he says, his voice low.

"Thank you. I want to make a good impression."

He crosses the room and surprises me as he takes my hands in his. He's been really tactile over the past couple of weeks, even more so the last few days, but it still surprises me when he takes my hand or kisses me on the forehead.

"My parents love you, Sophie—"

"They might have before…" I say, cutting him off.

"You're overthinking things."

"I'm not. I hurt you. Your parents aren't just going to forget that."

He drops my hands and pulls me against his chest. I go willingly, wrapping my arms around his waist. He smells incredible, and I inhale deeply, loving being in his arms. He holds me for a couple of minutes before brushing his lips on my head.

"I don't want you to get stressed about it. It's not good for the baby," he mutters, his lips still on my head.

I close my eyes and sigh. He's just concerned for the baby. Of course he is. Why would it be anything more? I need to stop hoping things mean more than they do. I'm going to drive myself crazy. I pull out of his embrace and take a step back.

"We should go." I turn away from him and pick my purse up off the bed.

"Are you okay?" he asks.

"I'm fine." I walk out and leave him in the bedroom. I know I'm being a bitch. I don't mean to be. He's being amazing, but it just reminds me of everything I've lost, and it hurts. It hurts so much to spend time with him when we can't be together. I think it would be easier to just go home. I'm not vomiting as often as I was. Maybe he can just come over to give me fluids occasionally. He can go back to work then too.

"I think I'll be okay to go back home now that I'm managing to eat a little," I say quietly as we drive toward his parents' place.

"You want to go home?" he asks, looking across the car at me.

I shrug. "I can't stay at your place forever. If I go home, you can go back to work."

"Work isn't a problem, Soph." His hands tighten on the steering wheel and his knuckles turn white. "I want you to stay."

"Why?"

He frowns. "So I can make sure you're both okay."

"I have to go home at some point, Cade."

"I know. Just not yet."

"I feel like I'm taking over your whole life."

"You're not."

"You've hardly been out since I moved in."

"There's nowhere I want to go."

"Surely you have friends you want to spend time with?"

"I am spending time with my friends. I'm spending time with you."

"I don't mean me."

"I'm good, Soph. I promise."

"Urghh, fine."

"So you'll stay with me?"

"Okay," I concede. "If you're sure."

"I'm more than sure."

We're silent for the rest of the journey, and my knee bounces nervously as Cade pulls into his parents' driveway. Nerves swirl in my stomach and tears fill my eyes as I look up at the impressive Brookes family's home. There are so many memories within those walls, all of them good, and it feels like I've never been away.

I'm pulled from my thoughts when Cade opens my door. "You ready?" he asks, holding his hand out to me.

I sigh. "As ready as I'll ever be." Placing my hand in his, he helps me from the car. I go to walk on ahead when he pulls gently on my hand.

"Sophie, wait." I turn around, and he keeps his hand in mine. "I wasn't just concerned for the baby earlier. I know that's how it came across. I hope what I said isn't why you want to go home."

I lift my shoulder in the subtlest of shrugs. "It's fine, Cade. I get it."

"You get what?"

"We're not together. Your interest is going to be in the baby. Not me."

He frowns. "I care about you too, Soph."

"I know," I whisper, holding his gaze.

He takes a deep breath and squeezes my hand. "Come on. Let's go inside."

"They know we're coming, right?" I ask as we walk toward the porch steps.

"They know I'm coming."

I stop walking, forcing him to stop with me. "You haven't said anything to them about me?"

"I didn't know what to say without telling them about the baby."

Before I can respond, the door swings open, and Tessa, Cade's mom, stands in the doorway. Her eyes widen before dropping to our joined hands.

"Sophie!" she exclaims, rushing down the steps and pulling me into a hug. "It's so good to see you." My arms wrap around her, and I hold her tightly. "Come inside." She steps out of the hug and reaches for my hand, pulling me along with her. I look over my shoulder at Cade, who's smiling. Maybe he was right and they aren't going to hate me.

"Do you want a drink?" she asks as I follow her into the kitchen.

"Just a water for me, please."

"Cade?"

"Same for me, Mom."

Tessa busies herself getting our drinks, her eyes flicking occasionally between me and Cade, a small smile on her lips. When we've all got a drink in our hands, she leads us to the living room.

"Henry's through here. He's going to love seeing you, Sophie."

I glance at Cade, who smiles reassuringly.

"Did I hear my name?" Henry asks as we walk in. When his eyes land on me, he stands and crosses the room. "Sophie. What a surprise. Come in and sit down."

"Hi, Henry. It's good to see you," I say shyly, taking a seat on the sofa. Cade sits next to me and tangles his fingers with mine. My heart pounds in my chest, and I'm sure everyone in the room can hear it.

"Have you two worked things out?" Tessa asks, her eyes going to our joined hands. I look to Cade, who smiles.

"We've talked things through if that's what you mean," he tells her.

"So you're back together?" she asks, excitement evident in her tone.

"No," I say quickly.

"We're not back together," Cade confirms. "But we do have something to tell you."

"Okay," Tessa says, sounding confused.

He squeezes my hand, and I fix my eyes on my lap. "We're going to have a baby," he says.

"What? But you just said you aren't together," Tessa says, and I look up to see her eyebrows pulled together in a frown.

"We're not, Mom, but Sophie's pregnant with my baby, and I'm going to be there for the both of them."

Her eyes go from Cade to me, then back to Cade. "So, you're having a baby, but you're not in a relationship, even though you still love Sophie and Sophie loves you?"

My stomach rolls. She thinks Cade still loves me? Has he told her that? And how does she know I still love him?

"Tessa, I think maybe it's their business whether or not they're in a relationship," Henry says, smiling sheepishly at me.

"It's not as simple as whether or not we love each other. A lot has happened. We're friends who are having a baby together. It's not something either of us planned, but it's where we are," Cade explains.

Despite him not denying he loves me, my heart fractures a little more at his words. I know we're only friends, but hearing him say it hurts.

"And you're both happy?"

"Yes," Cade says, looking at me.

"Sophie?" she prompts when I don't say anything.

ECHOES OF LOVE

Part of me wonders if I should just be honest and tell Cade I don't want to be his friend. I'll take friendship if that's all he's offering, but surely he knows I want more than that? Now isn't the time, though, and it's definitely not a conversation for in front of his parents. Instead, I give a small nod and try to ignore the knowing look Tessa's giving me.

"Sophie's staying at my place for a while. She's had a tough start to the pregnancy and she needs meds and fluids to help her get through it," Cade says, squeezing my hand again.

"I'm sorry to hear that, Sophie. It's not twins, is it?" Tessa asks. "I was so sick when I was first pregnant with Seb and Wyatt."

"No. There's just the one. I'm not sure how I'd cope with two on my own."

"You're not going to be on your own, Soph," Cade says, and I give him a small smile. I have no doubt he's going to help out when the baby comes, but he's not going to be there for the midnight feedings and diaper changes. That's going to be all on me.

"I'm going to be a grams," Tessa says, a wide smile on her face. She stands and pulls Cade up into a hug. She hugs me after Cade, and then we both get hugs from Henry.

"When's the baby due?" she asks.

"March twenty-seventh. Would you like to see a sonogram picture?" I ask, reaching for my purse that's on the floor.

"Yes, please."

Opening my purse, I take out the images and hand them to her. "It doesn't quite look like a baby yet, but Cade says it will on the next ultrasound."

"Oh my goodness," Tessa exclaims, and I look across to see tears running down her face. "That's my grandbaby."

Henry comes to stand next to her and slides his arm around her waist, kissing her softly on her head.

I was always in awe of their relationship. They've always been so in love. I never really saw that with my parents. They split up when I was five, and I didn't see much of my dad after that. Mom dated on and off over the years, but she never found anyone who loved her like she was their world. I wish she had. I glance at Cade to see him watching me. I know I had that once, but I lost it, and I don't think I'm ever going to get it back.

A wave of emotion crashes over me, and I suddenly need some space.

"Can I use the bathroom?" I ask, willing my voice not to break and my tears not to fall.

"Of course, sweetheart. You know where it is," Tessa says, her eyes still fixed on the sonogram pictures.

"Are you okay? Do you need me to come?" Cade whispers in my ear.

I stand up and shake my head, afraid if I speak, I'll lose it.

Rushing from the room, I quickly make my way down the hallway and into the bathroom, closing the door behind me. I drop down onto the closed toilet seat and the tears I'd been holding back finally fall. I sob into my hands, not caring that my makeup is going to be streaked down my face. After a few minutes, a knock sounds on the door and I reach for some toilet tissue to wipe my face.

"Hang on," I croak out as I quickly wipe my eyes.

"It's Tessa. Can I come in?"

"Erm... sure." Nerves swirl in my stomach as I stand from the toilet and unlock the door.

"Oh, sweetheart, please don't cry," she says when the door opens and she sees my tearstained face. After closing the door behind her, she reaches for me and pulls me into her arms. I'm tense for a few seconds before I relax and cry against her shoulder.

"I'm so sorry," I gasp between sobs. "I'm so sorry I hurt him. I never meant to, and now everything is such a mess."

"Shhhh. Everything is going to be fine. I promise."

I cry against her shoulder for a few more minutes before I pull myself together. Embarrassed, I step out of her embrace.

"I want you to know what happened."

"You don't have to tell me, Sophie. It's your and Cade's business."

"I want to tell you. I know I hurt you and Henry too."

"We still love you, Sophie. We were worried about you and devastated for you and Cade. No one hates you, despite what you think."

"Cade told you?"

She nods. "He said you were nervous to come here. I could never hate you, sweetheart. You were eighteen. We all make mistakes." She takes the tissue out of my hand and dries my tears. "Come on, let's go to the kitchen. We don't want to talk in the bathroom."

She takes my hand and leads me back down the hallway. We have to pass the living room on the way, and Cade jumps up from his seat as we walk past. He's by my side in a second.

"What's wrong? You've been crying." He reaches for my free hand, his fingers going to my puffy face.

"It's just hormones, Cade. You're in for a lot of tears in the next few months," Tessa says, pulling me away from him. "She's okay."

He takes no notice of her and follows us into the kitchen. "Sophie? *Are* you okay?" he asks, his voice laced with concern.

"I'm okay," I say quietly, my eyes dropping from his.

"We're just going to have some girl talk, Cade. Go and spend some time with your dad," Tessa tells him as she drops my hand and pulls out one of the chairs at the breakfast bar.

"You're sure you're okay? You're not feeling sick or dizzy?" he asks, his eyes sweeping over me.

"I'm okay. Really, Cade."

He stares at me for a few seconds. "I'll be in the living room if you need me."

"We won't," Tessa assures him, and I can't help a small smile pulling on my lips.

He walks backwards out of the room, and when he's gone, I turn to face Tessa.

"So, that's what you kids are calling a friendship these days?"

"What?" I ask in confusion.

She laughs. "Sophie, Cade might be my son, but there is no way that man wants to just be your friend."

I shake my head. "He's just concerned about the baby, that's all. I wish it were more, but it isn't."

"There's more there, sweetheart. Even if he won't admit it."

God, I so wish that were true. I want her to be right more than anything. I'm desperate to know what he's feeling, but I'm too scared to ask and too scared to hear the answer.

CHAPTER EIGHTEEN

Cade

Walking backwards out of the kitchen, my eyes are fixed on Sophie. I hate knowing she's been crying. I hope she really is okay and not just telling me she is. I don't want to leave, but my mom isn't giving me much of a choice.

When I get back into the living room, I flop down onto the sofa and sigh.

"Everything okay?" my dad asks.

"Sophie's upset."

"She'll be okay with your mom." He sits up in his chair and rests his elbows on his knees. "So, you're going to be a dad? How are you feeling about it all?"

I blow out a breath. "Well, it wasn't planned."

"I didn't think you two were speaking."

"We weren't. Not really. I was happily avoiding her until the day of the shooting. Seb asked me to go and check on her. One thing led to another and here we are."

"Happily avoiding her?" He raises his eyebrows in question, and I drag my hand down my face.

"Okay, unhappily avoiding her. I should have heard her out when she first came back to Hope Creek. Maybe things could have been different."

"You're okay with why she left?"

"It wasn't her fault. She got pregnant and thought I'd drop out of school if she told me. She ended up being really sick and had to end the pregnancy. She blamed herself and couldn't face coming back."

"I'm so sorry, Cade."

"Yeah, me too. She went through all of that on her own while I was here hating her. I should have tried harder to find her."

"This isn't your fault, son."

"Maybe not, but it wasn't hers either."

"And you're okay just being friends now?"

I sigh. "Honestly? No. I think I want more, but I don't know if it's too late for that."

"It's never too late. You should talk to her, see what she wants."

"I know what she wants. She wants to try again. What if we try and it doesn't work? We'll both end up getting hurt again, only now there's a baby to think about. It's a mess."

"Love is messy, son. It's rarely straightforward, but anything good is worth fighting for. You just need to decide if she's what you want."

"She's always been what I want, but is that enough? Sometimes we don't get what we want."

"Can you live your life knowing you never tried? What happens when she meets someone? Can you watch someone else love her?"

ECHOES OF LOVE

"I can't bear the thought of her with someone else. I think that's what's eaten me up all these years. I was sure she'd met someone else while I was away at school and she just never had the guts to tell me. Now I know that's not the case."

"I think you've just answered your own question, Cade." He stands and comes to sit on the sofa next to me. "Did you know she spent at least one night a week sleeping in your room while you were away? Sometimes she'd stay more than once."

I frown. "I never knew that. She never told me."

"I think she felt close to you here. She missed you. I know that much."

"I missed her too. I've always wanted to be a doctor, you know that, but I sometimes regret the choices I made. If I hadn't been away at school, I would have been here with her."

"You can't think like that, Cade. Everything happens for a reason, and you'll drive yourself crazy if you keep asking yourself *what if.*"

"That's what Soph said."

"She's likely been asking herself the same for years. It doesn't get you anywhere."

Before I can respond, the door opens, and Sophie and my mom walk in. They both look like they've been crying, and I stand up.

"Everything okay?" I ask, looking between them.

"Everything's fine," my mom assures me. My eyes lock with Sophie's, and when she smiles and nods, I let out a breath I didn't realize I was holding. "I'm going to make us all some lunch. What does everyone want?" my mom asks.

"Do you have Cheerios?" Sophie asks, and my mom gives her a small smile.

"Is that all you can eat?"

"It's pretty much all I've been able to keep down so far. I'm a bit scared to try anything else."

"I have Cheerios, sweetheart. Sit down and I'll bring you some. Do you want milk?"

"No. Just dry, please."

She nods. "Henry, can you come and help me?"

"Sure," he says, following her out of the room.

When it's just the two of us, I reach for her hand and guide her to sit on the sofa. "How did it go? Did you two talk?"

She nods. "Your mom's amazing, Cade." Tears fill her eyes and a single tear rolls down her cheek. My heart breaks when I see her crying again, and I reach my free hand up to wipe away her tears.

"Please don't cry."

"She was so understanding, and having her hug me reminds me just how much I miss my mom. I've felt so alone since she died. I might have been surrounded by people, but sometimes that just made me feel lonelier."

"Fuck. I'm sorry, Soph. I can't imagine how hard it's been for you being back in Hope Creek and having no one. I've been such an asshole."

"No, Cade. You haven't."

"I have. I've been a jerk to you at every opportunity. Look how I just walked out and left you after we slept together. I never once stopped to think about how you might be feeling. I was only thinking about me, and all the time you were dealing with…" I trail off. "I'm so sorry."

"You have nothing to apologize for. Hey, look at me." She stands, then kneels on the floor in front of me. "Cade?" Slowly lifting my head, I look down at her, my eyes meeting hers. "Did you hear me? You have nothing to apologize for."

"I heard you. I just don't believe you."

Her small hand reaches up and cups my jaw. I tilt my head and lean into her touch, my eyes closing. "I hurt you, Cade, and you had no idea why. Your defenses were always going to be up. You were protecting yourself."

"I should have let you explain. You tried often enough. I just never wanted to listen."

"Cade," she whispers, kneeling up between my legs so her face is level with mine.

"I miss you so much, Sophie."

"I miss you too."

I rest my forehead on hers before reaching for her hand and gently pulling her up. "We should talk later." She sits next to me and looks down at our joined hands.

"Okay," she whispers.

A few minutes later, my parents return with lunch for us all. I feel guilty eating a sandwich while Sophie eats dry Cheerios.

"Who else knows about the baby?" my dad asks.

"Everyone except Wyatt and Ash. Paisley was with Sophie when she got sick, and Seb called me while I was at the hospital. We wanted to tell you together, so we waited for Sophie to feel better."

"When are you telling Wyatt and Ashlyn?"

"Telling Wyatt what?" a voice asks from behind us. I turn to see Wyatt standing in the doorway.

"Hey. I thought you were at training," I say, standing up and pulling him into a hug when he comes into the room.

"I was. I've got a few more weeks and then I'll be back in Phoenix for pre-game prep." His eyes flick from me to Sophie. "Hi, Sophie. Good to see you." She puts down her Cheerios and stands up, brushing a kiss on Wyatt's cheek.

"Good to see you too, Wyatt."

He frowns. "Why are you eating dry Cheerios?"

Her eyes flick to mine, and I take her hand. "Sophie's pregnant. We're having a baby," I say, smiling when his eyes widen with surprise.

"That's incredible news! Congratulations!" Sophie laughs as he picks her up and spins her around. When he puts her down, he pulls me into a one-armed hug and slaps me on the back. "It's about time you two sorted things out. Don't think I didn't see you sucking face in Eden a couple of months ago."

I chuckle as Sophie's face turns pink. "Thanks for pointing that out, Wyatt. We're just friends right now."

Sophie's eyes find mine, and I wink at her. I also make the mistake of looking at my mom, who has tears in her eyes and the biggest smile on her face.

I groan inwardly. Maybe I shouldn't have said *right now*. I have no idea if we can make a go of things. I want to, but we've got so much to overcome. I don't want to get anyone's hopes up prematurely.

CHAPTER NINETEEN

Sophie

I'm throwing up as soon as we get back to Cade's place, and I don't know if it was the car journey or the weird smell in the elevator as we rode up from the parking lot. Whatever it was had me running to the bathroom.

Cade stays with me until the vomiting stops and then leaves me to get changed. I stand up and grip on to the vanity unit, staring at my reflection in the mirror. I look a mess. The eye makeup I'd worn to Cade's parents' house is long gone after my breakdown in the bathroom, and my eyes are red and puffy. My face is pale and my hair looks a little like a bird's nest, piled on top of my head by Cade while I was throwing up. Sighing, I brush my teeth and try not to gag. When I'm done, I remove what little makeup I have left on my face and head back into the bedroom. I take off my dress and toss it on the floor, reaching for my sleep shorts and tank. As I do, the bedroom door swings open.

"Shit! Sorry. I didn't realize you were getting changed," Cade says from the doorway, his eyes roaming all over me.

I pull my tank over my head and shrug. "It's okay. You've seen me in less."

"How are you feeling?"

"Okay. Tired." Slipping on my sleep shorts, I sit on the edge of the bed.

"Do you want to take a nap?"

"Yeah, I think I will."

"I'll be on the balcony if you need me."

"Cade."

"Yeah." He looks over his shoulder at me.

I bite down on my bottom lip. "Are we still going to talk?"

He turns and crosses the room, taking me in his arms. I wind my hands around his waist and let him hold me.

"Sleep first and then we'll talk. Okay?"

I nod, and he brushes a kiss on my cheek. He leaves the room, and despite being tired, I have no idea how I'm going to sleep when my stomach feels like a million butterflies are waiting to take flight in there. I shouldn't let myself hope that maybe, just maybe, I'm going to get a second chance with him, but I can't help that my racing heart is getting ahead of itself. Part of me worries he's just trying to keep me close because he knows I want to leave. I wish I didn't think like that, but I can't seem to stop myself.

* * *

MY EYES FLUTTER OPEN, AND I STRETCH MY ARMS ABOVE MY HEAD on a yawn. It's still light outside, so I don't think I've been asleep long, but I need to pee. I sit up slowly and swing my legs to the side of the bed. Sitting for a minute or so, I stand and pad silently into the bathroom. As I pull down my panties and sit on the toilet, fear crashes through me when I see a small amount of blood on the fabric. When I wipe with the tissue, there's more, and tears track down my cheeks.

"Cade!" I shout. "Cade!"

A few seconds later, the bathroom door flies open. "What's wrong?" he asks, his face a picture of worry.

"I'm bleeding," I whisper.

"Do you have cramps?"

"No. Nothing." My hand comes over my mouth and I stifle a sob.

Despite sitting on the toilet, he kneels in front of me and pulls me into his arms. "No pain is good. I'm going to see if I can call Dr. Black."

"I'm scared."

"Whatever happens, I'm going to be right there with you, okay?" I nod. "Come on. I'll help you get dressed."

Fifteen minutes later, we're both silent on the way to the hospital. Cade spoke to Dr. Black, who wants me to come in for an ultrasound. He asked to speak to me and tried to reassure me that bleeding in early pregnancy is very common, but with everything else that's happened, I'm terrified. I just want to know my baby's okay. My hand is nestled in Cade's, and he rubs his thumb in circles over my skin as he drives. Naively, I'd allowed myself to believe everything might be okay after getting the vomiting and dehydration under control. I should have known it wouldn't be that easy, and it feels like it's karma after what happened the first time around.

When Cade's parked the car, we walk hand in hand into the hospital and take the elevator to the third floor. Dr. Black is waiting for us by the nurses' station and guides us into a side room.

"How are you feeling, Sophie?" he asks as he gestures for me to sit on the examination bed.

"Scared," I admit.

He gives me a small smile. "How has the HG been?"

"The new anti-nausea meds seem to be working. I'm still vomiting most days, but not as much as before."

"She's having IV fluids every couple of days, more if she has a bad bout of vomiting," Cade explains.

"That's good. You're looking a lot better than you did the last time you were here. Cade must be looking after you well."

"He is," I tell him, my eyes flicking to Cade.

"Shall we have a look at what's happening?"

Blowing out a breath, I nod.

"We'll start with an abdominal ultrasound now that you're a little further along. We can always switch to an internal if we need to."

"Okay," I whisper, lying down on the bed and pulling my yoga pants down a little to expose my stomach.

"Ready?" Dr. Black asks, and I nod. "The jelly might be a little cold."

Cade stands to the side of me and takes my hand, squeezing reassuringly. I keep my eyes fixed on Dr. Black as he moves the wand around my stomach and concentrates on the screen, which is out of view. When the whooshing sound of our baby's heartbeat fills the room, I burst into tears.

"Your baby is fine, Sophie." He moves the screen around, and through my watery eyes, I can make out a wriggling baby. Even though we had an ultrasound a couple of weeks ago, the baby has grown and looks less of a blob and more like a baby. He points to an area on the screen. "There is a small hematoma sitting just under the placenta. That's the likely cause of the bleed."

"A hematoma?" I ask, my eyes going from Dr. Black to Cade. "What's that?"

"It's a small pocket of blood which, in your case, has formed by the placenta." My eyes widen, and he must see my reaction. "It sounds worse than it is. It's very small and will likely be reabsorbed. There's very little risk to the baby."

ECHOES OF LOVE

"Will I get more bleeding?"

"It's quite likely you will. At least until it's been reabsorbed. I know it must be scary to see, but at least we know where the bleeding is coming from. We can monitor you over the next week or so until it's gone."

"But the baby's okay?" Cade asks from the side of me.

"The baby's fine, Cade." He presses a button on the machine and the image converts from a two-dimensional image to a four-dimensional one, and I gasp.

"Oh my God! Cade, look," I exclaim.

It looks even more like a baby now, and I can't tear my eyes off the screen.

"I can't believe we made that," Cade whispers as he leans down and presses a kiss to my cheek.

Dr. Black chuckles. "I'll print you off some pictures and then make you an appointment to come back for a repeat ultrasound in a few days." He hands me a strip of images, along with some tissue to clear the jelly off my stomach. "I'll go and make you an appointment in a couple of days. I'll be back shortly."

"Thank you, Dr. Black," Cade says, holding out his hand.

"You're welcome, son." He shakes Cade's hand and leaves the room.

"Are you okay?" Cade asks, brushing a stray piece of hair off my face.

"I'm so relieved. Are you okay?"

"I'm relieved too," he whispers.

I can't stop myself from thinking that if anything happens to the baby, I'll lose Cade as well. We're just starting to get close again. While the baby is my number one priority, I'm not sure I'll survive if I lose him again. I shouldn't be thinking that way, but it's impossible not to.

"Here, let me help you."

He takes the tissue from my hand and gently wipes the jelly off

147

my stomach. He tosses it in the trash, and I pull up my yoga pants. Holding out his hand, he pulls me to sit up, and I close my eyes as a wave of dizziness comes over me.

"You okay?" he asks, sitting next to me.

"Just a little dizzy."

He takes my wrist and presses his fingers over my pulse. "Your heart is racing, but that's understandable with everything that's happened."

"It's passing now. Thank you." He keeps his hand in mine and reaches for the sonogram pictures. "They're amazing, aren't they? Do you think you could smuggle the portable ultrasound machine out of the room so we can see the baby whenever we want?" I ask with a giggle.

He laughs. "I think it might be a little big for me to smuggle into my car, Soph."

"That's a shame," I joke.

I watch his face as he studies the pictures, and my heart flips in my chest. There's a smile pulling on his lips and he shakes his head.

"What?" I ask.

"I still can't believe it." He pulls his hand from mine and places it over my flat stomach.

"Me neither. I don't think it will really sink in until I start showing."

"I can't wait to see your belly swollen with our baby."

My eyes widen in surprise. "You can't?"

"You and a family were all I ever wanted, Sophie. Is it too late for us?" His eyes search mine, and I can barely believe what he's saying.

"Cade—"

"Okay, then," Dr. Black says as he comes back into the room, seemingly oblivious to the fact that he's interrupting a moment

I've waited fourteen years for. "I've booked you in for another ultrasound on Friday at three."

"Thank you, Dr. Black," I say as I drag my eyes off Cade.

Hand in hand, we make our way silently out of the room and toward the elevators.

"Dr. Brookes," a voice says as we wait for the car.

We turn around, and a man walks toward us.

"Hi, Dr. Moore. Good to see you. This is Sophie. Sophie, Dr. Moore."

"Nice to meet you, Sophie."

"You too."

"I'm glad I ran into you. Harry wasn't very forthcoming with why you left. Just that you'd moved on. I was surprised, especially since you've only just made attending physician. You must have been offered something incredible to walk away from that."

My eyes widen at his words, and I look across at Cade, who won't make eye contact with me.

Did he walk out on his dream job to take care of me? He couldn't have. His whole career has been leading toward making attending physician. I know he must have worked so hard for that position. Surely, he didn't give it up for me?

CHAPTER TWENTY

Cade

I can feel Sophie's eyes on me, but I can't look at her. I know how she's going to feel when she finds out I gave up my job. I'm not even sure she knows I made attending physician. I've only been in the role a couple of months, and I know she always thought it was my dream. It was, but it isn't something I would ever put above her.

The elevator doors open, and the three of us walk forward.

"I'm actually between jobs at the moment," I say when we're inside the car. "I've got some personal stuff going on."

He presses the button for the first floor and looks down to my and Sophie's joined hands. "Well, I hope everything works out for you."

"Thanks."

We ride the elevator in silence, and he raises his hand in a wave when the doors open on the first floor and he heads in the direction of the ER. Once we're outside, Sophie stops walking and tugs on my hand.

"You gave up your job?" she asks quietly.

I sigh and pull her around the side of the building, away from the entrance. "I asked for some time off and they said no."

She frowns. "So you just quit?"

"Yes."

She shakes her head. "But that guy said you'd just made attending physician. That's everything you've ever wanted."

"No, it wasn't. You were everything I ever wanted, and you still are. You and this baby are more important than any job, Sophie."

"But—"

"No buts."

"I never wanted you to have to choose between me and your career. That's why…" She trails off.

"I know," I tell her softly. "And I know now you did that because you loved me." I take a deep breath and envelop both of her hands in mine. "I did what I did for the same reason, even if at the time I wouldn't admit it to myself."

Her uncertain eyes meet mine. "You still love me?"

"Yes. I've always loved you."

"I love you too," she whispers.

I pull her against me and wrap her in my arms.

"What does this mean, Cade?" she asks into my chest.

Leaning back, I lift her chin with my fingers so she's looking at me. "I want us to be together again."

"You do?" I nod. "Do you think we can make it work?"

"I don't know, baby, but I want to try. It's always been you, Sophie. Even after fourteen years. I know what it's like to live without you, and I don't want to live like that again." I slide one of my hands around her neck and my thumb gently strokes her cheek. Lowering my head to hers, I softly kiss her. "Tell me you're mine again?" I ask against her lips.

"I've always been yours, Cade. Even when I wasn't."

I close my eyes, and for the first time in fourteen years, I feel whole again. A piece of my soul was ripped away when she left, but having her back in my arms makes everything right again.

"Want to go home?" She smiles and nods.

Slipping my arm around her waist, I pull her against me and guide her back to the car. My fingers remain tangled with hers on the short drive back to my apartment, and every time I turn to look at her, she's watching me. She averts her gaze whenever I catch her staring, and I can't help but smile. We might have been together for three years in the past, but it feels brand new somehow, and my stomach dips and my heart races every time I look at her. We have to make it work this time. I've lived so much of my life without her, and I know being with her makes me a better person. She makes everything better.

Once we're back in the apartment, she kisses me on the cheek and goes to her room to get changed. I'm hoping she's going to want to sleep in my bed tonight. Sex is off the table for a while at least, but my arms were made for where she sleeps, and they've been empty for the past fourteen years. I want her back in them.

"What are you going to do about a job?" she asks when we're lying on the sofa a little while later. She's changed into tiny sleep shorts and a tank, and she's not wearing a bra. It's taking every-thing in me to keep my hands off her.

"I'll find something in a couple of months when I know you're feeling better."

"A couple of months? What about money?"

"I have plenty, baby. It's only ever been me, and I've got savings."

"Will you be able to find an attending physician position? I feel so guilty you gave everything up for me."

I pull her gently up my body so her face is level with mine. "I would do *anything* for you, Sophie. Just like you would for me. I don't want you to ever feel guilty. As much as I love my job, for the past few years, I've always finished my shift and come back to an empty house. I want more than that. My job isn't and never has been my everything. You're what's missing in my life and you always have been."

"Cade," she whispers, dropping her head onto my chest. "I'm so sorry I hurt you."

"Look at me." I wait until she lifts her eyes to mine. "I know how sorry you are, and I don't ever want to forget the little girl we lost, but everything else has to stay in the past, okay? You can't keep apologizing. We can't keep going backwards. We have so much to look forward to, baby."

"I love you."

"I love you too."

My mind wanders as I hold her against me. I've been giving some thought to family medicine. It's not something I'd ever really considered before, but if I stick to trauma, the hours are crazy. I want to be around when the baby's born. I can't wait to be a hands-on dad. I can't wait to be a family.

I'm pulled from my thoughts when my phone rings in my pocket. Sophie sits up, and I slide out my phone. Seeing it's Ashlyn, I accept the call and put the phone to my ear.

"Hey, Ash. What's up?"

"Hey, Cade. I just wanted to know what the plan was for next weekend."

I frown. "What's happening next weekend?"

"The Brett Young concert. You did book the time off work, didn't you?"

"Fuck," I mutter. I'd bought Ashlyn concert tickets for her birthday a couple of months ago. I was supposed to be driving her and her friend to Phoenix. With everything that's happened, it had completely slipped my mind.

"Did you forget? Ivy and I can make our own way there. It's fine."

"No! I just need to work some stuff out. Can I call you back?"

"Is everything okay?"

"Everything's good, Ash. Actually, can you hang on a sec?"

"Sure."

Taking the phone from my ear, I cover it with my hand and turn to Sophie. "Are you okay with Ash coming over if she's free, and we can tell her about the baby?" I ask quietly. "I feel kinda bad everyone but her knows."

"Of course."

I lean over and kiss her softly.

"Hey, Ash, are you busy?"

"Erm, no. I'm just at home."

"Can you come over?"

"Yes. Are you sure you're okay? You're freaking me out."

I chuckle. "I'm fine, I promise."

"Do you want me to come now?"

"Yeah. Just head over when you're ready."

"Okay. See you soon."

"Bye, Ash."

Sophie stands from the sofa. "I should get changed."

I reach for her hand. "You don't need to. It's only Ash."

She yawns. "If you think she won't mind, then I won't. I'm exhausted."

"Are you feeling okay?"

"Yeah, just tired and nauseous, but that's nothing new." She reaches for the bowl of Cheerios on the table by the sofa and takes a handful.

"Are you sure it's okay for Ash to stop by?"

"I'm sure. What did she call for?"

I sigh. "I bought her Brett Young concert tickets for her birthday. I was going to drive her to Phoenix next weekend. I need to see if Nash is free."

"You can still take her. I'll be fine here, Cade."

I pull her onto my lap, her legs straddling mine. "No. I'm not leaving you." My fingers skate under the material of her tank and come to rest on the bare skin of her waist. "I've only just gotten you back. I don't want to spend any time apart. Plus, I'd worry about you."

"Why don't I come with you, then?"

"What if you're not well?"

"Then I'll have the sexiest doctor I know to look after me."

I smile as she winds her arms around my neck. "Sexy, hey?"

"Hell yes, and if I didn't feel like I could throw up at any moment, I'd be showing you just how sexy I think you are."

I laugh and hold her gaze. "I think you're sexy."

"Oh, please. I'm a hot mess."

I shake my head. "You're carrying my baby, Sophie. There's nothing sexier than that."

She lowers her head and brushes her lips against mine. I tangle my hand into her hair and snake my tongue into her mouth. After a few seconds of kissing her, I pull back before it gets heated, conscious she isn't feeling great. She presses her lips to mine again before dropping her head into the crook of my neck as I hold her tightly against me.

After a few minutes, she sits up. "I need to use the bathroom."

"Okay, baby. Do you need some help?"

"I'm good."

She climbs off my lap, swaying when she stands up. "Whoa!" I exclaim, jumping up and winding my arm around her waist. "Are you dizzy?"

She closes her eyes and sags against me. "Yeah, a little. I think I got up too quickly."

"I think you might need some fluids again."

She pouts. "Can we wait until Ash leaves?"

"Sure." I scoop her into my arms and carry her through her bedroom and into the bathroom. "I'll wait right outside." I kiss her softly on the head and close the bathroom door. Just as I do, the intercom sounds. "That'll be Ash. I'll buzz her in and be right back, okay?"

"Okay."

Jogging to the entryway, I lift the intercom phone.

"Hey, it's me," Ash says.

"Come on up. The door's on the latch." Pressing the button to open the door downstairs, I open the apartment door and flick the latch before going back to Sophie.

"You okay?" I ask through the closed bathroom door.

"I'm bleeding again."

I close my eyes and drop my head onto the wood. "Can I come in?"

"Yes."

Opening the door, I cross the small space and kneel down in front of her. "I know it's scary, but Dr. Black said this might happen. Baby Brookes is a fighter."

She lifts her head and smiles. "Baby Brookes?"

"Or Baby Greene. Whichever you prefer."

"I like the sound of Baby Brookes."

"I like it too."

"Cade?" a voice shouts.

"That'll be Ashlyn," she says, finishing on the toilet and standing up.

"Be right there, Ash," I shout.

I wait until Sophie has washed her hands before scooping her into my arms again.

"I can walk." She giggles. "I just need to hold on to you."

"I like having you in my arms."

I carry her through the apartment and into the living room. I

ECHOES OF LOVE

smile as I see Ashlyn with her back to us, her head buried in the refrigerator.

"What are you looking for, Ash?"

"Wine. I've had a hell of a day at work. Do you have…" She trails off as she turns from the refrigerator and sees me carrying Sophie. "What's going on?" she asks, a wide smile on her face as she looks between us.

"We have some news," I tell her, gently lowering Sophie to the sofa and going to her in the kitchen. "Do you want a glass of wine?" I ask, taking an unopened bottle from the refrigerator door.

"Don't open the bottle just for me," she says. "You'll have a glass, won't you, Sophie?"

"None for me, thanks, Ash, but you have one."

I open the bottle anyway and pour a glass, handing it to her. I make my way back to Sophie, Ash following. Sitting down, I take Sophie's hand in mine. She looks between us again before smiling.

"Are you two together?"

"Yes," I say, tugging Sophie closer to me.

Ashlyn would only have been nine or ten when we were together before, and I have no idea what she remembers about what happened, but I know she and Sophie have become friendly in the last eighteen months.

"I'm so happy for you guys."

"Thanks. That's not our news, though," I tell her.

"There's more?"

I nod. "We're having a baby."

"Oh my God!" she shouts, putting her wineglass down. I stand up and she throws her arms around me. "Congratulations." I chuckle at her excitement and hug her back. When she pulls away, she wraps her arms around Sophie, who's still sitting on the sofa. "How long have you two been back together? You sure kept that quiet."

"Not that long. About two hours," Sophie says, laughing when she sees the confusion on Ash's face. "It's a long story."

"However it happened, I'm happy for you. I know how miserable you've both been lately. You belong together. Anyone can see that."

"Thanks, Ash," I tell her.

"Has Cade gone all protective and moved you in here already?" she asks Sophie, winking at me.

"Yeah, for a while at least. I've had some pretty intense morning sickness, so he insisted I stay with him for a few weeks so he can look after me."

"I'm sorry to hear you've been unwell. If there's anything I can do to help, you only have to ask."

"Thanks. I'm being well looked after." Sophie turns to me and takes my hand.

"I can't believe I'm going to be an aunt! Mom must be so excited! They know, right?"

"Yeah, we told them earlier. There were tears and everything," I tell her.

She laughs. "She's going to need that bigger dining table she's been talking about for years! I'm so happy for you guys." She reaches for her wine and swallows a mouthful. "How about I drive to the concert next weekend? Ivy and I will be fine."

"No. I'll still take you," I tell her. "Sophie is going to come with us if she's well enough. How do you feel about staying over? I think it's too far to go in one night if Sophie's coming."

"I am here, you know, and I'm pregnant, not dying," Sophie exclaims.

"Think of it as our second first date," I whisper, leaning across and brushing my lips with hers.

Ashlyn smiles before taking another mouthful of wine. "We could book a room in the Royal Palms," she suggests.

"The Royal Palms?" Sophie asks, a tinge of excitement in her

ECHOES OF LOVE

voice. We've been stuck inside for a while. I'm sure a trip anywhere would be appealing.

"Mom and I went there for a spa weekend last year. It's amazing!"

"That sounds good," Sophie says, looking at me with wide eyes.

"I'll book us two rooms," I say with a chuckle.

Thirty minutes later, Ashlyn stands. "I'd better get going, let you get some rest. You look tired, Sophie."

"Yeah. I'm a little wiped out."

Sophie stands, and Ashlyn pulls her into a hug. "Congratulations again, guys. I can't wait to meet my niece or nephew."

After a round of hugs, I walk Ash to the door and see her out. When I get back to Sophie, she's almost asleep. I want her to have some fluids, so I quickly sort out a cannula and the IV. She's asleep as soon as I've finished.

I sit and stare at her as she sleeps. I can barely believe we're where we are. It's like we've never been apart. I'm not going to let anything come between us this time. We're finally going to be a family. Something I've wanted since I was seventeen.

CHAPTER TWENTY-ONE

Sophie

It's Saturday, and I'm getting ready to go with Cade when he drives Ashlyn and her friend to Phoenix for a concert. I know Cade's worried about me going, but after two ultrasounds last week, I'm feeling much better about the pregnancy. Despite some more bleeding early last week, the hematoma Dr. Black found has gone and everything is looking good. The vomiting has been a little worse the past couple of days, but I'm hoping I can make the trip without throwing up everywhere. It will be nice to get out of the apartment for a while. As much as I love being here with Cade, I can't wait for a change of scenery.

"Are you almost ready, baby?" Cade shouts from the hallway before coming to stand in the doorway. After making things official between us just over a week ago, I've spent every night since then in his bed and in his arms. It still feels a little surreal we're back

160

together and having a baby, but everything is perfect between us. It's like we've never been apart. I still feel guilty, but I'm trying to do what Cade said and leave things in the past. It's just hard knowing how unhappy we both were. If I'd done things differently, I could have stopped the heartache for both of us.

"Yes, I think so."

"I have the IV fluids and your meds. I picked some more up from Dr. Black when we were there last week."

"I think I'll be okay for fluids. I'm feeling good."

"I'd rather take them just in case."

"Okay. I'm sorry we can't go out to a nice restaurant while we're there."

"I'm not. I booked a room which a huge tub. I can't wait to see you all wet and soapy."

I stand up and cross the room to him, winding my arms around his neck. "I hope you're going to be wet and soapy with me," I whisper in his ear before biting gently on his earlobe.

"Try and stop me."

We've done nothing other than make out since we got back together. With the bleeding, the vomiting, and the falling asleep every twenty minutes, I know I'm not a great catch, but my body aches for him. I want to touch him, and I desperately want him to touch me.

"What are you thinking about? Your breathing has quickened and your pulse is racing," he says huskily as his hand comes over the pulse point on my neck.

"You. I want you to make love to me tonight."

He drops his forehead onto mine and sighs deeply. "God, Soph, I want that too, but you're not well."

"Please, Cade. I'm not going to break. You can't not touch me for the next seven months. I have all these hormones racing around my body. I *need* you."

"Are you saying you're horny, baby?"

"Yes!"

"You're actually killing me," he groans.

I chuckle. "Is that a yes?"

He sighs again. "It's a maybe. I can't believe you're begging me for sex and I'm saying maybe," he mumbles under his breath. "Do you know how many cold showers I've taken since you moved in?"

I laugh. "I can imagine."

"We should get going before I strip you naked."

"Do you think we have time?"

His eyes widen. "I was joking."

"I'm not." I take his hand and pull him into the bedroom. I keep my eyes on him as I walk backward, climbing onto the bed when it hits the back of my legs. Dropping his hand, I reach for the bottom of my tank and pull it over my head, tossing it on the floor.

"What are you doing?" he asks, his eyes going to my black lace see-through bra.

"What does it look like?"

Reaching around, I undo the clasp and drag the material from my body, throwing it on the floor next to my tank. My eyes are still fixed on his as I undo the button on my jeans and push them down my legs. He kneels on the bed next to me, his hands tugging on the material. When he's removed them, he tosses them to one side, his eyes tracking all over me. He picks up one of my legs and lowers his head, pressing a kiss on my ankle. I watch him as his mouth peppers kisses up the inside of my leg. By the time his mouth reaches my thigh, I'm practically panting.

"Fuck, Cade," I mutter as I drop my head back on the comforter. He lowers my leg and comes over my body, his lips finding mine. When he kisses me, my body ignites and my fingers claw at his t-shirt in an attempt to get as close to him as possible. I snake my tongue into his mouth and he moans, rolling his hips against mine. I gasp as his jean-clad erection hits me right where I need him. Reaching up, I pull off his t-shirt and throw it off the side of the bed. I love his broad chest and shoulders. He always worked out, but he's thicker set now, and I love how it looks on him. Lifting my hands, I skate them over his toned chest.

"This isn't how I wanted our first time back together to be," he whispers against my lips. "I wanted to worship your body and kiss every inch of your skin, but my girl is needy and I'm more than happy to satisfy that need. Just know that tonight, I'm going to take my time and make you scream my name."

"Holy fuck," I mumble, heat pooling in my stomach at his words.

He slides his hand between our bodies, and I arch my back as his finger circles my clit. He drops his head and tongues my pebbled nipple. Standing, he makes quick work of removing his jeans and boxers before bringing his body back over mine.

"You okay?" he asks, stroking his fingers over my cheek.

I nod. "I love you, Cade."

"I love you too, baby."

He takes himself in his hand, pumping his erection before lining up with my entrance. He slowly pushes inside me, and I let out a long moan. Reaching up, I wind my arms around his neck and slide my fingers into his hair. He pulls out and gently pushes back inside me. As amazing as he feels, I need more.

"Harder, Cade."

"I don't want to hurt you."

"You're not going to," I gasp as he rolls his hips. "God, you feel so good."

"Fuck, so do you. You're so tight, Sophie."

His thrusts increase, and I move along with him. His eyes are

LAURA FARR

fixed on mine, and I've never felt as connected to him as I do right now. He lowers his head and captures my lips with his. Pushing my tongue into his mouth, I tug gently on his hair, loving how consumed by him I feel. My orgasm is building with every thrust, and I can tell from how he's breathing and moving against me that he's close too.

"I'm close, baby. I want you with me."

He reaches his hand between us and flicks my clit. Gasping, I arch my back as his fingers continue to play. When he begins to move faster, I come hard, crying out as wave after wave of pleasure crashes over me. My release must trigger his own, and he comes with a moan, his body shuddering. He drops his head into the crook of my neck and I wrap my arms around him.

When our breathing has evened out, he sits up, kissing me softly. "I can't wait to do that again." He smiles. "Are you okay?"

"Everything is perfect."

"You're perfect." He leans down and kisses my nose. "Wait there and I'll get something to clean you up."

He slowly pulls out, and I wince as a delicious sting is left behind. "Did I hurt you?" he asks, his voice laced with concern.

"No. It just reminds me you've been there. I like it."

He smiles and climbs off the bed. "Be right back."

I watch him walk naked to the bathroom, my eyes roaming over his perfect body. He returns a few seconds later with a washcloth and climbs onto the bed, gently wiping between my legs.

"We should get dressed, sweetheart. I think we're already late."

"You can blame me. I don't mind," I tell him on a laugh as I reach for my clothes.

"You want me to tell my baby sister we're late because you were horny?" he asks, a smile pulling on his lips.

"Hmmm, maybe not."

He laughs. "Don't worry. If I know Ash, she won't be ready anyway! She's late for everything."

ECHOES OF LOVE

* * *

THIRTY MINUTES LATER, WE'VE PICKED UP ASHLYN AND IVY AND we're heading to Phoenix. Cade was right. Despite us being almost half an hour late, Ash wasn't ready, and we ended up waiting another fifteen minutes for her. I didn't mind. At least I didn't have to tell her why *we* were late.

Ashlyn and Ivy insist we play Brett Young songs for the entire two-hour journey, and they sing the whole way. Cade keeps looking over at me and shaking his head.

"I don't think I thought this through. I should have just bought her a gift card," he mutters, and I laugh.

"Not a Brett Young fan, then?" I ask as I reach my hand across the center console and tangle my fingers with his.

"Sure. Just not when my tone-deaf sister is singing."

"Hey! I can hear you," Ashlyn exclaims from the back seat.

"Thank God we're here," he says, parking in the hotel parking lot. "I hope by tomorrow they'll have had enough of Brett Young and we can listen to something else on the way home."

"No way!" Ash and Ivy shout in unison from the back.

He rolls his eyes. "Come on. I need a drink," he says, turning the engine off and climbing out of the car. He opens my door and holds his hand out to me. "Not to mention getting you into that giant tub I was telling you about."

I take his hand as my cheeks flush with heat. I climb out of the car and he wraps me in his arms. "I can't wait," I whisper in his ear.

"You two are so cute. I wish I had a man!" Ashlyn says from behind us.

"Maybe you'll catch Brett's eye," Ivy says, bumping her shoulder into Ashlyn's. "We have seats near the stage."

"He's way too old for you," Cade says, dropping his arms from around me and pulling our luggage from the trunk.

165

Ashlyn sighs. "Aren't all the good ones?"

I frown, and before I can ask what she means, Cade beats me to it.

"What do you mean? Who are you talking about?" he asks.

Her cheeks flush pink and she drops her eyes. "No one, and Brett Young's not that old. He's only forty."

"You're twenty-five, Ash."

"It's fifteen years, Cade. It's not like I'm twenty and he's eighty. Age is just a number."

"He's too old," he says forcefully.

"I'm pretty sure Brett Young is married," I say with a chuckle, trying to dissolve the atmosphere that's building between them.

He snakes his arm around my waist. "I'm not sure it's him we're talking about, is it, Ash?"

She picks up her bag and takes Ivy's arm. "We're going to check in," she says, ignoring his question. Turning her back on him, she walks away.

"Ash," he shouts, and I put my hand on his arm.

"Leave her, Cade," I say gently.

"Do you know what she means? Has she said anything to you?"

"No. She's a grown woman, though. You can't protect her from everything. Would it be so bad if she met a guy who's a little older? Nash is older than Paisley."

"That's different."

"Why?"

"There's seven years between Nash and Paisley, not fifteen."

"Look, you're getting ahead of yourself. It was likely just a passing comment."

He sighs. "Yeah, maybe."

All of the Brookes brothers are fiercely protective of Ashlyn. They always have been, even when she was little, and probably

ECHOES OF LOVE

more so now that she's older. They're a little over the top. I'm not sure any guy would be good enough for her, no matter what age he was.

"Let's check in. That tub has my name on it," I say, hoping to get his mind onto something else.

He leans down and brushes his lips with mine. "Hmmm, sounds good to me."

As we wait to check in, I hang back and dig my phone from my pocket. Finding Ashlyn's number, I send her a message.

Me: You okay?

I watch as three dots flash on the screen, telling me she's typing a reply. I don't have to wait long for a message to come through.

Ashlyn: I'm okay. I love all my brothers, but sometimes they drive me crazy. I swear a prince wouldn't be good enough!

Me: They love you, Ash. Maybe we need a girls' night soon? You, me, and Paisley?

Ashlyn: I would love that. As soon as you're well enough, we'll have to arrange something.

Me: Have a great time tonight, and forget about Cade.

Ashlyn: Don't worry, I will. You have fun too.

Seeing Cade heading toward me, I push my phone into my pocket and walk to meet him. "All checked in?"

He nods and holds up a room key. "Come on. Let's get that tub filled up," he says with a wink.

LAURA FARR

Nervous excitement pools in my stomach as we walk to the elevator. We weren't much more than kids when we were together before, and although we went on dates, we never came to a hotel. It was picnics by the lake and movies at the theater. I loved all of those times with him, but I can't wait to have a second first date. I never thought I'd get the chance.

CHAPTER TWENTY-TWO

Cade

I hold my breath as I open the hotel room door and step aside to let Sophie enter. I've booked one of the penthouse suites. I hope she likes it. She's had a rough few weeks, and she's amazing to have coped with everything that's been thrown at her with this pregnancy. She deserves to be spoiled for a night.

"Cade," she gasps as she spins around to face me. "This room is beautiful." She walks toward me and goes up on her tiptoes, brushing a kiss on my cheek. "You didn't need to book a suite."

"I wanted to make our second first date one you'd never forget." Her bottom lip trembles and tears fill her eyes.

"It's perfect," she whispers, her voice breaking.

"You're not allowed to cry. Not tonight," I tell her as I pull her into my arms.

Her hormones are all over the place and she cries most days, normally over nothing. She couldn't find her phone yesterday and burst into tears. She was sitting on it. We ended up laughing about it, but I hate to see her cry for any reason.

"These are happy tears," she mumbles, her face buried in my chest.

I tangle my hand into her long blonde hair and hold her against me. After a few minutes, I take her hand and lead her farther into the room. I sit down on the edge of the bed and bring her to stand in between my legs. Pressing a kiss on her stomach, I look up to see her watching me.

"I never thought I'd be this happy again."

"Me neither, Soph."

"Do you remember our first date?"

"Of course I do. I was so nervous."

"You were?" she asks, surprise lacing her voice.

"God, yes! Why do you sound so surprised?"

She moves from between my legs and climbs on the bed, lying down on her side. I scoot backwards and lie facing her.

"You were the most popular guy in school. I was a nobody and two years younger. I didn't even realize I was on your radar."

I smile and trace my fingers up and down her arm. "Our moms were friends. How could you not have been on my radar?"

"They might have been close, but we weren't."

"I remember seeing you talking to Nash at school the first day back after summer break. I hadn't seen you all summer, but when I saw you that day, you took my breath away. I couldn't take my eyes off you. It was like I was seeing you for the first time."

"That was the summer I spent with my aunt. There was some trouble at the shelter that year and my mom didn't think it was safe for me to be around."

"I never knew that. What happened?"

"The husband of one of the women staying there found out where she was and kept showing up and causing trouble. She

ECHOES OF LOVE

didn't want me witnessing it." She frowns. "Hang on. You didn't ask me out until almost Christmas. What took you so long?"

"You were fifteen. I wanted to wait until you were a little older."

She smiles. "I was still fifteen when you asked me out."

"I know. I couldn't wait any longer. I was afraid someone else would beat me to it. I was so nervous asking you."

"You didn't need to be. I was never going to say no."

"You weren't?"

"No. I'd liked you for a while. I just didn't think I had any chance with you."

"You were gorgeous, Sophie. You're even more beautiful now."

I smile as her cheeks flush pink. "I don't think we saw any of the movie at the drive-in."

"I don't even remember what movie was playing."

"It was *The Day After Tomorrow.* I thought you were crazy taking me to a drive-in movie in December."

"I kept you warm, didn't I?"

She laughs. "Was that your plan all along?"

"Of course it was. I was seventeen and I'd waited what felt like forever to ask you out. I *loved* having you pressed against me in my battered old truck." She bites down on her bottom lip, her eyes dropping to my mouth. "Are you thinking about what I think you're thinking about?"

"What do you think I'm thinking about?" she asks, a smile pulling on her lips.

"That night at the lake, in the back of my truck?"

She nods. "I never knew a teenage boy could be so romantic."

I roll over onto my back and stare up at the ceiling. "We'd been together eight months and I was so in love with you. I wanted to make our first time together special."

She moves next to me and leans over my chest. "You did make

it special, Cade. It was amazing. You'd gone to so much effort with the picnic and making the flatbed of the truck comfy with the pillows and the comforter." She smiles. "You'd even hung battery-powered lights around the truck. It was perfect."

"You were perfect."

"I wish we could go back," she whispers, dropping her head on my chest. I wind my arms around her and hold her close.

"Back to the lake, or back in time?"

She sighs. "Both."

"I can make one of those things happen." We lie in silence for a few minutes. "I want us to do everything we were going to do that summer I never came home, Soph. When you're feeling up to it, I want to make those memories and new ones with you." She lifts her head off my chest and her eyes find mine. "What do you say?"

"I'd love that."

"As soon as you're better, it's a date."

"I can't wait."

She drops her head back onto my chest and I hold her close. "Do you think we're having a boy or a girl?" I ask quietly, my lips brushing on her hair.

"I think maybe a girl," she whispers.

"Why do you think that?"

"I don't know. Just a feeling."

"Do you want to find out at the next ultrasound?" I ask, looking down at her.

"I don't know. Maybe we should have a surprise."

"I think a surprise is good. This whole pregnancy has been a surprise, so it makes sense for the gender to be as well." She grins at me, and I grin back. "If it's a girl, though, I hope she looks just like you."

"If it is a girl, she's going to have the most protective daddy and uncles, isn't she?" she asks with a chuckle.

"She definitely is. No boy is getting anywhere near her!"

"I'm sure her aunt Ashlyn will have her back."

"Is Ash mad at me?"

She sits up and gives me a small smile. "A little, but she knows you love her. You have to let her make her own mistakes, though, Cade. All of you do. She *is* going to meet someone someday, and you're going to have to deal with that. Surely you want her to be happy?"

"Of course I do. I just don't want her to get hurt."

"But sometimes love *does* hurt. You can't protect her from everything."

I sigh. "I know. I'll apologize in the morning."

"I think she'll appreciate that."

"Enough about Ash. Now that I have you here, what *am* I going to do with you?" I ask, reaching over and cupping her face with my hand.

"Where's that huge tub you were telling me about?"

I smile and climb off the bed. "Wait there and I'll go and fill it up." Leaning down, I press my lips to hers. I'm just about to pull away when her hand fists my shirt and she pushes her tongue into my mouth. "Fuck, Soph," I mutter against her lips as I drop my forehead onto hers. "Hold that thought." I kiss her once more, my eyes fixed on hers as I back away from the bed. Dragging my eyes off her, I turn and head into the bathroom, adjusting my hardening cock as I go.

The online pictures of this place don't do it justice, and as I walk into the bathroom, I take in the amazing space. I can't wait for Sophie to see in here. She's going to love it. A huge sunken tub sits in the middle of the room with a floor-to-ceiling window looking out onto a private balcony. Turning on the faucet, I let the water run as I go back to where I left Sophie.

"It's going to take a while to fill. It's enormous. Do you want something to eat while we wait?"

She screws up her nose and shakes her head. "I think I'll eat after our bath in case I feel sick. I don't want to ruin our date."

"Baby, you aren't going to ruin our date. If you're hungry, you should eat."

"I'm good." She smiles and beckons me over with a crook of her finger. "How long do you think we have?"

I narrow my eyes, a smile pulling on my lips. "What do you have in mind?" I climb onto the bed and push her gently onto her back, my fingers tracing up and down her arm.

"I think you know."

Her breathing is already labored, and I've hardly touched her. She was always receptive to my touch, and it's no different now. I love how affected she is by me. I bring my body over hers, careful not to put my weight on her stomach.

"Well, I did promise to make you scream my name. I think we have time to see if I can manage that."

I drop my lips to hers and kiss her, pushing my tongue into her mouth. Her arms come around my neck and her fingers wind into the hair at the base of my neck. As our tongues dance together, she pulls sharply on my hair and moans into my mouth. Pulling out of the kiss, I brush my lips around her jaw and down her neck. She tilts her head to give me better access, and my teeth nip at the skin under her ear before I soothe it with my tongue. After kissing down her neck, I pull my lips from her body only long enough to remove her shirt. When she's free of it, I tug down the material of her bra and circle my tongue around her nipple.

"Cade," she moans as she arches her back. Reaching around, I undo the clasp and pull the thin fabric of her bra from her body. Tossing it on the floor with her shirt, my mouth goes back to her nipple. "God, I think I could come from just your mouth on me."

Smiling, my hand goes to her other breast, and I pull and roll her bud between my fingers. I want to test her theory, and I suck her nipple into my mouth, eliciting a moan from her lips. I

ECHOES OF LOVE

increase my assault on her breast, and I can tell she's close when her breathing changes and her body begins to twitch underneath me. My name falls from her lips as her orgasm washes over her, and her nails dig into my back. When she relaxes back into the comforter, I release her nipple from my mouth with a pop and kiss up her neck, my lips finding hers.

"Seems you can, baby. That was hot."

"Fuck," she mutters, dropping her hands from around my neck. "I've never come like that before."

"I wonder how many other ways I can make you come," I whisper in her ear, feeling her shiver at my words.

"I can't wait to find out." She captures my lips with hers and pushes me gently onto my back. She reaches for the bottom of my t-shirt and tries to pull it over my head. Sitting up, I remove it for her and throw it over the side of the bed. Her hands go to my jeans and she slides them down my legs, along with my underwear. I kick them off, and she pushes me onto my back and climbs off the bed. I watch her as she removes her jeans, leaving her in just a pair of white cotton panties. My cock hardens as she slides the material down her legs. Stepping out of them, she kicks them to the side and climbs back onto the bed, straddling my lap.

"Do you know how fucking sexy you look sitting there?" My fingers dig gently into her waist and she smiles before leaning down and kissing me.

"You make me feel sexy," she mutters against my lips before rolling her hips against my erection as her tongue pushes into my mouth. Winding one of my hands into her hair, I tug gently as her kisses consume me. "I want to feel you," she says as she pulls out of the kiss and reaches down, gripping my cock. Her small hand pumps my length, and I drop my head back onto the pillow. When she lifts her body and sinks onto me, I gasp as her wet heat envelops me.

"God, you feel good." My hand drops from her waist and fists the comforter as her hips move against mine. I watch her as she closes her eyes and arches her back, her hands going behind her to rest on my thighs. Needing to touch her, I reach up and roll her nipples between my fingers, making her movements erratic. Her walls flutter around my cock, and I can feel the familiar pull in the pit of my stomach as she moves against me.

"Are you close?" I gasp as she rolls her hips.

"Mmmm," she mutters, and I smile, taking that as a yes. Reaching between us, I circle her clit with my finger and she cries out, her body shuddering. She drops her head onto my shoulder, and I hold her as she comes down from her orgasm. When her breathing evens out, I flip her onto her back and gently move inside her. She feels incredible, and I want to stay like this forever.

"I want you to come again," I whisper into her ear as I nibble her earlobe.

"You're trying to kill me." She giggles.

"You haven't screamed my name yet."

I roll my hips and she gasps. "Oh, God. Keep doing that and I just might!"

I smile as I continue to pound into her. My orgasm is right there, but I hold back, wanting her to come again. Her walls are strangling my cock, and my jaw clenches as I try not to come. Sliding my hand between us, I pinch and flick her clit. Lowering my head, I take her nipple into my mouth, and as I circle it with my tongue, her breathing becomes erratic. Releasing her nipple, I kiss around her jaw and up to her ear.

"I can feel you pulsing around my cock. Come for me, Sophie. Let go."

"Oh, fuck, Cade!" she cries as her body arches off the bed and she comes. Her release triggers my own, and I groan, dropping my forehead to hers.

I've been with a few women in the years we've been apart, but

ECHOES OF LOVE

none of them came close to making me feel how I feel when I'm with her. I feel whole, and like I'm exactly where I'm meant to be.

We're both slick with sweat and breathing heavily as we hold each other. When we've both caught our breath, I press my lips to hers.

"I'll be right back, baby."

I gently pull out of her and climb off the bed, heading to the bathroom. I grab some toilet tissue and go back to her, gently wiping between her legs.

"You okay?" I ask, lying next to her and pulling her into my arms.

"I'm good. I think you broke me." She giggles.

I smile. "How about that soak in the tub?"

"Mmmm, that sounds good."

"I'll go and check it's ready."

I kiss her softly on the head and make for the bathroom again. The tub is finally full, and I turn off the faucet and swirl my hand in the warm water. I pick up some rose petals that sit in a basket on the side of the tub and toss a handful into the water.

Padding back into the bedroom, I stop when I see she's fast asleep. Chuckling, I cross the space and lie on the bed next to her, covering her with the comforter. She's going to be annoyed she's fallen asleep, but I'm not going to wake her. She needs all the rest she can get. The tub can wait.

CHAPTER TWENTY-THREE

Sophie

I open my eyes to a dark room, the only light coming from the flickering of the TV on the wall. It takes me a couple of seconds to realize where I am, and when my stomach rolls, I jump off the bed and run in the direction of the bathroom.

"Sophie," Cade shouts after me.

I don't stop until I drop to my knees in front of the toilet, throwing up in the bowl. Seconds later, Cade kneels next to me and scoops my hair away from my face as I continue to throw up. After a few minutes, the worst has passed and I sit back.

"You okay?" Cade asks, passing me some toilet tissue.

I nod, tears streaking down my cheeks. It doesn't seem to matter how many times I'm vomiting, I always end up crying. "I need to brush my teeth."

"I'll get your bag."

Cade stands, brushing his fingers over my cheek before leaving

ECHOES OF LOVE

the bathroom. It's only now that I look around at the stunning room. An enormous sunken tub sits in the center of the room and is filled with water and rose petals. Huge windows look out onto a stunning rose-filled private balcony, and I stand, pressing my nose to the glass as I look out into the darkness. Fairy lights illuminate the space, and it really is beautiful. I can't believe I fell asleep. I must have been asleep a while if it's dark.

"Why didn't you wake me?" I ask when Cade returns with my toiletry bag. He places it on the vanity and reaches inside for my toothbrush and toothpaste.

"I wanted you to rest. I felt guilty for wearing you out." He smiles sheepishly and squeezes some toothpaste onto my tooth-brush before handing it to me.

"I've slept through most of our date," I say as I lean over the vanity and brush my teeth. His hand comes to rest on my back, and I find his eyes in the mirror.

"It doesn't matter. There's going to be plenty more dates, Soph."

"I really wish you'd woken me," I tell him after I've finished brushing my teeth.

"Well, you're awake now. Do you still want to take a bath?"

"Isn't the water cold?"

"Probably, but I can fix it."

"Okay. I'm sorry I've ruined your plans."

He turns me around and pulls me gently into his chest. "You haven't ruined anything. I don't care where we are as long as we're together."

"Even if I'm asleep?" I ask incredulously.

He chuckles. "Even if you're asleep."

He kisses me softly before turning and leaning over the tub. Releasing some of the cold water, he waits before turning on the hot faucet.

"Have you eaten?"

He shakes his head. "I wanted to wait for you. I thought with your anti-nausea meds beginning to work, you might want to try something other than Cheerios, but now that you've thrown up..." He trails off, and I sigh.

I would love to try *anything* other than Cheerios, but the thought of throwing up all night fills me with dread. I know I can't survive for the next few months on dry cereal, though.

"What about some mashed potatoes?" he suggests. "I'm sure the restaurant will be able to make you some."

My stomach rumbles at the prospect of eating proper food, and I know Cade hears it when he smiles.

"Are you hungry, Soph?" I nod. "I'll make a call."

"Thank you."

He disappears, and I can hear him talking to someone on the phone. When he appears a few minutes later, there's a wide smile on his face.

"Two portions of mashed potatoes coming right up."

My eyes widen. "You don't need to eat mashed potatoes. You could have a steak! I bet it's good here."

"I'm not going to sit and eat a steak in front of you. Plus, I love potatoes!"

"You're incredible, you know that?"

"It's just mashed potatoes, Soph," he says with a small shrug.

"It's so much more than that."

He wraps his arm around me and brushes his lips with mine. "I think the tub is ready." He winks at me, ignoring my compliment. He always hated compliments, and it's clear nothing has changed. He is incredible, though, and I know I wouldn't have gotten this far without him. Just like I didn't last time.

I step out of his embrace, and he holds my hand as I climb into the tub. I moan as the warm water envelops me. It's so deep only my head is out of the water when I'm sitting down.

"Aren't you getting in?" I ask when Cade sits down on the closed toilet seat.

"I'll wait for the food to get here. I've never eaten mashed potatoes in the tub. First time for everything."

I smile and drop my head back. "This is perfect," I mutter as I close my eyes.

When a knock sounds on the door a few minutes later, Cade stands. "Be right back."

When he walks back in, he's naked, two plates of mashed potatoes in his hands. My eyes widen as I take him in.

"Well, that's something I never thought I'd see." My eyes track over him, and his cock jumps at my perusal. "Get that cute ass in here," I tell him, sitting on my knees and holding out my hand for one of the plates.

He chuckles as he passes me one and climbs into the tub. Picking up the fork that sits on the side of the plate, I load it up with mashed potatoes and swallow down a mouthful.

"God, that tastes good," I moan, my taste buds coming alive. Even though mashed potatoes are pretty bland, after what feels like weeks of only dry cereal, it tastes like the best meal I've ever had. I clear my plate, hoping I don't regret it later. Cade takes it from me, placing both plates on the side. When he's done, he opens his arms.

"Come here."

I slide across the massive tub and settle between his legs, my back to his chest. His arms wrap around me and my head falls onto his shoulder. I smile as his hands come to rest on my stomach and his thumbs gently stroke my skin.

"I can't wait until I can feel our baby moving," he mutters into my hair.

I tilt my head and brush my lips against his. "I can't wait for that either. When will I be able to feel movements?"

"Anytime from around twenty weeks, I think." He laughs. "My

obstetrics rotation was a while ago, so I might have the weeks off a little. We can ask at your next appointment."

"Can you believe that this time next year we're going to be parents?" I look down at where his fingers are still drawing circles on my stomach.

"It is pretty crazy. We need to think about where we're going to live when the baby comes."

It had crossed my mind that we'd need to talk about what we're going to do. Cade's apartment is beautiful, but I don't think it's all that child-friendly. Plus, I have the shelter to run, but I'm not sure how appropriate it is to have a guy living there. A lot of the women who come to me are wary of men. I have no idea how we're going to work out the living arrangements.

"What are you thinking?" I ask, wanting to know where his head is at.

"I'm not sure, but I know I want us to be together. You could move into my place, or I could move in with you. Or we could sell both our places and buy somewhere together. What do you want to do?"

"I can't sell the shelter." I feel him tense behind me, and I frown. Sitting up out of his embrace, I turn around to face him.

"You still want to keep running the shelter?"

I raise my eyebrows in surprise. "Yes. Why wouldn't I?"

"I just thought with the baby coming, you wouldn't want to put yourself in any dangerous situations."

"Dangerous situations?" I ask in confusion.

He sighs and drags his hand through his hair. "Yeah. You never know who's going to show up and what trouble they might bring with them. It's unpredictable. I know from Nash you've had to call him out a couple of times since you took the place over. I don't want you or our child in any danger."

"You want me to give up the shelter because I'm having a

ECHOES OF LOVE

baby?" I ask quietly, my heart sinking at his words. "I grew up there and I'm okay."

"I know you are, but you didn't always like growing up in a shelter. I think it's something we should talk about."

"The shelter has been a part of my life forever, Cade."

"And it was a part you hated." He closes his eyes and blows out a breath. "It's not just that it can be unpredictable. I don't see how we can make the shelter a home when there's a constant stream of people coming through the door. I can't ever imagine being comfortable leaving you and the baby alone there."

I stare at him, panic swirling in my stomach.

"It seems like you've given it a lot of thought," I whisper, devastated that, although he's asking me to discuss it, it sounds like he's already made up his mind.

His voice softens. "Sophie, I think what you do at the shelter for those women is incredible..."

"But?" I ask when he trails off.

He sighs. "Is it wrong that I want a different life for us?"

"You seem to have forgotten that your mom needed the help of the shelter when she first arrived in Hope Creek."

"I haven't forgotten. Just like I haven't forgotten what it was like to live there. A shelter is no place for a child. It's no place for *our* child. I want this baby to have a childhood that's filled with love and family, not strangers and the cops showing up at the door every other week."

His words sting, and tears cloud my vision. Not only is he judging my childhood, but the choices my mom made too. It hurts. The shelter is all I have left of my mom. How can I just walk away from that? I don't have the big family unit that he has. It was always just Mom and me. I feel close to her at the shelter, and I know what it would mean to her to know I was carrying it on. He doesn't even seem to acknowledge that.

"Did you ever stop to consider that my mom loved the shelter and maybe I feel obliged to carry it on in her memory? You more than anyone should know how it feels to be obligated, Cade." I drag in a shaky breath. "I think I'm going to get out," I tell him, my heart hurting. I stand and climb over the side of the tub. Reaching for one of the white fluffy robes hanging on the back of the door, I slip it on and go to walk out.

"Fuck! Sophie, wait."

"No, Cade. Clearly you have no idea what the shelter means to me."

"Sophie—"

I shake my head. "I need some space."

Leaving him in the tub, I go into the bedroom and sit down on the edge of the bed. The comforter is still rumpled from earlier, and my clothes are tossed on the floor from when Cade removed them. I can't pretend I'm not hurt, and tears prickle behind my eyes. I bite the inside of my cheek, willing the tears not to fall. I quickly get dressed and grab my bag. Cade's still in the bathroom, and I take out my phone, sending him a message.

Me: I'm going to see if there's another room available.

He doesn't have his phone with him, and I know running out on him probably isn't the greatest idea, but I just need some time to think. A voice inside my head whispers that maybe I'm so upset because a part of me knows what he's saying is right. It's a part I can't bring myself to fully acknowledge, though, and I push down the voice, blocking it from my mind. The shelter is all I have left of my mom, and I'm just not ready to let go of that yet.

CHAPTER TWENTY-FOUR

Cade

I watch Sophie walk away and then close my eyes, dropping my head back on the edge of the tub. That wasn't at all how I expected the conversation to go. Was I naïve to think that she would agree with me about the shelter? The Sophie from years ago would have. Maybe I don't know her as well as I thought I did, or maybe she's just not the same person anymore. Fourteen years is a long time, and I guess both of us are different people now. This just highlights that we really don't know each other anymore. I do know I've hurt her, though. I didn't mean to.

I stand by what I said about the shelter. I will always want to protect her and our child. Nothing will change that. I lived in a shelter for over a year. I might have been young, but I remember. It's no place for a child. Not any child that has a choice, anyway.

I give her as much space as I can before climbing out of the tub. Despite wondering if we're moving too fast, I need to know

185

she's okay. Drying off, I wrap a towel around my waist and pad into the bedroom. When I'm met with an empty room, I frown. Fear creeps up my spine when I realize her bag's gone.

"Fuck!" I cry, sitting down heavily on the edge of my bed. Snatching my phone off the nightstand, I unlock the screen to call her, only to be met with a message notification. Clicking into it, my heart drops.

Sophie: I'm going to see if there's another room available.

Hitting the call button, I press the phone to my ear. When it rings and goes to her voicemail, I end the call, my fingers flying over the screen as I type out a reply.

Me: Baby, I'm so sorry. Where are you?

I stare at the screen, hope igniting in my chest as three small dots appear, telling me she's typing out a reply.

Sophie: I checked into another room. We'll talk in the morning.

Me: I don't want us to go to sleep on an argument. Which room are you in?

Sophie: Just leave it for tonight, Cade. We'll talk in the morning.

Me: No. I want to talk now. Which room are you in?

I watch the screen for a couple of minutes but get no reply. Pressing on her name, I hold the phone to my ear, but it goes straight to voicemail again. I toss my phone onto the bed and flop backwards, staring at the stark white ceiling.

I drag my hand through my hair and stand. I get dressed quickly and head out of the room to the elevator. I need to talk to

ECHOES OF LOVE

her, and if I have to knock on every door in the hotel, then I will. I'm hoping that won't be necessary, though, and someone at the check-in desk will tell me which room she's in.

When the elevator doors open, I cross the large lobby and choose the check-in desk with a pretty brunette behind the counter. Nash isn't the only Brookes brother who can turn on the charm.

I come to a stop in front of the desk, my eyes dropping to the name tag pinned to her shirt. "Hi, Abigail."

When she looks up from her computer, she smiles, her eyes all over me. "Good evening, sir. How can I help you?"

I lean on the counter and flash her a smile. "I was hoping you could do me a favor?"

She raises her eyebrows in surprise and her smile widens. "What did you have in mind?" she asks suggestively.

"I'm here with my sister and we've had an argument. She stormed out when I was in the shower. She's checked into another room." I grimace. "Honestly, I was an asshole, and I want to make sure she's okay. I was hoping you could give me her room number."

She frowns and shakes her head. "I really shouldn't. Have you tried calling her?"

"Yep. She's not answering." I lean over the counter a little more and lower my voice. "Are you sure you can't make an exception?"

Her eyes hold mine until she blows out a breath and nods. "Okay. Just this once, but don't tell anyone. You'll get me in trouble."

"My lips are sealed." I mimic zipping locked my lips and wink at her.

She smiles. "What's your sister's name?"

"Sophie Greene."

Her eyes drop to the screen in front of her and her fingers fly over the keyboard. "She's only just checked in. Room twenty-two on the second floor."

"Thank you. I really appreciate your help."

"I hope you sort things out with her. Maybe we could go for a drink sometime?"

"Maybe. Thanks again, Abigail."

I turn and run to the elevator, pressing the button for the second floor when I'm in the car. I feel a little bad that I tricked Abigail into giving me Sophie's room number. I just hope she's not working when we check out tomorrow.

The doors open on the second floor, and I follow the corridor until I come to room twenty-two. Taking a deep breath, I knock lightly on the wood. When the door opens, Sophie's eyes widen.

"What are you doing here, Cade?"

"I wanted to check you're okay."

"I'm fine."

"Can I come in?"

She sighs. "I guess. How did you know which room I was in?" She turns and walks into the room, and I follow her, closing the door behind me.

"I asked at the check-in desk."

"So much for confidentiality," she mutters, sitting down heavily on the edge of the bed.

"You wouldn't answer your phone."

"Maybe that's because I don't want to talk to you."

I blow out a breath and sit down next to her. "I'm sorry if I upset you."

"Are you?"

"Of course I am. I never want to hurt you."

"Well, you did. You basically said my childhood was shit, Cade."

Her fingers fiddle with the edge of the comforter and her head is down. I reach across and take her hand.

"I never said that."

She pulls her hand from mine. "It's what you meant."

"It isn't, Sophie, I swear." I drag in a breath and run my hand through my hair.

"I don't know where we go from here, Cade. I took the shelter on when my mom died, not expecting to be trying to raise a child while doing it. I admit it's not ideal, and I can understand some of what you're saying, but I don't think I can walk away. Not yet, anyway."

I take her hand again, holding it tighter this time. She was right when she said I didn't realize what the shelter meant to her. It's only now, with her reaction to what I said, that it's becoming clearer. We're not going to resolve this tonight. We're at total opposites. We both need to take some time to think. "We're going to work this out, baby. I promise you. We don't have to make any decisions tonight. Okay?"

"Okay," she whispers. "I'm sorry I stormed out. Maybe I over-reacted."

I shake my head. "I was a jerk. I should have known my words would have hurt you and that's the last thing I wanted. I'm the one who's sorry." She gives me a sad smile. "Can I ask you something?"

She nods.

"What did you mean when you said that I more than anyone should know how it feels to be obligated?" I ask, our conversation from earlier playing on a loop in my head.

She sighs and stands. Crossing the room, she looks out of the window, her back to me.

"Sophie," I prompt when she stays silent.

"I heard you on the phone at the hospital," she says quietly.

I frown. I have no idea what phone call she's talking about, and I wrack my brain trying to think. That whole day and night have become a blur, and from memory, the only person I spoke to while I was at the hospital was Seb.

"What did you hear?"

She's still facing the window, and I wish she'd look at me. "That you felt it was your obligation to be there for me because I'm carrying your child. That you wish you could change what happened." Her voice is low, but I can hear the dejection in her tone.

I close my eyes, the conversation with Seb coming back to me. I stand and go to her at the window. "Sophie, I spoke to Seb just after I found out you were pregnant. My head was all over the place. I wasn't thinking straight." I sigh deeply. "Look, maybe we've rushed into things and we need to take a step back. If this is going to work, I think we have to take things slowly."

She finally turns to face me, her eyes wide. "What do you mean?"

I take both her hands in mine and guide her gently to the edge of the bed. I sit down and pull her to sit down next to me. "I want us to be together more than anything, but maybe we need to go back to the beginning."

"Back to the beginning?"

"Yeah. We should date. Get to know each other again. Fall in love again. We've been apart for fourteen years. We're different people now."

Her eyes are focused on our joined hands, and when she looks up, she gives me a small smile. "I think that could be good," she says quietly.

"Me too. We have someone else to think about now, and I want to get this right." I reach down and place my hand over her flat stomach. "We have to for them."

"Anything good is worth fighting for, right?"

"Definitely, baby." I pause and stare at her. "We're good, right?" She nods. "Will you come back to our room?"

"Okay."

I snake my hand around her neck and pull her lips to mine, kissing her softly. I'm going to fight. I'm going to fight harder than I've ever fought for anything. I want so badly for this to work. I've waited fourteen years for her to be mine again, but it's hit me today like a smack in the face that just because we love each other, it doesn't mean we're going to get our happy ever after. Sometimes wanting it isn't always enough.

CHAPTER TWENTY-FIVE

Sophie

$\mathcal{I}$ wake up the next morning feeling exhausted. After talking to Cade last night, I'd gone back to our room with him, but I'd struggled to find sleep. His words had played on a loop in my head, and as hard as it was to admit, a lot of what he'd said made sense. The shelter *isn't* the ideal place to bring up a child, and it was my mom's dream, not mine.

Turning my head, I watch him as he sleeps. His dark hair is messy from running his fingers through it, and I'm loving the dark beard that he's allowed to grow over the past few weeks. His tanned chest rises and falls as he sleeps, and I'm so in love with him. The pain of being back in Hope Creek these past eighteen months and having him hate me was crippling. I'd put on a brave face, but I cried myself to sleep more times than I could count. It hurt every time I saw him, but it was nothing compared to the pain of being away from him.

Despite our talk last night, I'm still not sure what's happening with us. I know we're taking things slowly, but I don't know how that's going to work if we're living together. We can hardly take things slowly when we're together twenty-four hours a day. Maybe I need to think about going home. I don't want to, but I can't see another way.

A few minutes later, Cade begins to stir. When he wakes up, he turns his head, his eyes finding mine.

"Morning," he says quietly.

"Morning."

He stretches his arms above his head and turns onto his side.

"Is everything okay?"

"I was thinking I should go home when we get back."

"Oh," he says, his eyebrows pulled together in a frown. "Is that what you want?"

I give a small shrug. "No, but if we're taking things slowly, I don't think we have any choice. We're together all day every day at your apartment. That's the opposite of taking things slowly."

He sighs. "I guess. What if you're unwell?"

"Then I'll call you."

"You promise?"

"I promise."

"Okay."

He sounds dejected, and I wish I knew what he was thinking. It was him who suggested we take a step back. I'm only doing what he asked.

"I'll order us some room service."

He stands from the bed and reaches for the phone on the nightstand. When he's ordered breakfast, he heads to the bathroom for a shower. Sighing, I close my eyes, my heart heavy. It feels like he's slipping away from me and I hate it.

. . .

LAURA FARR

CADE

I STEP UNDER THE HOT SPRAY AND TIP MY HEAD BACK, LETTING THE water cascade over my face. Despite knowing Sophie and I need to take things slowly, I don't want her to go back to her place. I hate that she's going to be there on her own. I know I have no choice, though, and hopefully taking a step back now is going to bring us closer together in the future. I just wish I could press fast-forward and speed up the time we're going to be apart.

I'm quick in the shower, wanting to spend as much time with her as soon as possible. After I've dried off, I wrap a towel around my waist and go into the bedroom. Sophie's still lying on the bed, and her eyes flash with heat as they track over me.

"Exactly how slowly are we taking things?" she asks, her voice low.

I smile and sit on the bed next to her. "Well, we waited eight months to sleep together the first time around. Maybe we should follow the same timeline again?"

Her eyes widen and her mouth drops open. "You want to wait eight months?"

I burst out laughing and tug her onto my lap, her legs straddling mine. "Sophie, I couldn't go eight days without touching you. There's no way I could wait eight months." I pause, my eyes finding hers. "Unless you want to wait?"

"No! I don't."

"Neither do I." I stroke her cheek with the back of my hand, and she leans into my touch. I drop my lips to hers and kiss her softly. Her hands wind into my hair, and as I push my tongue into her mouth, she pulls gently on the hair at the base of my neck. My cock hardens beneath the towel, and she moans into my mouth when she rolls her hips and my erection pushes against her. I pull my lips from hers and pepper kisses around her jaw and down her

ECHOES OF LOVE

neck. My tongue licks over her pulse point, and she rolls her hips again. This time it's me who lets out a moan. I push my hand into her robe and she gasps as I roll one of her hard nipples between my fingers.

"Fuck, that feels good."

I pull my mouth off her and gently lay her down. I can't take my eyes off her perfect body as I open her robe, finding her naked underneath. I drop my head, my tongue circling her nipple. Her back arches and pushes her hard bud further into my mouth. Dragging the wet towel from around my body, I blindly toss it off the bed, not wanting to release her nipple from my mouth even for a second. When I've worked her up to boiling point with my mouth, I remove myself from where I was lying between her legs and pull the robe off her body. I roll her gently onto her side and lie behind her, my chest pressed against her back and my arm under her shoulder. She lifts her leg in the air, and my fingers come around, sliding through her wet folds. As I slip a finger inside her, she moans and pushes her ass into my hard cock. I groan and drop a kiss on her shoulder.

"Please, Cade. I need you."

"I've got you, baby," I assure her.

Removing my finger, I palm my erection before lining it up with her entrance and pushing gently inside her. My eyes roll as I feel how hot and wet she is, and it's like she's pulling me inside her and holding me hostage. Taking the weight of her leg, I slowly rock against her as the fingers of my free hand pull and roll her nipple. She feels incredible this way, and it's taking everything in me to hold back. I want to take my time with her.

"Oh, God, that feels so good," she moans, tilting her head back and brushing her lips with mine.

"Touch yourself," I whisper in her ear.

Her hand comes between her legs, and she circles her clit with her finger. She brushes my cock every time I thrust against her, and as I continue to roll and flick her pebbled nipple, her breathing increases. The familiar pull in the pit of my stomach increases with each movement, and I know I'm close.

"Come for me, baby," I mutter against her shoulder.

I pinch her nipple and that pushes her over the edge. She shudders in my arms, and I continue to pound into her, my orgasm right there. I come hard, her name falling from my lips in a gasp. Dropping her leg, I wrap my arms around her and hold her close as we both come down from our orgasms.

"I love you," she says quietly, and I squeeze her tightly.

"I love you too, Sophie."

"I'm not losing you, am I?" she asks quietly, and I can hear the uncertainty in her voice.

"God, no. Not ever, baby." I use my fingers to tilt her chin so she's looking into my eyes. "Not ever." I hold her gaze and hope to God she believes me. I mean every word.

We're both silent as we lie in each other's arms, and I don't want to let her go. I know we have to slow things down between us, but it's going to be strange being at my apartment without her. She might only have been there a few weeks, but I love having her in my space, and I'm not ashamed to say I'm going to miss her.

CHAPTER TWENTY-SIX

Sophie

It's been a couple of weeks since we got back from Phoenix, and things between Cade and me have been a little strained. Despite him assuring me he'll never let me go, it feels like he's pulling away. I'm back home now, and while we see each other every day, I don't really know how to act around him. I want him to hold me and kiss me, but he rarely does. It doesn't feel like we're dating, but maybe that's because I've been too sick to go anywhere. He planned a date last week but had to cancel when I couldn't stop vomiting. He stayed at my place that night and held my hair and rubbed my back while I spent all night throwing up. As amazing as he was, it feels a little like he's my caregiver rather than my boyfriend, and I miss him.

It's Saturday night, and we're finally managing to go out. Cade's arranged to meet Nash, Paisley, and Ashlyn at Eden, and thankfully, other than the ever-present nausea, which is manageable, I'm feeling good and looking forward to getting out of the house for a couple of hours. It's been a hellish few weeks, and I can't wait to be *normal* for a bit. I just hope Cade isn't distant with me.

I look in the full-length mirror in my bedroom and smooth down the material of the dark blue maxi dress. I turn to the side and place my hand over my tiny baby bump. I'm only fourteen weeks pregnant, but because I've lost such a lot of weight due to the HG, my stomach seems to have popped out, and I love that I'm starting to show. To anyone who doesn't know me, I probably look like I've just eaten a big meal, but I know what my swollen stomach really is, and I can't keep my hands off it.

I slip on my heeled pumps and fluff my hair in the mirror one last time. It feels like forever ago that I got dressed up to go anywhere, and I've curled my long blonde hair and put on more makeup than normal. As much as I'm looking forward to tonight, I'm nervous. I'm so desperate for things to work with Cade. I know I'm going to have to talk to him about how I'm feeling. I just hope we can get past whatever this awkward stage is.

"Hey, Sophie. Are you ready?" a voice shouts from downstairs, and what feels like a million butterflies erupt in my stomach hearing Cade. I'd given him the combination to the coded lock on the front door when I'd moved back home, knowing I'd need him to be able to get in if I was too unwell to open the door.

"Be right down."

I pick my purse up from the dresser and head to the stairs, stopping on the top step when I spot Cade waiting in the entryway. My eyes track over him and heat pools in my stomach as I take him in. He looks gorgeous. He's wearing dark gray dress pants and a white button-down shirt. The buttons are open at the collar, and my mouth waters as my eyes drop to the small section of skin I can see. I move slightly and the wood creaks beneath my feet. He looks up, his eyes meeting mine.

"Wow. You look stunning."

"You look good yourself," I tell him, descending the stairs. I stop in front of him and hesitate for a second before I wind my arms around his neck. I have no idea what's happening between us, but I know I want to be in his arms. When only one of his hands comes to rest on my waist, my eyes drop to his other. "Are they for me?" I ask in surprise, gesturing to the huge bunch of stargazer lilies in his hand. I'd been so busy staring at him when I was at the top of the stairs, I'd completely missed the flowers in his hand.

He smiles. "Yes."

"Thank you. They're beautiful."

I press my lips to his and wind my fingers into his hair. He's still sporting a beard, and I love the feel of it on my face as he kisses me. When he bites down on my bottom lip, I open up to him, our tongues sliding together. It's been days since he kissed me like this, and I've missed him. After a few seconds, he pulls out of the kiss and leans his forehead on mine.

"Stay at my place tonight? I miss you and I want to fall asleep with you in my arms."

I smile, thinking he pretty much read my mind. "I miss you too."

"Is that a yes?"

I nod, and he kisses me softly again. I step out of his embrace and he takes my hand, tugging me toward the kitchen.

"I'll put these in water if you're staying with me," he says, holding the flowers up. "Do you want to pack an overnight bag?"

"Yeah, I'll grab some stuff." I go up on my tiptoes and brush my lips over his. "There should be a vase in the top cupboard. I'll be right back."

I go to leave the kitchen when his hand reaches for mine. "Wait," he says, turning me to face him. His eyes drop to my slightly rounded stomach and he places his hand there. "When did this happen?"

I chuckle. "It just sort of appeared overnight."

"God, you look so beautiful, Sophie."

"Thank you."

I smile and leave him in the kitchen while I go back upstairs. Grabbing an overnight bag, I throw in some clothes along with my hairdryer and toiletries. When I've got everything, I make my way downstairs, finding Cade waiting in the entryway. He takes the bag from my hand and slips his other one in mine.

"Ready?"

"Ready."

He drives us the short distance into town and parks outside Eden. He climbs out of the car and jogs around the hood, opening my door for me. I take his hand, and he helps me out and guides me toward the entrance, but I tug on his hand, making him stop. He turns around, worry etched on his face when he sees me staring at him.

"Sophie?" he asks, his eyes searching mine.

"Are we okay?" I ask, my voice betraying how unsure I feel.

He frowns and takes a step toward me. He drops my hand and winds his arms around my waist, pulling me into his chest. Nerves prickle up my spine as I ask the question I've been dreading.

"If you're having second thoughts—"

"I'm not," he says, cutting me off. He leans back and uses his fingers to tilt my chin so I'm looking at him. "I've *never* wanted anything more than I want you or this baby." He sighs and closes his eyes. "I was the one who suggested we take things slowly, but I have no idea how to do that." He opens his eyes, his gaze locking on mine. "I don't know how slow I should go when going slow is the opposite of what I want. I guess I've been holding back because I didn't know what you wanted."

"I just want you, Cade," I whisper. "I want you to hold me and kiss me. It feels like tonight's the first time you've touched me in days." Pain flashes across his perfect face.

"God, I'm so sorry, Sophie. The last thing I want is you doubting my feelings for you. I love you. I've always loved you."

"I love you too, but we need to communicate if this is going to work. You have to tell me how you're feeling. I can't lose you again." My voice catches, and I know he hears it when his hold on me increases.

"You're not going to lose me. I'm not going anywhere, baby. I should have talked to you. I'm sorry."

I go up on my tiptoes and brush my lips with his. Relief courses through me. I should have talked to him days ago. It seems we were both walking on eggshells when, really, all we wanted was each other.

"We should go inside. We're late," I tell him, stepping out of his embrace and tangling my fingers with his.

"If I have to share you…" He drops his lips to my neck, and I whimper.

"You have me all to yourself tonight," I remind him, my voice breathless.

"I can't wait."

Smiling widely, we walk together across the sidewalk. When we get inside, Eden is busy. Cade keeps his hand nestled in mine as we cross the crowded bar.

"Sophie, Cade," a voice shouts, and I squeeze Cade's hand as I see Paisley waving from a booth in the corner.

Cade turns to me, and I point to where they are. He nods and leads us to them. When we get to the table, Paisley stands and pulls me in for a hug.

"You look great, Sophie."

"Thanks. So do you."

After hugs from Nash and Ashlyn, I slide into the booth while Cade and Nash go to the bar for drinks.

LAURA FARR

"How are you feeling, Sophie?" Ashlyn asks. "You look so much better than the last time I saw you."

"I'm doing good. As long as I'm careful what I eat, then I'm okay."

"That's great. You've moved back home, right?" I nod. "How come?"

"We're just taking things slowly. A lot has happened since we were last together and we want to get things right this time."

"That makes sense," Paisley says, taking my hand and squeezing it gently. "I'm glad you're doing better."

"Thanks. How was your and Nash's trip?" I ask Paisley, knowing they rented a log cabin in the mountains a couple of weeks ago.

"It was incredible," she gushes. "There was a hot tub on the porch. We didn't get dressed the whole time we were there." She giggles, and her cheeks flush pink.

"Eww, that's not a vision I need in my head," Ashlyn exclaims, and I laugh.

"It sounds great. You'll have to let Cade know where this cabin is," I tell her with a wink.

"What cabin?" Cade asks as he slides into the booth next to me and hands me my Diet Coke.

"The cabin Paisley and Nash went to in the mountains. It sounds amazing."

He slips his arm around my waist and scoots me closer to him. "I think we could fit in a weekend away at a secluded cabin before the baby arrives," he whispers in my ear, his hot breath on my skin making me shiver. I smile at him, and he kisses me softly.

"We have some news," Nash says, pulling me from my Cade haze, and I turn to look at a grinning Nash and Paisley.

"This sounds intriguing!" Ashlyn exclaims. "Tell us, then!"

Nash laughs. "This beautiful woman has *finally* agreed to move in with me." He wraps his arm around Paisley and kisses her head.

"We might have spent almost every night together since we started dating, but now we're making it official."

"That's great news. Congratulations, guys," Cade says, reaching across and shaking Nash's hand.

I catch Paisley's eye and smile. She deserves every bit of happiness that comes her way after everything she's been through. Their connection had been easy to see as their relationship developed, and I'm excited to see what's next for them. Being an only child, I've never had a sister, but I've become close to Paisley in the few months she's been in Hope Creek. I'm so happy she's found Nash.

"We're having a family barbeque the weekend after next to celebrate. Wyatt doesn't have a game, so we hope everyone can make it," Paisley says.

"Count me in!" Ashlyn exclaims. "I think we need some champagne to celebrate. I'll go to the bar."

"I'll come and help you," Paisley says, standing from the booth. As soon as they're gone, Nash turns to me.

"Now that Paisley is out of earshot, I need to ask you a huge favor," he says.

"Sure. What is it?"

"I've arranged for her friend from Pittsburgh to come to the barbeque. They haven't seen each other since Paisley left, and I know how much she misses her. It's a surprise, but I need to find her somewhere to stay. I was wondering if she could stay with you? I think she's planning on sticking around for a couple of weeks. I can ask my parents, I'm just conscious their place is a little out of the way and she's not going to have a car."

"Of course she can stay with me. I have plenty of space. It'll be nice to have some company in the house again."

"Thanks, Sophie. What's happening with the shelter now that you're pregnant? Are you going to get someone to take over?"

Cade tenses beside me, and I'm acutely aware that, after our argument in Phoenix, neither of us has mentioned it again.

"I'm not sure what's happening yet," I tell Nash, squeezing Cade's hand. "I'm not taking referrals right now, but it doesn't feel good that I've had to turn women away while I haven't been there."

"I'm sure everyone understands, especially with how sick you've been."

"I guess," I say, not wanting to get into it with Nash when Cade and I still need to discuss it. I know he's right, but that doesn't stop me feeling guilty. The nearest shelter is three towns over, and I know they don't have as many bedrooms as I do. They must be full by now.

Before anyone can say anything, Paisley and Ash return to the table, followed by Seb, who's carrying a bottle of champagne and some glasses.

"I hear we're celebrating," Seb says as he puts the champagne on the table and pulls Paisley in for a hug. "Congratulations, guys."

"Thanks, Seb," Paisley says, hugging him back.

He steps out of her embrace and his eyes go from her to Cade's hand on my thigh. I haven't seen him since I found out I was pregnant. As well as getting close to Ashlyn in the last eighteen months, I've also built a good relationship with Seb. He'd been so good to me in the weeks after the shooting and would often call or message to check I was okay. I haven't heard from him in weeks, but I've been too unwell to do anything about it.

"Hey, Seb," I say as I stand from the booth and hug him. He hesitates for a second before winding his arms around me and hugging me back.

"Congratulations on the baby," he whispers in my ear. His voice sounds weird, and I lean out of his embrace. He smiles, but it doesn't quite reach his eyes.

"Are you okay?" I ask, my eyes searching his.

ECHOES OF LOVE

He nods, but I don't believe him. "Let's get the champagne opened," he says, moving away from me and picking up the bottle.

I sit back down in the booth and watch as Seb pours the champagne, laughing and joking with Ashlyn. It feels like he's putting on a front, though, and I can't help but wonder what's wrong.

"Do you think Seb's okay?" I whisper to Cade.

"Yeah. Why?"

"He just seems a little off."

"He looks okay to me," he says as he watches him talking to Nash.

"Yeah, maybe." I push away my wayward thoughts, vowing to try and get him alone to check he really is okay.

When everyone has a glass of champagne in their hand—everyone except me, who has a Diet Coke—Cade stands and raises his glass in the air.

"To Nash and Paisley. You found each other against all the odds, and I wish you both a lifetime of happiness."

"To Nash and Paisley!" everyone shouts in unison, and I smile as tears streak down Paisley's face. Nash puts his glass down and wraps his arms around her.

"They're happy tears, I promise," she says into Nash's chest as he holds her close. He chuckles and presses a kiss on her hair.

After a few minutes, Seb disappears. It's busy tonight, and I guess he's needed behind the bar. Wanting to talk to him, I lean across to Cade and whisper in his ear.

"I'm going to check Seb's okay," I tell him, and he frowns.

"I'm sure he's fine, Soph."

"I know, but he's been a good friend to me and I want to be there for him too."

"Okay, baby. Do you want me to come?"

"No, I'm good. I won't be long."

"Wait," he says as I stand. He stands too and wraps me in his

205

arms. "I'm sorry Nash asked about the shelter," he whispers in my ear.

"It's okay," I tell him, leaning back slightly and searching his eyes. "He didn't know it was an awkward question." I give him a small smile. "I know we still have to talk about it, and we will, just not yet."

He nods and drops his lips to mine, kissing me. I still feel torn over the shelter. I don't really want to give up running it, but if I don't, how can we make things work as a family? I have no answers and I'm not sure Cade does either.

Leaving Cade in the booth, I head to the bar. It's crowded when I get up there, and I go on my tiptoes to look for Seb. When I don't see him, I make my way toward his office. It's quieter here, but I can still hear the music from the bar, so I knock loudly on the door, hoping he hears me.

"Come in," he shouts.

I open the door, and his eyes widen in surprise when he sees me. He stands from behind the desk he's sitting at and comes to me.

"Sophie. Are you okay?" he asks, his voice laced with concern. He takes my hand and tugs me gently into the room, closing the door behind me. The sounds of the bar fade away as he leads me into the room and gestures for me to sit on the worn leather sofa across from the door.

"I'm fine. I wanted to check that you're okay."

"Me?" he asks in surprise.

"Yeah. You just seemed a little… distracted earlier."

His eyes drop from mine. "I'm good, Soph."

I frown. "Are you sure?" He nods. I don't believe him, but I can't force him to talk to me. "What have you been up to? I haven't spoken to you in a while."

He drags his hand through his hair and sits on the edge of his desk. "I'm sorry I haven't been in touch. It's been crazy busy here."

"It's okay. I understand."

"Cade said you'd been unwell. Are you feeling better now?"

I nod. "Today is a good day, and I'm finally in a place where I have more good days than bad."

"I'm sorry you've been so sick…" He trails off. "So, you and Cade are together now?"

"Yeah. We're taking things slowly, but things are good." My hand drops to my stomach and his eyes follow.

"I'm happy for you, Soph. I know how much you wanted this." The tone of his voice betrays the meaning of his words, and when we make eye contact, he looks… sad. I wish I knew what was going on with him.

"Thanks, Seb," I say quietly.

A strange silence descends, and despite speaking to him, I'm still not sure he's okay. Something's wrong, I just don't know what. I thought we were friends, but maybe in his eyes we're not that close, or maybe he knows what I did fourteen years ago and it's changed the way he sees me. I really hope it's not that latter, but either scenario makes me sad.

CHAPTER TWENTY-SEVEN

Cade

I frown as I watch Sophie go after Seb. I'm only just realizing how close they've become in the eighteen months since she's been back. I know he'd been concerned about her after the shooting, and I was surprised when I'd found her at his place later that night. I know it's only friendship on Sophie's part, but I can't help wondering if that's how Seb sees their relationship.

She's only been gone a few minutes when I see her heading back. Standing, I meet her halfway and pull her into my arms.

"Everything okay?" I ask, brushing my lips against hers.

"I guess so. He says it is."

"You don't sound convinced."

"I'm not. Maybe he'll open up when he's ready."

"Maybe." I kiss her again. "Dance with me?" I mutter against her lips as a slow song starts.

"No one else is dancing." She giggles.

"I don't care. I want to dance with you."

"Okay."

She winds her arms around my neck and rests her head on my chest. I hold her close as we sway to the music. I don't think we ever danced like this other than at prom. Neither of us was old enough to go to bars when we were together last time, and I'm loving having her in my arms. When the song ends, we head back to the table.

"Looks like you're having fun," Paisley says as we slide into the booth.

"We are," Sophie says. "It's nice to be able to get out now that I'm feeling a little better."

"It must have been so tough," Ashlyn says. "I can't even imagine."

"It's going to be worth it," Sophie says, placing her hand over her stomach. My hand comes over hers, and we tangle our fingers together.

"She's been amazing," I tell them. She turns and smiles at me before pressing her lips to mine.

"I couldn't have gotten through those first weeks without you."

"I'm so glad you two sorted things out. Are you coming to Mom and Dad's on Thursday?" Nash asks.

"Can we?" Sophie asks, her face lighting up. She always loved our big family meals; it was something she never had when it was just her and her mom.

"Sure. I'll message Mom to make sure she's making mashed potatoes," I tell her, tickling her side.

"Ha ha!" she exclaims, smacking me on the chest.

Laughing, I hold her hand over my heart. "Can I take you out tomorrow, just the two of us?"

"I'd love that. Where are you taking me?"

"It's a surprise."

LAURA FARR

She smiles widely. "I'm intrigued."

While Sophie was talking to Seb, I spoke to Nash about borrowing his truck. Although Nash's truck is fairly new, and not at all like the battered one I had when I was eighteen, it's going to be perfect for what I have planned. I can't wait to show her.

An hour or so later, Sophie yawns for the second time in five minutes.

"You ready to go home?" I ask quietly.

She shakes her head. "No. It's still—" Before she can finish her sentence, she yawns again. "Early," she finishes, and I chuckle.

"It's not that early, and if you're tired, you should sleep."

"I don't want to ruin your night."

"You're kidding? The best part of my night is going to be falling asleep with you wrapped around me. I can see these guys anytime," I tell her with a wink.

She smiles. "Okay. I am pretty tired."

"Let's get out of here."

I stand from the booth and hold my hand out. Her fingers entwine with mine, and I pull her up.

"We're going to call it a night, guys," I say, interrupting everyone's conversations. "Nash, I'll come by your place late afternoon to sort out that thing we discussed."

"What thing?" Sophie asks, squeezing my hand.

"Wait and see," I tell her, dropping a kiss on her nose.

After a round of goodbyes, we head outside to my car. I've only had one beer, so I'm good to drive back. By the time I pull into the underground parking garage, Sophie's asleep. Not wanting to wake her, I go around to the passenger side and scoop her up into my arms.

"I can walk," she says sleepily, her eyes still closed.

"Looks like it." I chuckle and press a kiss on her head, which is nestled against my shoulder. I don't mind carrying her. I'll jump at any chance to have her in my arms. I'm making up for the fourteen years I've missed.

When we get into the apartment, I carry her straight into my bedroom and lay her gently on the bed.

"Do you want some help with your dress?"

"Please," she mutters, sitting up and pulling the dress from underneath her ass. She lifts her hands in the air and I pull the material up and over her head, leaving her in just a black lace bra and matching panties. My eyes track over her and my cock jumps as her swollen breasts spill out over the material. My eyes drop to her slightly rounded stomach, and my heart flips in my chest as I stare at her. She's fucking perfect.

"Fuck, you look hot, baby."

Her cheeks flush pink, and she drops her eyes from mine. She reaches around her back and unclips her bra, pulling the material away from her body.

"I can't sleep in that. It's too uncomfortable."

I should offer her one of my t-shirts to wear, but I don't. I want to feel her skin next to mine. Climbing on the bed next to her, I take her in my arms and she drops her head on my chest. I want to touch her and do all sorts of unspeakable things to her body, but she's tired and I know she needs to sleep. I can make up for it in the morning. Having her in my arms is more important than anything else right now, and I hold her tightly against me.

"Get some sleep, baby. I can't wait for our date tomorrow," I whisper as I lean over with her still in my arms and turn off the lamp on the nightstand.

"I can't wait either," she mumbles, already half asleep. "I love you."

"I love you too."

Within minutes, her breathing has evened out and her body relaxes into mine. I'm tired, but I want to make the most of having her close, so I fight sleep to enjoy the moment. I'd felt like the biggest jackass when she'd asked me if we were okay earlier. I had to admit I'd been a little distant with her over the past couple of weeks, too stuck in my own head worrying about how I should be around her. In hindsight, I should have just talked to her. I hate that she thought I was having second thoughts about our relationship. I need to get out of my head and trust that we're exactly where we need to be.

When my eyes begin to feel heavy, I finally give in, falling asleep tangled up with the woman who I know for sure owns my heart.

* * *

I WAKE UP THE NEXT MORNING, MY HANDS REACHING FOR SOPHIE. When I feel the cold, empty bed next to me, I sit up, my eyes scanning the room. She's not there, though, and I swing my legs to the side of the bed and make my way to the living room. The smell of pancakes invades my senses the closer to the kitchen I get, and I stop and smile as Sophie stands at the stove with her back to me, swaying her hips to the music playing softly from the radio.

I watch her for a few minutes as she flips the pancakes and stacks them on a waiting plate on the counter. She's wearing one of my t-shirts, which falls mid-thigh, and my eyes are drawn to her toned legs. Needing to touch her, I move silently across the room and wind my arms around her waist, resting my hands on her tiny bump. A scream escapes her lips, and she jumps in my arms.

"Shit," she says with a laugh. "You scared me. I didn't hear you over the music."

"Sorry, baby. I didn't mean to make you jump. I woke up and you were gone."

She removes the last pancake from the pan and turns in my arms. "I wanted to make you breakfast. You've done so much for me these past few weeks."

I lower my head and brush my lips with hers. "You didn't need to, but thank you. They smell great."

I drop my arms from around her and she reaches for the plate, bringing it to the breakfast bar. "Do you want some coffee?" she asks.

"You sit down. I'll make it." I flick the coffee machine on and pass her the maple syrup. "Are you going to have some?"

"No. I'll stick to Cheerios. I don't want to feel sick for our date."

I give her a sympathetic smile before taking down the box of Cheerios and pouring some into a bowl for her.

"I feel bad I'm eating pancakes while you're stuck with dry cereal."

"Don't. I'm good."

She kisses me before sitting at the breakfast bar. After making myself a cup of coffee, I slide into the seat next to her.

"So, what do I need to wear today? Where are we going?"

I smile. "I'm still not telling you." She sticks her tongue out at me and I laugh. "You don't need to dress up."

"I'm going to need some more clothes soon. All of my pants are getting tight."

"I can take you shopping one of these days."

She leans over and presses a kiss on my cheek. "I'd like that. Thank you."

I can't stop stealing glances at her as I sit and eat my pancakes. She's beautiful, and I love having her in my space. I think I've gotten away with my perusal of her until she smiles and turns to look at me.

"Do I have something on my face?" she asks, her voice tinged with amusement.

"What?" I ask innocently, swallowing down a mouthful of pancake.

LAURA FARR

"You keep looking at me. I wondered if I had something on my face."

I turn in my seat and pull her stool toward me so her legs fit between mine. I run my hands up her bare thighs and smile as she shivers under my touch.

"You have nothing on your face. You're beautiful, and I can't stop looking at you."

Her face flushes pink and she drops her eyes from mine. She's embarrassed by my compliment, but she doesn't need to be. I'm only speaking the truth. She's even more beautiful now than when we were together before, and my desire for her all these years later is just as strong, if not stronger. I can't imagine *ever* not wanting her. I only hope she feels the same.

CHAPTER TWENTY-EIGHT

Sophie

I feel my face flush with heat as Cade tells me I'm beautiful. Despite receiving more than one compliment from him since we got back together, I'm still not used to it. It's not something I'd been used to when we were apart. I'd dated on and off over the years, but there was no one I saw more than once or twice, and definitely no one who made my heart pound and my body come alive the way Cade does.

When we've finished eating and cleared away the dishes, Cade takes my hand and helps me down from the breakfast bar.

"I should get in the shower," I tell him, going up on my tiptoes and kissing his cheek. "Is there time for you to wash my back?" I ask, wriggling my eyebrows.

He chuckles. "Feeling needy again, baby?"

I feel my cheeks flush with heat. "Always lately. Maybe I have a sex addiction." I giggle.

LAURA FARR

"I think it's more of a Cade addiction." His voice is cocky, and I roll my eyes.

"You keep telling yourself that."

Laughing, he pulls me along with him to the bathroom.

Almost an hour and a half later, after spending far too long in the shower, we're finally in the parking garage of his apartment, ready to go on our date. I still have no idea where we're going, but I hope my jeans and shirt are appropriate. I hadn't brought anything dressier with me.

As Cade pulls out of the garage, I look across at him. "Are you going to tell me where we're going now?" I ask as he drives away from Hope Creek.

"You're relentless, you know that?" His voice is laced with humor.

"Does that mean you'll tell me?"

He rolls his eyes and laughs. "Fine! We're going to the fair in River Falls."

When I don't say anything, he reaches across the car and tangles his fingers with mine. Tears fill my eyes and I turn to look at him.

"The fair in River Falls?" I repeat. He nods and squeezes my hand. "I didn't even know they still had an end-of-summer fair."

"They do."

"Have you been again since…" I trail off.

"No. The fair was always our place. I've never wanted to go again without you."

The tears that were threatening to fall slip down my cheeks, and I wipe them away with my free hand.

"Shit!" he says when he sees me crying. "Maybe taking you there is a bad idea. We can go somewhere else."

"No! I want to go. I always loved the fair."

"I know. I should have told you so it wasn't a surprise."

"I love that we're going, Cade. It just brings back memories."

"Good memories?"

"The *best* memories."

He squeezes my hand again, and I drop my head back onto the comfy leather seat of his car.

Cade had taken me to the fair in River Falls the first summer we'd been together. My mom had taken me when I was a kid, but I'd never been there with a boy. We'd been dating for around eight months, and I knew I was head over heels in love with him. I hadn't told him yet, too afraid he didn't feel the same, even though he'd given me no reason to think that. At the top of the Ferris wheel as the sun set over Lake Serene, he told me he loved me. I'd smiled and flung my arms around him, rocking the car so much we'd almost fallen out. I told him I loved him too, and we'd made out until the car reached the bottom. Later that night, Cade and I had slept together for the first time under the stars in the bed of his truck. It had been the perfect night, and one I'd thought about often when I was away from him.

We'd only made it to the fair once after that first year, and I couldn't wait to go with him again. Although I'd gotten emotional when he'd first told me, what I'd said was true. Every memory from there had been good, and I was looking forward to making more amazing memories with him.

"Maybe next year we can bring this little one?" I say quietly, bringing my hand over my tiny bump. "We could make it a family tradition like Thursday roast?"

We're stopped at a stoplight, and he leans over, placing his hand over mine.

"I love that idea, baby," he says, pressing a kiss to my lips. "I hope you're going to take a ride on the Ferris wheel with me."

"Try and stop me."

"I think we should make out the whole way around," he says, leaning back in his seat as the light turns green.

I smile. "Do you?"

He nods. "It'll be our last chance to. Baby Brookes will be with us next year."

My eyes widen. "And what, once the baby comes you're never going to kiss me again?"

"Of course I'm going to kiss you once the baby's born, but we can hardly make out for the whole of the Ferris wheel ride with a baby sitting on your knee."

"No. Maybe not." Excitement swirls in my stomach. "I can't wait to hold Baby Brookes on the Ferris wheel," I whisper, barely believing that I am actually going to get to hold our son or daughter. Although the HG is still present, and I have to take each day as it comes, I think the worst is over. I've made it to fourteen weeks, two further than I made it last time. It's all because of Cade and everything he's done for both of us.

"Thank you," I say softly, my eyes fixed on my hands.

"What for?"

"For taking care of us. I know we wouldn't have gotten this far without you."

"You would. You're the strongest person I know."

I chuckle. "I'm not sure about that."

"I am."

"I love you."

"I love you too."

CHAPTER TWENTY-NINE

Cade

Standing in line for the Ferris wheel, I wrap my arms around Sophie, her back to my chest. She's clutching a stuffed bear I won for her on one of the shooting games. I smile to myself as I remember her face lighting up just like it had all those years ago when I'd won her something similar. The fair doesn't seem as big as I remember, although it's probably the same as it's always been and my memories of it are distorted. For a long time, I'd blocked out the memories of being here with her all those years ago. It just hurt too much. It was easier to try and push them from my mind. It was hard to forget, though, especially when deep down I never wanted to.

When we reach the front of the line, I hand over our tickets to the attendant and help Sophie into the car. As the wheel turns, we get closer to the top, and Sophie gasps.

LAURA FARR

"Wow. I'd forgotten just how incredible the view is from up here."

I follow her gaze to be met with the stunning Arizona landscape. You can see for miles, and with the mountains and Lake Serene in the distance, she's right. It's beautiful.

"Will you tell me about Boston?" I ask as I lean back in my seat and turn to face her. As hard as it's going to be to know, it's a part of her past. If we're going to have a future, it's something I need to hear. "I want to know about your life when we were apart."

"Okay. There's not much to tell."

"You were away for twelve years, Soph."

She shrugs. "Maybe in body. My heart was always here, with you."

I pull her against me and drop a kiss on her head. I can't help but think back to when we slept together after the shooting at Eden. She told me she hadn't been with anyone the whole time she'd been away, but surely she dated? Guys must have been interested in her. She's beautiful.

"When I finally pulled myself out of the hole I found myself in after the termination, I applied to Boston University." She sighs. "As much as I loved you and Hope Creek, I needed to put some distance between us. It was the only way I could survive. If I'd stayed close by, I would have wanted to see you. Being a plane ride away meant I couldn't."

I increase my hold on her and blow out a breath.

"Did you have the whole college experience?" I ask, wanting to lighten the mood. "Did you live on campus?"

"Yeah, I shared a dorm room." She laughs. "My roommate was nice, but a little crazy."

I smile. "How so?"

"She was a year or so younger than me and *loved* to party. She used to bring guys back to the room and I'd have to listen to them

ECHOES OF LOVE

having sex. Let's say I spent a lot of time in the library!" She sits up out of my arms and stares off into the distance. "She could never understand why I didn't want to date and was always trying to fix me up with someone."

"You never dated?" I ask quietly, knowing that not sleeping with anyone doesn't mean she hadn't come close. My stomach churns as I wait for her answer.

"Not in college."

"But afterwards?" I ask.

She turns back to face me and gives me a sad smile. "On and off. Nothing that ever lasted or meant anything. I tried to move on. A huge part of me wanted to. I thought there was no way we could be together again after what I'd done, and I desperately wanted that closeness with someone. I couldn't get you out of my head, though, and any guys I did date soon lost interest when I wouldn't sleep with them."

Despite not wanting her to have been with anyone else in the years we were apart, I hate that it sounds like she was lonely, especially in a city where she had no family. I hope she had friends.

"What happened after college? Did you stay in Boston?"

She nods. "I did an internship during my second year with a large accounting firm. They offered me a permanent position after graduation, and I rented a tiny apartment in the city. I stayed there until I got the call from my mom's neighbor telling me..." She trails off, and her voice breaks. Pulling her into my arms, I hold her tightly.

"I'm so sorry about your mom, Sophie," I say quietly, acknowledging that I've never said those words to her. If I'd been a better man, I would have said them eighteen months ago when she came back to bury her, but I was selfish and still consumed with love and hate in equal measures. It's something I regret and always will.

"I should have been here. I hadn't seen her in over a year. I just never thought anything would happen to her, you know?" She looks up at me. "I know that sounds ridiculous. I knew she was getting older, but I never saw it. I didn't even get to say goodbye."

"I'm sorry, baby. She knew how much you loved her."

"I really hope so."

We're silent for a few minutes, and I know she's thinking about her mom. I can't imagine how much she misses her, especially with not having any other family in Hope Creek. I can't help but wonder if her need to keep the shelter running is more out of guilt for not being here when she died rather than something she actually wants to do. She never showed any desire to run the shelter when we were together before. In fact, it was the complete opposite. She'd almost come to resent it and how much time it asked of her mom. Her comment in Phoenix about feeling obligated to keep the shelter going swirls in my mind, but I don't want to bring the shelter up now.

"Tell me about your friends in Boston," I say, wanting to get her mind on something else.

She grimaces. "I had a few friends, but I was a bit of a loner. My best friend, if you could call her that, lived in the apartment next door."

"Do you still keep in touch?"

"Occasionally. She got married about a year before I came back home. They bought a house just outside Boston and I didn't see her as much after that."

"What about friends at work?"

She nods. "Yeah, there were one or two. No one I really saw outside of work drinks though."

While we've been talking, the Ferris wheel has made its way around a couple of times and we're back to stopping and starting as people begin to get off.

"Do you want to go around again?" I ask, conscious that we've talked the whole time, rather than making out like I'd planned.

ECHOES OF LOVE

"Okay. I'd like that." She drops her head on my shoulder and sighs. "What about you?" she asks quietly.

"Me?"

"Yeah. What was your life like while we were apart?"

Lonely is the first word that comes to mind, but I don't tell her that. I know she feels guilty enough about what happened. I don't need to make it worse. I was lonely, though. So fucking lonely I sometimes thought I'd go crazy. I had plenty of family around me, but even in the most crowded of rooms, I felt alone. Work was my savior. I threw myself into medicine and somehow that got me through.

"Cade," she prompts when I don't answer her question.

Pulled from my thoughts, I squeeze her shoulder. "I worked. I took as many shifts as my body would allow. It left little time for anything else, but that was fine by me. If I was working, my mind was occupied." *And not on you*, I want to add, but I don't.

"Did you date?" Her voice is barely audible, and I know it's a hard question to ask. I can't lie to her, though. I can't pretend I haven't had meaningless encounters over the years. I wish I could say there had been no one since her, but I'd be lying.

"Yes, but no one that really meant anything. There's been no one since you came back to town."

"Except Elise," she whispers.

I sigh. "Except Elise."

"Do you think you'd still be with her if I hadn't gotten pregnant?"

"I don't know. Maybe." I feel her tense beside me, and I know I have to explain. "Sophie, look at me." I wait until she lifts her head off my shoulder. She's still not looking at me, though. "It's not what you're thinking. It's not because I was in love with her, or even anything close to that." I drag my hand through my hair and notice how her eyes are fixed on her hands as she twists them together in her lap. I take one of her hands and squeeze it gently, waiting until her eyes meet mine. When they do, they're swimming with uncertainty, and I hate that what I'm telling her put that look in her eyes.

"It's okay. You don't have to explain."

"I do. After we slept together, I thought I should move on. I thought after fourteen years, I could let you go and try to be happy. Elise was nice, and she'd hinted that she liked me, so I asked her out. We went out five or six times, and if you hadn't gotten pregnant, I might still be with her." She goes to say something, but I hold up my hand to stop her. "As nice as Elise was, she wasn't you. Eventually, I *know* I wouldn't have been able to stay with her. My heart wasn't mine to give away. You've owned it since I was seventeen and us sleeping together just cemented that for me, even if I wouldn't let myself admit it."

I'm still holding her gaze, and she bites down on her bottom lip. She looks nervous.

"Can I ask you something?"

"The answer to your question is no," I say softly, preempting what she's going to ask.

"I can't ask you something?" Her eyes are wide as she takes my answer the wrong way.

I shake my head. "You can ask me anything, Sophie, but I know what you're going to ask, and no, we didn't sleep together."

Her cheeks flush pink and she drops her eyes. "I'm sorry."

"You never have to apologize, baby. I have a past. I can't pretend I don't. I was just trying to lose myself and forget you. It never worked, though, and I'm glad. I never wanted to forget you, I just thought I did."

She sighs. "I know this pregnancy wasn't planned, but I can't help feeling that it was meant to be. I was on birth control, after all, yet I still got pregnant."

"And not just this time. You were on birth control when you were eighteen. Maybe I have super sperm!"

She laughs and smacks me gently on the chest. "Well, you'll have to wrap it up once this baby's born. I'm not keen on having any more after all the vomiting! You're good with one, right?"

Although we never talked about having children when we were younger, it was always a given that eventually we would. I guess at eighteen and twenty it wasn't something we needed to think about. I always wanted a big family, though. I love how close to my siblings I am, and I think Sophie knew that, but watching her go through what she has, there's no way I'd ever expect her to do it again.

"As long as I have you, I'm good."

She looks at me, her face full of uncertainty. "You're sure? I know you love being part of a big family…" She trails off.

"That was before I knew how hard it would be for you. Sure, a big family would be great, but not if it puts you in danger. I would never ask you to do that."

"I always wanted at least two children. Growing up as an only child was lonely, and I never wanted that for my child."

"Our child won't ever be lonely, Sophie. They'll never get the chance with all of my family to dote on them, and if I was a betting man, I'd say they'll have a cousin or two to play with in a couple of years."

"Paisley?" I nod. "Yeah, I'd say that was a good bet."

"I think we've done enough talking," I tell her, my voice husky. "Kiss me."

"So bossy," she mutters, a smile on her face.

She leans into me and I wrap my hand around her neck, my fingers curling into her hair. Our lips meet, and I lose myself in her. We make out just like we did the last time we rode the wheel, and it's as though all of the years apart just fall away. Nothing else matters other than right here, right now. I don't think I've ever been more in love with her than in this very minute.

CHAPTER THIRTY

Sophie

It's late afternoon by the time we leave the fair. I feel like I'm floating on air as Cade and I walk back to where he parked the car, his hand nestled firmly in mine. Despite a pretty intense conversation on the Ferris wheel, I feel closer to him now than I ever have. It was a difficult conversation, but a long overdue one, and I feel better now that it's done. There's no way we could move forward together without discussing the past, no matter how hard it was to hear.

When we're in the car and heading away from the fair, I turn to Cade. "I've had the best time. Thank you."

He glances across at me and smiles. "I've had the best time too, but our date isn't over yet."

"It isn't?"

"Nope." He pops the p on the word nope and winks at me.

ECHOES OF LOVE

"Where are we going?" I ask, intrigued by what else he has planned.

"Your place. You need to get changed. I'll pick you up in an hour."

I frown. "You aren't going to wait?"

He shakes his head. "I have something I need to do."

I'm even more intrigued now. "What should I wear?"

"Something pretty. A dress maybe."

"Okay. Where are you going?"

He smiles again. "You'll find out later."

He reaches across the center console and laces his fingers with mine. We drive in comfortable silence as Cade's thumb rubs circles on the back of my hand. When he pulls up on my driveway, he turns to me.

"I'll walk you inside."

He releases my hand and climbs out, coming around the hood to open my door. When we climb the porch steps and stop outside my door, I fist his shirt and pull him close.

"Don't be long," I mutter against his lips before I kiss him.

"I won't be," he says, his voice husky.

He waits while I key in the code for the lock and open the door. I watch from the entryway as he jogs back to his car, waving as he pulls out of the driveway. Closing the door, I drop my head back on the wood, a stupid grin on my face. So far, today has been perfect, and I can't wait to see what else he has planned.

Once I'm in my bedroom, I walk into my closet and pull three or four dresses from the hanging rail. I haven't worn any of them since I found out I was pregnant, and I've no idea if they'll fit. With the weight loss from the HG and my expanding stomach, I've lost track of my dress size. Tossing them onto the bed, I slip out of my jeans and shirt and reach for my favorite dress out of the pile. It's a black lace bodycon dress with sheer lace sleeves. The material has a bit of give to it, and I'm hoping it will stretch over my rounded stomach and my larger-than-normal breasts. I slip it over my head and tug the material down. I'm surprised when it's not as snug as I thought it would be.

I look in the floor-length mirror and smile as I turn to the side, loving how the tight-fitting dress wraps around my bump. It's a little shorter than normal because of my swollen stomach, and it hits my legs mid-thigh. It's a little tight across my chest, but not too tight. My breasts seem to be growing daily, much to Cade's enjoyment.

I don't even bother trying on the other dresses. I know this is the one, and for the first time in weeks, I feel good about myself. I move across the room and sit at the vanity unit. I spend some time curling my hair, pinning up the sides when I'm done so it's off my face. Then I reapply my makeup, paying extra attention to my eyes. I make them smoky before applying some mascara. I finish off with a swipe of lip gloss. Slipping on some black heeled pumps, I take one last look in the mirror and head downstairs.

Looking at the clock in the entryway, I see it's been around forty-five minutes since Cade dropped me off, so I know it won't be long before he's back. I head into the kitchen and take some anti-nausea meds, not wanting my HG to rear its ugly head tonight. I want to enjoy every second with Cade, and I hope the medication lets me do that.

I've just swallowed the tablets when a knock sounds on the door. Smiling, I walk from the kitchen into the entryway, swinging the door open. My breath catches in my throat as I stare at Cade. He looks gorgeous, and my eyes track over him. He's wearing dark denim jeans and a navy-blue shirt, which is stretched tight across his chest. His sleeves are rolled up, and I can't take my eyes off his sexy arms.

"God, Sophie," he whispers, pulling me from my perusal of him. Looking up, my eyes find his. "You look incredible, baby. That dress…" He trails off, his eyes all over me.

I smile. "You look good too," I tell him. He takes a step toward me and pulls me against him.

"I can't wait to peel this dress off you later," he mumbles against my neck.

Heat pools in my stomach as I tilt my head, giving him better access to my neck. My pregnancy seems to make every part of my body super sensitive, and I want to strip my dress off right here so I can feel his hot mouth all over me. I moan as he bites gently on my earlobe, and I reach my hand down to the zipper of his jeans. I can feel his hard cock pushing against the material, and I palm him through his pants.

"Fuck, Sophie," he gasps, pushing against my hand.

"How about we just stay here?" I ask, my voice not hiding how turned on I am.

"God, I want to, but I want to take you out too." He pulls his lips from my skin and takes a step back, my hand falling away. "Maybe we can pick this up later?" he asks, dragging his hand through his hair and taking a deep breath.

I smile. "We'd better, Dr. Brookes."

He grins and takes my hand, pulling me onto the porch. "Like I can keep my hands off you."

I close the door behind us and let him lead me to the driveway. I stop in my tracks when I see Nash's truck parked where his car should be.

"Where's your car?"

"I asked Nash if I could borrow his truck. It's a little nicer than the truck I had when we were kids, but it's as close as I could get."

"Are we going to the lake?" I ask excitedly, my mind drifting back to the times we used to spend making out in the bed of his truck as the sun set over Lynx Lake.

"Yes, but we're going somewhere else first."

"Where?"

"Franco's. I booked us a table. I know you haven't been eating much more than cereal and mashed potatoes lately, but I thought maybe some pasta would be okay."

Franco's is the Italian restaurant in town. It's been run by the same Italian family for as long as I can remember. Cade went to school with the owner's son, and while I was in Boston, he took over the running of the restaurant from his aging father. I haven't been there for years. The last time had been with Cade. I hadn't wanted to go on my own after I'd returned to Hope Creek.

"I love it at Franco's."

"I remember."

He takes my hand and helps me into the passenger seat of Nash's truck. As he shuts the door, I glance over my shoulder, my eyes widening when I see a load of pillows, blankets, and comforters filling the back seat. When Cade climbs in, I raise my eyebrows in question.

"Dr. Brookes, are you hoping to get lucky tonight?" I ask, a smile pulling on my lips.

"I think I already got lucky, baby."

He leans across the cab and kisses me, his hand cupping my jaw. When he pulls away, we're both panting.

"What are all the comforters for?"

"I want to watch the stars with you from the back of the truck."

My heart squeezes in my chest, and I reach my hand up, stroking my fingers over the dark beard on his jawline.

"Like before?" I ask, referring to our first time together when I was sixteen. He nods. "I can't wait."

He holds my hand on the drive to Franco's, and when he parks, I wait for him to help me down from the truck.

When we walk into the restaurant, Cade gives his name to the server, and we follow him through the packed space. Halfway across the room, I feel Cade stiffen next to me. Following his line of sight, my stomach churns as I see Elise having dinner with

ECHOES OF LOVE

another woman. Her eyes meet mine briefly before she looks away. I groan inwardly when the server leads us to a table right next to her.

"What can I get you both to drink?" the server asks as he pulls my chair out for me.

"Just a water for me, please," I tell him as I sit down.

"And for you, sir?"

"I'll get a Coke."

The server nods his head and passes us a menu each before leaving us alone. My eyes drop to the menu as I try and concentrate on what to order. Of all the people to be sitting next to in a restaurant, it had to be Cade's ex-girlfriend. Maybe she'll ignore us.

"Hi, Cade," Elise says quietly.

Okay, so maybe she won't ignore us. I look up from the menu to see her staring at him.

"Hi, Elise. How have you been?" he asks.

"I'm okay. I'm back at work. I was only off for a couple of weeks in the end. The family decided not to take things any further."

"That's great. I'm glad everything worked out for you."

She looks from Cade to me, giving me a tight smile. "You're looking much better than the last time I saw you, Sophie."

"I'm feeling much better, thank you," I tell her.

She almost ignores my reply and focuses back on Cade. "If you want to come back to work, you should talk to Harry. He hasn't found anyone to replace you."

"He hasn't?" Cade asks, surprise evident in his voice.

"No. He's interviewed a few people, but no one stacked up to you, apparently."

She flashes him a smile and Cade chuckles. "Maybe I'll give him a call. I'm not sure I want to go back to trauma medicine right now, but it is tempting."

I raise my eyebrows in surprise. *He isn't sure he wants to go back to trauma medicine?* That's the first I've heard about it. That was all he ever wanted to do. Why doesn't he want to do it anymore? Is it because of me and the baby? Is he sacrificing his career for us? These and more questions swirl in my mind as I listen to the rest of their conversation.

"It would be great to have you back. It hasn't been the same since you left," Elise says.

My stomach rolls as I think of him spending a fourteen-hour shift with Elise. I hadn't thought much about it until now. I'm not normally a jealous person, but the way she's looking at him… maybe it's my hormones, but I want to lean across the table and scratch her eyes out to stop her looking at him like she wants to tear his clothes off.

"I thought Harry might have brought in Parker while he looked for someone more permanent," Cade says, turning in his chair to face her.

She bursts out laughing, and I want to strangle her. It's completely irrational, but it's the way I feel.

"There was no chance of that happening! Don't you remember the last time he was called in to cover Mendez? He had half the nursing staff in tears. The guy's a jerk!"

"God! Yes! I'd forgotten about that. Chell and Rachel were ready to walk!"

He laughs along with her, and I feel like a third wheel. I have no idea what they're talking about, and other than answering Elise's question when we first sat down, I haven't uttered a word. I stare at the menu, trying to make it look like I'm not bothered that they're chatting like old friends. I am bothered, though, and mortified to feel tears prickling at my eyes.

"I'm just going to use the restroom," I say, interrupting their catch-up and standing before Cade can say anything. Picking up my purse, I rush across the restaurant. When I'm safely in a stall, I sit down on the closed toilet seat and drop my head in my hands as I try to calm my racing heart. Embarrassment washes over me, and I don't want to go back out there. Not when I practically ran from the table. I'm an idiot. A jealous, hormone-fueled idiot. I know it's crazy to be jealous. Cade's here with me, and I know he loves me, but still, I can't help how I feel. I've never had to see him with someone else, and while I know he isn't *with* Elise, he used to be, and I hate that he was.

CHAPTER THIRTY-ONE

Cade

Frown as I watch Sophie practically running through the restaurant to the bathroom. Sitting at a table next to someone I was dating very recently can't be easy for her, and I'd been praying the server wouldn't seat us near Elise when I'd first spotted her. Of course, luck wasn't on my side, and when he'd shown us to our table, I didn't want to cause a scene by asking for somewhere else to sit. Now I wish I had. I realize how insensitive I've been, talking and laughing with Elise. I can see how that's going to look to Sophie. I'm a fucking idiot.

Elise is still talking, but I haven't heard a word she said. When I suddenly stand, she looks up at me in surprise.

"Cade? Is everything okay?"

"No, but it will be. Will you excuse me? I need to go."

I don't give her time to answer as I toss some bills on the table to cover our drinks and head toward the restrooms. When I reach

234

the women's bathroom, I stand outside for a few minutes, waiting for anyone who's in there to finish up and come out. When no one does, I push on the door and walk inside. The bathroom's empty, but one of the stall doors is closed. Crossing the room, I stand in front of the closed door.

"Sophie," I say softly.

"Cade?" I hear movement on the other side of the door and the click of the lock before the door opens. "What are you doing in the women's bathroom?"

"Apologizing."

"What for?"

"For being a jerk. I know how uncomfortable me speaking to Elise would have made you. I'm sorry."

She shrugs and drops her eyes from mine. "It's okay."

"It's not." I know she's only saying that to make me feel better. I can see from her eyes that she's upset. She has every reason to be. I know I'd be pissed if she was laughing and joking with her ex while we were on a date.

I take her hand and pull her gently out of the stall. "Come on, we're leaving."

"What about dinner?"

"Screw dinner."

I lead her out of the bathroom and toward the exit. When we're out on the sidewalk, she pulls back on my hand.

"Cade, wait." I turn to face her, and she's biting down on her bottom lip. "I need to apologize too. I overreacted and let my jealousy take over. I've never had to see you with anyone else," she says quietly.

My heart stutters in my chest as I look at her. "No, baby. You didn't overreact. I would have hated it if it were the other way around. You know Elise means nothing to me, right?" She won't look at me, but I'm desperate for her to know that.

"I know," she whispers, her eyes fixed on the ground.

LAURA FARR

I tilt her chin. "You're all I've ever wanted since I was seventeen, Sophie. Hell, you're all I've ever wanted since the first day I met you when I was six years old, I just never realized it at the time."

She smiles. "I'm yours, Cade. I've always been yours."

"Let's get out of here. I want you all to myself."

I'm nervous as I drive from the restaurant toward the lake. I wanted everything to be perfect today, but I've already messed up. I don't want anything else to go wrong. We're both silent on the short drive, and I can't help but wonder what she's thinking. Needing to know, I reach over and lace her fingers with mine.

"What are you thinking about?" I ask, squeezing her hand gently.

"You never said you were thinking of moving away from trauma medicine."

I groan internally, knowing she's referring to my conversation with Elise. I hadn't talked to her yet about looking into family medicine. As tempting as it is to go back to the ER doing what I know, I don't want Sophie to feel uncomfortable if I'm working with Elise.

"It's just something I'm considering. I was always going to talk to you about it. The hours in trauma are long, and I want to be around when the baby's born."

"But you love the ER. What will you do instead?"

"I was thinking about family medicine. The hours will be better and I can set up my own practice eventually."

"But what about becoming attending physician? Wasn't that always the dream?"

"It was, but things change, and it doesn't have to be forever. I can go back to the ER when the baby's older."

I pull off the highway and slow the truck as we near the lake. It's just falling dark as we park a little way back from the water. I turn in my seat and pick up her other hand.

ECHOES OF LOVE

"This is my second chance at the life I've *always* wanted. I'm not going to miss out on being a husband and a dad because I'm at work every hour. I want to be there for the two a.m. feedings and the diaper changes. I don't want to work a fourteen-hour shift and be too exhausted the next day to take my son or daughter to the park. I love trauma medicine, but I know I'm going to love being a dad more."

She stares at me with wide eyes as tears roll down her cheeks. I drop one of her hands and gently wipe under her eyes with my fingers.

"This baby might have been an accident, but God, Sophie, it's the best accident I've ever had."

"You want to be my husband?" she whispers through her tears, and I chuckle.

"All you got from my heartfelt speech was that?" I ask, my voice teasing. Her cheeks flush pink, and I cup her face. "I'm joking, baby, but yes, I want to be your husband. I can't wait for you to be my wife."

"I thought we were taking things slowly."

"Fuck that. I couldn't go slow with you if I tried. I've waited too long."

"I want you to have everything you said, Cade. The two a.m. feedings, the diaper changes, the playdates at the park. If that's what you want, then I want it too."

I lean across the cab and capture her lips with mine, her salty tears on my tongue. I slide my hand from her cheek into her hair and hold her mouth to mine. When I swipe along her bottom lip, she opens up to me and her tongue duels with mine. I pour everything I feel for her into that kiss, wishing we weren't squashed in the front seat of Nash's truck. Pulling away, I rest my forehead on hers.

"Will you wait here while I do something?"

"Okay."

I kiss her again before climbing out of the truck and grabbing all the comforters, blankets, and pillows from the back seat. Tossing them into the flatbed of the truck, I jump up and lay them all out, putting the pillows against the back of the cab and making it as comfortable as possible. I place the lilies I've brought her in the middle of the comforter and turn on the battery-powered lights I've fixed all around the edge of the truck. Jumping down, I smile as I take in my work, memories of years ago flooding my mind. I can't wait for Sophie to see. I'm sure she's guessed what I'm doing after seeing everything on the back seat, but I'm still excited to show her.

I jog to the passenger door and open it. She slips her small hand into mine.

"Close your eyes," I tell her.

She smiles and closes her eyes. I don't trust her not to peek, though, and I cover her eyes with my free hand.

"I'm not going to look." She giggles.

"I'm just making sure." Guiding her around the back of the truck, I stand her in front of the flatbed and brush a kiss on her cheek. "Ready?"

"Ready," she whispers, her voice breathy.

Removing my hand, I watch as her eyes flutter open and she takes in what's in front of her. Her face lights up in a smile and she turns to me, throwing her arms around my neck.

"It's exactly like before," she gushes, holding me tightly.

I chuckle and scoop her up, my hands going under her legs. She squeals and giggles as I lift her into the air and place her gently onto the pile of blankets and comforters. I climb up behind her and hand her the flowers.

"They're beautiful. Thank you." She looks around the truck and gestures to the twinkling fairy lights. "Does Nash know what you've done to his truck?"

"He does. It was him who helped me set it all up."

ECHOES OF LOVE

"I'll have to remember to thank him."

"Come and lie with me," I tell her, lying down and opening my arms.

She scoots backwards and presses herself into my side. My arms wind around her and we both stare up at the darkening sky above us. It's a clear night, and what looks like a million stars twinkle above us. This area of the lake is secluded and there's no one here but us. It's unlikely anyone else will show up. I hope no one does. I want the night to belong to us alone.

"It's incredible, Cade," Sophie exclaims. "I'd almost forgotten how incredible."

I'd almost forgotten too. I'd avoided coming here since she left. I hadn't always been able to avoid it, though, as it was a favorite of my family's. We'd had birthdays and gatherings here over the years, but I'd certainly never been here like this with anyone else. I hadn't wanted to.

Sophie turns her head, her eyes fixing on mine.

"Thank you. It's perfect."

"You're welcome. I'm glad you like it," I whisper, moving so her body is pinned beneath me.

I drop my head to hers and kiss her, snaking my tongue into her mouth. She moans into the back of my throat and my cock jumps in my pants. I pepper kisses along her jaw and down her neck, eliciting more moans and whimpers from her. My hand skates up her thigh and under the soft material of her dress. When I reach her panties, she gasps as I stroke her clit through the lace material. She raises her hips and pushes against my fingers, her hands gripping my shoulders as I continue to kiss around her neck.

"Please, Cade," she whimpers, her nails digging into my skin.

Slipping my hand under the material of her panties, I slide one and then two fingers inside her. Her tight, wet heat pulls my fingers in, and my cock strains against my pants.

"Fuck, Sophie. You're so ready for me, baby," I mutter into her ear as I move my fingers in and out of her. She whimpers as my thumb circles her clit, and I'm desperate to sink inside her. Her breathing is labored, and as my fingers continue to work her over, I kiss her, swallowing her moans and cries. I want to take her dress off so I can get my mouth on her breasts, but I don't want to stop touching her, and from the sounds she's making, she doesn't want me to stop either.

"Oh, God," she mumbles against my lips, and I can feel her walls fluttering around my fingers.

Moving my lips to her ear, I whisper, "Come for me, baby."

I increase the pressure on her clit, and that pushes her over the edge, her body shuddering as she cries out, my name falling from her lips in a moan. I continue to move my fingers, pulling the last of her pleasure from her body. When her body relaxes back into the comforter, I remove my fingers and bring them to my mouth, licking them clean.

Sophie watches me, her eyes dropping to my mouth.

"God, that's hot," she mutters. She reaches her hand up and fists my shirt, pulling me down to her. "I need you."

"Here? Are you sure?" I ask in surprise. We might have had sex here as teenagers, but I didn't think she'd want to now that we're older.

"Yes! I'm sure!" Her fingers pull my shirt from where it's tucked into my pants. When it's free, her hands go to my zipper. I gasp when she takes my erection in her hand and pumps my shaft.

"Jesus, Soph," I groan, my head dropping into the crook of her neck. Heat swirls in my stomach as she moves her hand faster and faster. "This is going to be fast, baby," I tell her, tugging her hand off my cock and pushing her dress up. I drag her panties down her legs and waste no time pushing inside her. She gasps as I fill her and my eyes roll in my head as her body pulls me in. She feels incredible. She always does, but even more so when it feels

ECHOES OF LOVE

like we're doing something we shouldn't. I roll my hips and she moves her body with mine.

"Harder, Cade. Please," she begs, and I pull almost all of the way out before slamming back inside her.

She cries out and locks her legs around my body. Her heels push on my back as she drives me inside her. The familiar pull in my stomach begins to build, and I continue to rock against her, my thrusts becoming jerky as I get closer to a release. Sophie's breathing is labored, and I can feel her walls gripping me tightly. Her eyes flutter closed, and her soft whimpers get louder as I increase my thrusts. I want us to fall over the edge together. Reaching between us, my finger circles her swollen clit, making her moan.

"I'm going to come, Sophie. Come with me, baby."

"Oh, God! Yes! I'm coming! Don't stop!"

I have no intention of stopping, and I slam harder against her, my finger still massaging her clit. Suddenly, her body tenses, and she trembles beneath me as her orgasm hits her. Her jerks and moans seem to last forever, and watching her come pushes me over the edge. I come on a groan and drop my forehead onto hers. Despite being outside, my body is slick with sweat, and I hold Sophie close as we both come down from our orgasms.

I swear sex with her just gets better and better every time we're together, and I wish I could stay buried inside her forever. Lifting my head, I kiss her softly.

"I don't have anything to clean you up with. I didn't imagine we'd be doing this, so I didn't bring anything," I tell her with a chuckle.

She raises her eyebrows in surprise. "You didn't?"

"No. Why do you sound so surprised?"

"I thought that's what all the blankets and pillows were for."

I laugh. "I told you, I wanted to stargaze with you." Her

cheeks flush pink. "What?" I ask, intrigued to know what she's thinking.

"I thought that was code for hot outdoor sex!" She brings her hand over her face and covers her eyes.

"Hey, I'm not complaining. That *was* hot outdoor sex, but I never expected it."

"I think I was right earlier," she says, shaking her head.

"Right about what?"

"I think I have a sex addiction!"

"I thought we decided it was a *me* addiction?"

She bursts out laughing. "I think that's what *you* decided!"

I pull her close and wrap her in my arms. "As irresistible as I am, it's all the hormones. It's pretty common to have an increased sex drive in the second trimester, and I'm more than happy to help out with that."

She pushes me away and smacks my chest. "I bet you are! I'll remind you of that when I'm waking you in the night to satisfy my needs!"

"I swear I'll be fine with it!" She rolls her eyes, and I laugh.

When she starts to shiver a few minutes later, I reluctantly pull out of her and pass over her discarded panties. She slips them on and adjusts her dress. I redress myself and pull her into my arms, throwing a comforter over us.

"Can I ask you something?" I draw lazy circles on her arm as I wait for her to answer.

"Anything," she says.

"Did you sleep in my room when I was away at school?"

She lifts her head off my chest, and even in the dim glow of the fairy light, I can see her face flush pink.

"Yes. Sometimes. How did you know?"

"My dad told me."

"When?"

"The day we told them about the baby."

"He never said anything before?" I shake my head. "Your bedroom smelled of you and I loved falling asleep in your bed."

"Why didn't you ever tell me?"

"I didn't want you to think I was weird. I just missed you and always felt close to you there."

"I would never have thought that. I would have loved knowing you were falling asleep in my bed."

"I can't believe your parents never said anything. I just assumed you knew and chose not to mention it."

She drops her head back on my chest and I increase my hold on her. I always knew she missed me when I was away at school, but I don't think I realized just how much. I missed her too, of course, but school kept me busy and I know she was the one who was left behind, which is always harder.

"I love you," I tell her, kissing her gently on her head.

"I love you too."

We lie together until she falls asleep in my arms, and I stare down at her. I can't wait to finally start my life with her. The life we both wanted all those years ago.

CHAPTER THIRTY-TWO

Sophie

The past two weeks with Cade have been the best yet. Despite vowing to take things slowly, we've spent nearly every night together. If possible, I'm even more in love with him now than I was when I was eighteen. There's no denying I loved him then, but my feelings now are so much more. Maybe it's because I know what it's like to be without him. Although I never took our relationship for granted, I know I never want to feel like I did when we were apart.

My HG has gotten better, and even though I throw up every morning, it's rare that I do it again. I've even become a little more adventurous with what I'm eating too, and I can finally eat a normal meal now. Our next ultrasound is in a couple of weeks and we're both excited to see our baby again.

After falling out in Phoenix over where we're going to live once

ECHOES OF LOVE

the baby's born, it hasn't been mentioned since. I know it's a conversation we need to have, and soon. The weeks seem to be flying by, and we need to decide where we're going to live. We can't keep going between places, which is what we're doing at the moment. A part of me is scared that we'll fall out again, but I know we won't always agree on everything. Still, it's a huge decision and I hope we can work it out.

Last night was the first night Cade and I had spent apart in two weeks. Paisley's friend, Taylor, arrived from Pittsburgh, and we'd had a movie night. Despite only spending a few hours with her, I can see why Paisley loves her. She's easy to talk to and so excited to see Paisley. It's clear from how she talks about her that she misses her. She's asked a lot about Hope Creek, and I might be wrong, but I wouldn't be surprised if she ended up moving here. I know from Paisley that her mom has recently passed, so there's nothing keeping her in Pittsburgh other than her job.

I'm in my bedroom getting ready for the barbeque at Nash and Paisley's when the doorbell chimes. I'm not quite ready, but I know Taylor is downstairs. Popping my head out of my walk-in closet, I shout to Taylor. "Taylor, would you mind answering the door?"

"Sure," she shouts back.

I'm expecting Cade, but he knows the code, so if it is him, I don't know why he'd be ringing the bell. When I hear footsteps on the stairs, I wonder if I'm wrong and it is Cade.

"Knock, knock," Cade says, and I hear my bedroom door open.

"I'm in the closet," I call out. "You could have just used the keycode to get in."

"I didn't want to startle Taylor." His voice gets closer, and I know he's in the closet doorway when I hear him gasp. "You look beautiful, baby."

I turn around and smile. "Thank you," I tell him, smoothing

LAURA FARR

down the material of the floral maxi dress I'd chosen. "You're looking pretty good yourself, Dr. Brookes."

He's wearing dark jeans and a white button-down shirt. He looks so sexy with his sleeves rolled up and his jeans pushed into lace-up boots.

He chuckles. "Are you ready to go?"

"Yes. I just need to get my purse."

When I have everything, Cade leads me downstairs. Taylor is sitting in the living room, watching something on the TV.

"Hey, Taylor, we're going to head out. Are you sure you're okay walking to Nash's place in a bit? Cade can always come back and pick you up."

She stands from the sofa and comes to us in the entryway. "I'm sure. It's not far from what you said, and I like to walk."

"Okay. You have my number if you need anything. I can't wait to see Paisley's face."

"Me either! She's going to be so surprised."

After saying goodbye, we leave Taylor and head to Cade's car in the driveway.

"Why don't you stay here tonight? We can walk to Nash's and you can have a drink then?" I suggest.

"Sure. That sounds good."

We walk hand in hand to Nash's place, arriving just as everyone else does.

"You look beautiful, Sophie," Tessa says, taking me from Cade's side and pulling me into a hug. "How are you feeling now?"

"Really good. I still have the occasional bad day, but overall, the morning sickness is much more manageable."

"I'm so glad."

"Hey, Soph," Ashlyn says, pulling me in for a hug. "We can arrange that night out now that you're feeling better," she suggests, obviously overhearing my conversation with her mom.

ECHOES OF LOVE

"I'd love that. We can invite Paisley and Taylor too." Everyone other than Paisley knows Taylor is surprising her today and we've all been sworn to secrecy.

She nods. "Great. I'll get something organized."

Leaving Ashlyn and Tessa, I make for Seb, who's talking to Wyatt.

"Hey, guys," I say, hoping I'm not interrupting. I haven't seen Seb since our strange conversation at the bar a couple of weeks ago. I've texted him a couple of times, and while he always replies, it's not like it used to be. I wish he'd talk to me.

"Hi, Soph," Wyatt says, leaning down to brush a kiss on my cheek.

"Are you home for the weekend?" I ask, knowing the football season is underway.

"Not even that long. I can only stay for a couple of hours, then I need to head back to Phoenix."

"Well, it's good to see you."

"You too, Soph."

He walks past me to talk to Cade, leaving Seb and me alone. I move toward him and press my lips to his cheek before pulling him in for a hug. He tenses for a second before hugging me back. He might only have hesitated briefly, but I noticed. He was the same when I hugged him at Eden a couple of weeks ago.

"Are you okay?" I ask as I take a step back.

He nods. "How have you been?" he asks, giving me a small smile.

"Good. I'm feeling much better."

"That's good. You look great. Pregnancy suits you."

"Thanks."

It's awkward between us, and I wish I knew what I'd done. It can only be that he knows about the termination and sees me differently now. I want to ask him, but as we head around the side of Nash's place and into the backyard, I know now isn't the time.

247

LAURA FARR

This is Nash and Paisley's day, and I don't want anything to detract from that. I'll talk to him another time.

After a round of hellos, we're all settled on the outdoor sofa with drinks in our hands when Max barks, signaling that someone is at the door. I smile to myself as I see Paisley stand.

"I'll get it, babe," Nash calls, and she nods and sits back down. She's talking to Ashlyn, and I watch her until Nash returns a few minutes later. "Paisley, there's someone here to see you."

Tears pool in her eyes and her hand flies to her mouth as Nash steps to one side, revealing Taylor. She jumps up from where she's sitting and runs across the backyard, pulling Taylor into a hug. I can't hear what's being said, but I can see that both of them are crying as they cling to each other. I'm so happy Nash was able to do this for her. I know how it feels to have no one. While the whole Brookes family has taken her in like she's one of their own, having her best friend here must mean everything to her.

Paisley takes Taylor around, introducing her to everyone. When she gets to where Ashlyn and I are sitting, she sits down, pulling Taylor to sit with her.

"Sophie, this is Taylor, my best friend from Pittsburgh." She turns to Taylor. "Sophie is dating Cade, Nash's brother."

Taylor laughs and gives me a small wave.

"Hi, Sophie."

"Hi, Taylor." I grin at her.

"Okay, what am I missing?" Paisley asks, her voice laced with confusion.

"Taylor's staying at my place," I tell her. "Nash arranged it a few weeks ago."

Her eyes widen in surprise. "Did *everyone* know she was coming?"

"Pretty much!" I laugh.

She shakes her head. "I can't believe he did this for me."

"He loves you, Paisley," I tell her simply.

ECHOES OF LOVE

"Can you give me a minute? I just need to go and thank him."

"Of course," Taylor says. "Take your time."

Paisley pulls her into a hug before running across the backyard and throwing herself at Nash.

"I've never seen her so happy," Taylor says as she watches her. "She deserves every second."

"Nash adores her," Ashlyn says, her voice wistful. Taylor takes a deep breath before lifting her wineglass to her lips and swallowing down a mouthful. "Have you got a boyfriend?" Ash asks. I smile to myself. Only Ash would ask someone she met five minutes ago about their personal life.

"No. I spent every spare second I had with my mom. Not that I'm complaining. I'd do the same again."

"Paisley said you'd lost your mom. I'm sorry," she says.

"Thanks. I know she's at peace now." She takes another sip of her wine. "What about you? Do you have a boyfriend?"

She lets out a humorless laugh. "I wish! Having four older brothers makes dating a nightmare."

"I can imagine!" She looks around the yard. "I probably shouldn't say this, especially in front of the both of you, but seriously, how are all four brothers so good-looking? It's like they all have the perfect gene or something."

Ashlyn bursts out laughing. "Trust me, after growing up with them, I can assure you they are far from perfect." She wrinkles up her nose in disgust. "I'm going to grab a drink. Does anyone want anything?" We both shake our heads and she disappears inside the house.

"The Brookes brothers have always had that *something*," I tell her. "Although, it's only ever been Cade for me."

"Is it Seb or Wyatt with the tattoos? I've met everyone, but it was a little like information overload." She chuckles.

"That's Seb."

"He's beautiful."

I follow her gaze and smile. She's right. Although beautiful sounds like a strange way to describe a six-foot-three tattooed man, it somehow fits. He is beautiful inside and out.

"Seb's a great guy. The whole Brookes family is amazing."

"Yeah, I'm beginning to see that."

I look around the backyard, taking in just how close this incredible family is. Aside from welcoming me back after twelve years away, they've opened their arms and their hearts to Paisley when she showed up in Hope Creek, broken and battered. She's been in Nash's life for six months, but already they love her like they've known her for years. I know how lucky I am to be a part of this family, and now more than ever, I can't wait to create a small extension of that.

"You should talk to him. He's single, you know," I tell Taylor, wiggling my eyebrows at her.

She laughs. "How is a guy like that single?"

I shrug. "Maybe he hasn't met the right girl yet."

My mind wanders back to the conversation we had months ago at his apartment when he said he was too busy for love. I don't believe that for a second. No one's too busy for love, and if they are, then they've got their priorities wrong. I probably shouldn't be playing matchmaker, not when I don't know if Taylor plans on sticking around, but Seb's a good friend and I want to see him happy. Something tells me he's not happy at all right now, and I wish I knew why.

CHAPTER THIRTY-THREE

Cade

"Hey, baby. I wondered where you'd gone. Are you okay?" I ask into Sophie's ear as my arms slide around her waist. I pull her gently back against my chest. I'd seen her heading inside and followed her.

She tilts her head and smiles at me. "I'm good. I just wanted some water." She holds up a bottle before taking a mouthful.

"Are you having fun?"

She turns in my arms and nods. "We've just arranged a girls' night out. Me, Ash, Paisley, and Taylor."

"That sounds like fun."

"You should meet up with the guys. Have a boys' night."

"Yeah. I'll talk to them." I lean down and brush her lips with mine. "Are you about ready to head out? Wyatt's leaving, and Mom and Dad are going too."

"Sure. Let's say goodbye."

LAURA FARR

It takes us a while to get around everyone, and it's almost thirty minutes later when we finally leave. Taylor wants to stay a while longer, and Nash is driving her back when she's ready.

It's early evening, and despite the heat of the sun earlier, there's a chill in the air as we walk back, and Sophie shivers.

"Are you cold?" I ask, releasing her hand and wrapping my arm around her.

"Better now," she says as I pull her into my side, enveloping her in the heat of my body.

"So, I have something I need to talk to you about," I say quietly as we walk along the sidewalk.

She looks up at me, her eyebrows raised in question. "Is everything okay?"

I nod and squeeze her waist. "Doc Morris wants to retire next year. He's looking for someone to take over his half of the partnership."

Doc Morris runs the medical center in Hope Creek. I'd heard from a colleague at the hospital that he was looking to retire, and after he put in a good word for me, I went to see him earlier in the week.

"I know you said family medicine is what you want to do, but are you really sure? You're okay with walking away from everything you've worked so hard for?"

"I'm not walking away, just changing direction."

"But it's definitely a direction you want to go in? If I wasn't pregnant, would you be thinking about it?"

"Well, no, but—"

"I just don't want you to have any regrets," she interrupts.

"I'll have regrets if I don't do this, Soph." I stop walking, forcing her to stop with me. Reaching for her hands, I hold them in mine. "What I want has changed. I'm doing this for me as much as I am for us. I want to be a doctor, I can't deny that, but I want a family too. This way, I can do both."

"You're sure?"

"I'm sure, baby."

"When is he retiring?"

"He's going to reduce his hours before finishing completely, so he wants me to work alongside him for a few months before taking over."

She smiles and holds my gaze. "If this is really what you want, then it sounds perfect, Cade."

"Really? You're okay with this?" She nods, and I grin. "It is what I want. I'll tell him yes on Monday, then."

We've continued to walk as we talk, and when we turn the corner, Sophie's house comes into view. It's falling dark, and I squint as I see someone sitting on the porch swing. Sophie notices too and squeezes my hand.

"Who's that?" I ask.

She shakes her head. "I'm not sure." As we get nearer, Sophie gasps. "Lyra? Are you okay?"

I know from Sophie that Lyra's somewhat of a regular at the shelter, and I can tell by looking at her that she isn't okay at all. One of her eyes is red and swollen, while the rest of her face is deathly pale. She's sitting slumped forward with her hand clutching her stomach. I drop Sophie's hand and follow her up the steps. The security light illuminates the porch, and Sophie gasps as she sees the full extent of her injuries.

"I'm sorry, Sophie. I didn't know where else to go," Lyra says through her tears.

"It's going to be okay," she tells her, kneeling in front of her. She looks over her shoulder at me. "Do you have your bag in the car?"

"No, it's at home. Let's get her inside and I'll check her over. I think she might need to go to the hospital."

Lyra's eyes widen and fear crosses her face when she hears my voice. Despite her obvious pain, she shrinks back.

"Lyra, this is my boyfriend, Cade," Sophie says quickly, trying to reassure her. "He's a doctor. Can he take a look at you? He won't hurt you. I promise."

"No!" She shakes her head and tries to stand, wincing as her hand remains over her stomach. Sophie stands with her and reaches for her free hand.

"Do you trust me?" she asks her. She hesitates before nodding. "Then you know I wouldn't lie to you. Cade is one of the good guys. Will you let him help you?"

Her cautious eyes go from Sophie to me, and I can see she's terrified. After a few seconds, she nods slowly. I reach for her bag that sits by her feet and go ahead of them to punch in the code and unlock the front door. I hold the door open while Sophie guides her into the entryway.

"Let's go into the living room," I say from behind them.

Sophie takes her through and helps her to sit on the sofa. She keeps her hand nestled in Sophie's, who sits next to her.

"Hi, Lyra," I say softy as I sit on the coffee table in front of her.

"Hi," she whispers, finally lifting her eyes to mine.

"Can you tell me what happened and where it hurts?"

"Trent… he got laid off. He was drunk." She lets out a sob as she brings her hand from her stomach over her mouth. It's then I see just how much blood is on her shirt.

My gaze flicks to Sophie, whose wide eyes meet mine. She's seen the blood too.

"Lyra, what happened to your stomach? Can I take a look?" I ask gently.

She hesitates before nodding. "He had a knife," she whispers. "I managed to get from the living room to the kitchen after he hit me. He followed me though and grabbed a knife off the counter."

"I'm so sorry, Lyra," Sophie says quietly.

"I should have listened to you, Sophie. You were right about him." She takes a deep breath and grimaces as she repositions herself on the sofa. "I so wanted it to be different this time."

"I wanted that for you too." She gives her a sad smile. "I'll help you to lie down so Cade can look you over."

"Okay," she agrees, her voice shaky.

Sophie stands, and Lyra winces as she lifts her legs and maneuvers herself so she's lying on the sofa. Even more blood oozes onto her shirt, and Sophie steps aside so I can take a closer look.

"I need to open your shirt, Lyra. Is that okay?" I ask, knowing she's wary of me.

She nods and closes her eyes as I undo the buttons on her shirt. When I pull the material back, I see the source of all the blood. There's an inch-long wound to the left of her belly button.

"Sophie, can you get me some clean towels and call 911? We're going to need an ambulance." Lyra lets out a groan as I press my hand over the wound to stem the steady trickle of blood. "I'm sorry that hurts, Lyra. I need to try and stop the bleeding."

Sophie walks quickly up the stairs, and I hear her talking into her phone.

"My friend's been stabbed. I need an ambulance," she says, returning a few minutes later with a handful of towels and handing them to me.

She gives over the address, and I press one of the towels over the wound instead of my hand.

"Sophie, tell them it appears to be a shallow abdominal trauma with possible internal bleeding," I tell her.

She relays the message before telling me the EMTs are on their way. The emergency dispatcher must be asking her questions about Lyra's condition, and she answers as best she can. As we wait for the ambulance, the bleeding has slowed considerably, although Lyra still looks pale and terrified. Sophie holds her hand while we wait, and I see her breathe a visible sigh of relief when we hear sirens in the distance. She leaves us in the living room while she goes outside to let them in.

When the EMTs arrive, I give them a brief history before stepping away to allow them to work on her. Sophie follows me into the kitchen and waits while I wash the blood off my hands. When I'm done, I go to her and pull her into his arms.

"Are you okay?" I ask. "You're shaking."

"Am I? I hadn't noticed. I'm okay."

I take a step back and frown, my eyes searching hers. "Are you sure? Here, sit down." I pull out a stool that sits under the kitchen counter and guide her to sit on it.

Even when she's sitting down, her whole body trembles. I stand in front of her and she rests her head on my chest, her arms going around my waist. I know this has affected her; she can't hide it from me. This is why I want her to take a step back from the shelter. Even if I end up moving in, I'm not going to be here all the time. What if she's here with the baby and someone shows up like this? What if the abusive boyfriend shows up? I need to talk to her again. Surely she can't still think running the shelter is a good idea? Now isn't the time, though. Our talk will have to wait until later.

"I'm so glad you're here, Cade. I don't know what I would have done if I'd been on my own." She sits up, her eyes finding mine.

"So, she's never shown up like this before?"

"No, never. A black eye once or twice, but never this bad. I hope she finally kicks him to the curb for this. He could have killed her."

"I should call Nash. Do you know where this Trent lives?"

"I did have an address the first time she was referred here. I don't know if that's still where he lives, but it's worth a try. It'll be in my office."

"Are you sure you're okay?"

"I'm okay. Just worried about Lyra."

She stands, and I follow her out of the kitchen. She unlocks the door to the office and searches through some files, quickly finding Lyra's information. Using my phone, I take a picture of the address she has and wait for her to lock the office.

"Go back to Lyra, baby. I'm just going to call Nash."

She nods and brushes a kiss on my cheek. Going back into the kitchen, I pull up Nash's number and call him. After filling him in on what I know, I forward him the picture with what I think is Trent's address. I hope they get the bastard.

"We're taking her to the emergency room now. Is anyone coming in the ambulance with her?" one of the EMTs asks as I walk back into the living room.

"You go, Soph. I'll follow in the car."

She nods and the EMTs wheel Lyra through the entryway and outside. "Did you talk to Nash?"

"Yes. He's going to get a team together and head over to the address you gave me. Hopefully, they'll find him."

"I hope so. I'll see you at the hospital."

I brush a kiss on her lips and follow her outside, pulling the front door closed. She follows Lyra to the waiting ambulance and climbs in, the doors closing behind her. I dig my car keys from my pocket and slide into my car. This isn't how I thought today would end when we left Nash's place an hour ago. I thought by now I'd be in bed with a naked Sophie wrapped around me. Instead, we're heading for a long night in the ER. I hope Sophie's okay. She must be exhausted, but I know she won't be thinking about herself right now. She wouldn't let Lyra go to the hospital alone. From what Sophie's told me about her, she has no one, and I know she'll want to be there for her.

CHAPTER THIRTY-FOUR

Sophie

"I need to get you home, baby," Cade says. "You can barely stand. Lyra's in good hands now that she's been admitted. We can come back and see her tomorrow."

I'm not going to argue with him. I'm so tired I can't see straight, and waves of nausea wash over me.

When I arrived in the ambulance with Lyra over an hour ago, she was taken straight into trauma and it was touch and go whether she'd need surgery. Thankfully, she didn't, but they did admit her to keep an eye on her blood pressure, which was low due to all the blood she'd lost. I'd been able to see her briefly and assured her I'll be back in the morning. Now, I'm more than ready to go home and fall asleep in Cade's arms.

"I'm ready to go home. I'm exhausted."

I let Cade take my hand and follow him blindly through the

hospital to the parking lot. I have no idea how I make it back to his car when I can barely put one foot in front of the other, and I lean heavily on him.

"My place or yours?" he asks as he pulls away from the hospital.

"We'd better go back to mine. I don't know if Taylor will still be with Paisley, but I don't want her to go back to an empty house."

He nods and reaches across the center console to tangle his fingers with mine. I drop my head back on the seat and close my eyes. When I open them, he's parking on the driveway.

"God, I can't wait to get into bed. I'll have to clean up tomorrow when I've got some energy," I say as I climb out of the car and let Cade guide me up the porch steps.

"I'll clean up in the morning. I don't want you to worry about it."

I smile as I lean against him while he keys in the code to the front door. He guides me straight upstairs, not letting me see the mess the EMTs have undoubtedly left in the living room.

When we get into my bedroom, I strip my clothes off and climb straight into bed. I should brush my teeth, but I really don't think my legs will hold me up a second longer. My eyes close as soon as my head hits the pillow, and I feel the bed dip and Cade's arms wrap around me.

"Night, baby," he whispers in my ear, brushing a kiss on my hair.

"Night, Cade," I mumble, sleepily.

I'M DRAGGED FROM SLEEP BY AN INCESSANT BEEPING. I'M NOT FULLY awake and my confused brain can't work out if the noise is from my dreams or reality. As I open my eyes and the noise continues, I realize it's no dream. My hand goes over my mouth, and I choke as I try to take a breath. The room is dark, but the light from the moon streaks through a gap in the drapes, and as my eyes adjust, panic washes over me when I realize the room is full of smoke. It only takes seconds for my eyes to sting, and my lungs scream out for clean air.

"Cade," I choke out. "Wake up. I think the house is on fire." My hand that isn't over my mouth goes to his shoulder and I shake him roughly. I cough again as the thick smoke hits the back of my throat.

"Fuck!" Cade exclaims as he sits up, his eyes wide. He too begins to cough, and fear swirls in my stomach. "We need to get out of here." He looks around the room, his eyes landing on the small balcony off my bedroom. "The balcony. We can climb down."

He pulls his t-shirt over his head and slips it on me. I hadn't considered that I'd fallen asleep naked apart from my panties.

"We need to call 911," I tell him, searching blindly for my phone. Finding it, I snatch it up.

"We need to get out first. Pull my t-shirt up over your mouth," he instructs, and I do as he says. He takes my hand and we climb off the bed, making for the balcony.

"Wait!" I exclaim, the t-shirt slipping from over my mouth as I cough. "Taylor! Did she come back from Nash's place?"

"Shit! I don't know."

He tugs on my hand, pulling me toward the balcony. "Stop!" I cry. "We have to check her room."

"I will, but I need to know you're safe first. Please, Sophie."

I look over my shoulder at my closed bedroom door. With all the smoke in the room, I can't even begin to imagine what it's like beyond that door. I hope to God she decided to stay with Paisley.

Within seconds, we're outside on the tiny balcony, and I drag

ECHOES OF LOVE

in mouthfuls of fresh air, my lungs burning after breathing in the smoke. As I turn around and look at the house, I gasp as smoke and flames lick the building on the first floor.

"Are you okay?" Cade asks, taking my face in his hands, his eyes searching mine. Tears stream down my cheeks, and I nod, knowing we're not out of danger yet. We're stuck on a second-floor balcony and I've no idea how we're going to get down.

"I'm going back in for Taylor. Call 911."

He moves away from me and I grab his hand. "Maybe we should wait for the fire department."

"There's no time."

"Please be careful."

He presses his lips to mine. "I love you."

"I love you too."

I let out a sob as he goes back inside, terror flooding my body. Lifting the phone that's nestled in my hand, I'm just about to call 911 when I see a message from Paisley. Clicking into it, I quickly read it.

Paisley: Taylor's staying on the sofa tonight. Nash told me what happened. I hope Lyra's okay.

"Fuck, fuck fuck. Cade, she's not in there!" I shout into my bedroom. "Cade!" When I'm met with silence, I drop to my knees and dial 911 for the second time tonight.

"911, what's your emergency?" the dispatcher says.

"My house is on fire."

"What's your address?"

"419 Bramble Lane, Hope Creek."

I can hear her fingers flying over the keyboard, and I go to the balcony door, my eyes searching for Cade. Smoke billows out of the door, and I cough, moving backwards.

"What's your name? Are you somewhere safe?"

"It's Sophie. I'm outside on a second-floor balcony at the back of the house. My boyfriend's gone back inside looking for our friend. Please hurry."

"My name's Amy. The fire department is on the way. I'm sending the EMTs as well. I want you to stay on the phone with me until they arrive. Okay, Sophie?"

"Okay."

"What's your boyfriend's name?"

"Cade," I tell her, my voice breaking.

"How long has he been inside, Sophie?"

"I don't know. A few minutes. Taylor's not home. She's staying at a friend's house. He didn't know and went back in for her."

Before she can respond, there's a loud explosion, and the windows on the first floor shatter. I scream and grip tightly on to the metal railings of the balcony with my free hand as the whole house shakes.

"Cade," I shout into the night, my voice swallowed up by the sounds of the fire.

"What's happening, Sophie? Talk to me," the dispatcher says.

"There… there was an explosion. The windows have blown out. I need to go in and find Cade. He should be out by now."

"No, Sophie! You need to stay where you are. The fire crews are two minutes out."

"Cade might not have two minutes."

"Soph—"

I cut her off and end the call. Tossing my phone on the floor, I pull my t-shirt up and over my mouth, and after taking a deep breath, I go back into my bedroom. The smoke is heavy in the room, and I drop down as low as possible, crawling along the floor. When I get to the door, I can just make out a figure lying in the hallway. My lungs feel like they're on fire, but I push forward, ignoring how difficult it is to breathe. Flames are beginning to lick

ECHOES OF LOVE

up the wooden staircase, and I know I have one shot at getting him out of here.

"Cade," I say, coughing uncontrollably as I get to him. He's unconscious, and I drop the material covering my mouth so I have both hands free. Finding a strength I didn't know I had, I grab on to his arms and drag him across the hallway and back into my bedroom. When I get him clear of the door, I drop his arms and shut the bedroom door. I reach for the comforter off the bed and wedge it under the door to stop more smoke entering the room. Picking up Cade's arms again, I pull him closer to the balcony door and the fresh air we both so desperately need. He's breathing, thank God, but he's still unconscious.

When I hear sirens, I breathe a sigh of relief. A minute later, I hear someone calling my name.

"Sophie, it's the Hope Creek Fire Department. Can you hear me?"

"We're around the back," I shout, reluctantly leaving Cade in the doorway and stepping out onto the balcony. "Please hurry. My boyfriend needs help."

The security light illuminates the backyard as a firefighter comes into view. He acknowledges me with a wave of his hand before turning and shouting to someone behind him.

"Get the ladder, now!"

Within minutes, firefighters are carrying an unconscious Cade down the ladder, laying him on a waiting gurney. He's rushed around the side of the house and out of sight. I manage to hold it together until my feet hit the ground, and I collapse to the floor, tears tracking down my face.

The firefighter who rescued me scoops me into his arms and takes me to the front of the house to the waiting EMTs. There are two crews; one for Cade and one for me. When I'm transferred to the back of the second ambulance, panic begins to overwhelm me and my breathing becomes frantic.

LAURA FARR

"Hey, I need you to calm down," the EMT says, trying to get me to keep the oxygen mask on my face. My head knows she's trying to help me, but my heart just needs to know that Cade's okay.

"Cade," I gasp out, pulling the mask off again.

"Cade is in good hands, I promise. Let us look after you. Sophie, are you pregnant?" she asks, lifting my shirt. When I don't answer, she stands in front of me and takes my face in her hands. "Sophie, I need you to look at me." She holds my face until my eyes meet hers. "Good. That's good," she encourages as my breathing begins to even out. "Are you pregnant?"

"Yes," I whisper, more tears tracking down my face.

"How many weeks?"

"Almost seventeen."

She nods. "We need to get you checked over at the hospital."

My breathing accelerates again, and I fight to get away from them. I have to see Cade. "No! What about Cade?"

"Look, if you stay here and keep your mask on, I'll go and see if I can get an update, but you *have* to keep the mask on." I nod, and she squeezes my hand. "I'll be right back."

I watch as she steps off the ambulance and closes the door behind her. There's another EMT with me, and he smiles reassuringly as he checks my vitals. My stomach is churning as I wait for her to return. A few minutes later, the ambulance door opens, and I burst into tears as Cade steps on board.

"Are you okay?" he asks, his face a picture of concern. He turns to the EMT. "You know she's pregnant?"

The EMT nods. "Yes, she told us. We need to get both of them checked over at the hospital. You too. You really should have stayed in the ambulance. You need to be on oxygen."

I'm still sobbing as he kneels on the floor next to me. "I need to be with my girlfriend."

"You're really okay?" I ask from behind the oxygen mask. He nods, and I lift the mask and press my lips to his. "God, I was so scared. I thought I'd lost you."

"I'm fine, I promise."

"Taylor stayed at Nash and Paisley's. She was never in there," I tell him, my voice breaking. "You went back in there for nothing. I shouted to you, but you didn't hear me."

"Hey, it's all over now. I'm okay, Soph."

"When the windows blew out, I thought you were dead. I went in and found you unconscious on the floor. I knew I had to get you out."

"What? You got me out? I thought it was the fire department."

"There was no time to wait for them."

"Thank you. You saved my life." He drops his forehead to mine before pulling me into his arms. I go willingly, clinging tightly to his shoulders.

"I'm sorry, but we really need to get Sophie to the hospital. You too, Cade. I'll take you back to the other ambulance," the EMT says.

"Can't I just travel in this ambulance with Sophie?" Cade asks.

She frowns. "We really shouldn't…"

"Look, I'm a doctor. I'm fine, really."

She smiles knowingly. "That makes a lot of sense."

"What does that mean?"

"We all know doctors make the *worst* patients."

He smiles. "Is that a yes?"

She rolls her eyes. "Fine, but you need to wear this." She places an oxygen mask over his face before he can argue with her. "And you need to get properly checked over once we get to the hospital. You were unconscious until five minutes ago."

"Okay," he concedes from behind the mask. He tangles his fingers with mine, and I drop my head back against the gurney, suddenly exhausted. My free hand rests over my stomach and more tears prickle my eyes. It suddenly hits me how close I came to losing *everything* I care about, and that terrifies me. I've lived a life without Cade. I know what it's like, and I never want to live a life like that again.

CHAPTER THIRTY-FIVE

Cade

It's been a few weeks since the fire, and after getting the all-clear from the hospital, we're officially living at my place. It's not like Sophie had much choice. The house was completely destroyed, along with pretty much everything inside. I've never seen her as upset as she was in the days after the fire. The shelter had been her home, and it made me realize what it meant to her and how close she felt to her mom there. I had hoped there would be some of her mom's belongings that we could salvage, but everything was gone.

The fire department opened an investigation when it became clear that an accelerant had been used to start the fire. The glass in the back door had been broken and traces of gasoline had been found in all the rooms downstairs. The fire chief told us that with the amount of gasoline used, we'd been lucky to get out alive.

It was over, though. Trent, Lyra's boyfriend, had been picked up a couple of days ago and charged with the attack on Lyra and starting the fire at Sophie's place. They'd found a can of gasoline in the trunk of his car and glass from the back door lodged in the soles of his sneakers, which placed him at the scene. He'd eventually confessed to everything, and Nash assured us he'd be going away for a long time. Lyra was also being looked after and had been offered a room in a shelter a few towns over after being discharged from the hospital.

The insurance company had agreed on a settlement, and Sophie decided to go for a rebuild. I'd tried to talk to her about what she wanted to do with the house when the work had been carried out, but each time, she changed the subject. I think deep down she knows moving on from the shelter is the right thing to do, but understandably, she's struggling with letting go.

"Are you almost ready, Cade? We're going to miss our flight."

I smile as I stand from the sofa. I've been ready for nearly an hour. It's her who's packed and unpacked everything in her closet twice. We're heading to Vegas for the weekend. It was Sophie's idea. She wanted to get away from everything for a while, and after the few months we'd had, a trip away just the two of us sounded like bliss.

"I'm ready," I call out as she wheels her enormous suitcase into the entryway. My eyes widen. "We are only going for three nights, right?" I ask, looking at her bag.

She waves her hand dismissively. "Yes, but I couldn't decide what to take, so I've got more than I need."

"No shit," I mutter.

She glares at me, and I can't help but laugh. "Give it to me," I say, gesturing for the bag.

As I take it from her, the intercom sounds. "That'll be our ride," she says, reaching for the phone and buzzing them in. "Let's meet him at the elevator."

ECHOES OF LOVE

I smile at her. She's had a tough few weeks, and I'm so happy to see her smiling.

I close the apartment door behind us, and we walk side by side to the elevator. As the doors open, Nash smiles.

"Eager to get going?" he asks, winking at Sophie.

"Something like that," she replies, walking into the elevator and kissing him on the cheek. "Thanks for offering to drive us."

"No need to thank me. Paisley's in the truck. She decided to come along for the ride."

"Oh, good," Sophie says.

When we reach the first floor, we follow Nash outside to his truck. Paisley waves from the front seat and Sophie gives her a wave back.

"Pass me the bags and I'll throw them in the back," Nash says, taking the cases from my hand.

"I'll help."

"I got it."

"Can you help me into the truck, Cade?" Sophie calls, and I leave Nash with the bags to help her up.

"Sure, baby."

The ride to the airport is full of laughter and talking, and the two-hour drive flies by. When the airport comes into view, Nash parks rather than dropping us at departures.

"You can just drop us off if you want to get back," I tell him, climbing out of the car and helping Sophie down.

"It's okay, we'll come in with you," Paisley says, linking her arm with Sophie's.

Nash has got the bags from the trunk before I can help him, and I take them from him as we follow the girls across the parking lot and into the departures hall. It's busy, and I reach for my phone, pulling up the e-tickets.

"It's check-in desk five, Sophie," I call out, and she nods, heading for the line. There's not much of a wait when we get

LAURA FARR

there, and Nash and Paisley wait with us. When we've checked in, we say goodbye to them, and I see Paisley whispering in Sophie's ear. They both giggle, and I wonder what they're talking about.

"What do you think that's all about?" I ask Nash, gesturing to them. He looks at Sophie and Paisley and shrugs.

"I have no idea. They're likely plotting something!"

I laugh and pull him into a one-armed hug. "Thanks for the ride."

"No problem. Have a great time."

After waving them off, we head through security and into the departure lounge. I'm more than ready to get this vacation started.

* * *

A FEW HOURS LATER, SOPHIE GASPS AS THE CAB PULLS UP OUTSIDE the Bellagio hotel in Las Vegas. Coming here was always something we'd wanted to do, and while it might be almost fifteen years later than planned, it somehow feels even more special.

"Wow, this is incredible, Cade," she says, her voice full of awe.

"It really is."

I pay the driver and climb out of the cab, turning and offering my hand to Sophie. She takes it, and I slip my arm around her as she gets out, her eyes fixed on the impressive building in front of us.

"I can't believe we're here."

I kiss her softly on her hair and drop my arm from around her waist to pull the bags from the trunk. I groan as I pick up her huge case.

"God, Soph, what do you have in here? It feels like you packed your whole closet."

Her cheeks flush pink and she drops her eyes from mine. "I had so many new clothes after replacing everything the fire took. I couldn't decide what to bring."

ECHOES OF LOVE

I chuckle and shake my head. "You do know I'm planning on keeping you naked most of the weekend anyway, right?"

"Cade!" she exclaims, smacking me on the chest as the cab driver overhears me. She walks toward the entrance, leaving me to carry the bags. I follow her, as impressed with the place as she is. Despite living my whole life a short flight away from Vegas, I'd never been. I'd never wanted to, knowing we'd always planned to come together. I'm glad I waited.

Sophie checks us in while I wait in the lobby. She's taking a long time talking to the woman at the check-in desk, and I hope there's nothing wrong. I'm just about to head over when she turns and starts to walk toward me. Holding up the keycard, she grins.

"All checked in."

"Is everything okay?"

"Everything's great."

Our room, if you can call it that since it's more like a suite, is stunning, and Sophie excitedly goes from room to room, her eyes wide.

"This is even more amazing than I thought it would be," she gushes.

"Let's unpack and we can grab dinner."

"No!" she exclaims, and I look at her in surprise. "I mean, let's not waste time unpacking. Let's explore."

I chuckle. "Okay. Let's get out of here."

When we've eaten dinner and explored the casino, we decide to call it a night. I can see Sophie's tired, even if she won't admit it. Coming to Vegas isn't exactly a relaxing vacation and I don't want her to overdo it.

After we both shower, I pull Sophie into my arms as we lie in the massive California king bed. I swear you could get another four people in here with us. Not like that will ever happen. There's no way I'm sharing her.

Her breathing has evened out, and she's asleep in my arms

already. I'm more than happy to just hold her; it's my favorite place for her to be.

I can't wait to explore Vegas with her tomorrow. I know she's wanted to come here since she was a kid. I hope everything lives up to her expectations. I want everything to be perfect for her.

CHAPTER THIRTY-SIX

Sophie

erves swarm in my stomach the second I open my eyes and remember where we are. I'm nervous, but excited too. Seeing that Cade is still asleep, I slip from the bed and grab my phone, making for the bathroom. When I've silently closed the door behind me, I sit on the edge of the bath and send a message to Paisley.

Me: Is everything good to go?

I stare at the phone as I wait for a reply. I only now check the time and groan when I realize it's early. Really early. I hope I haven't woken her. Knowing she won't reply for a while, I decide to take a bath. It's likely Cade won't be awake for a while either, but I'm too excited now to go back to sleep.

As the tub fills with water, I use the toilet and pad silently into

273

the bedroom to grab my suitcase. I'd managed to convince Cade not to unpack yesterday, not that he took a lot of persuading, but if he'd opened my bag, the whole surprise I'd set up for this weekend would have been ruined. Dragging the heavy case into the bathroom, I close the door and dig out my toiletry bag before zipping the case closed again.

As I brush my teeth, I go through in my head the plan for this morning. After breakfast, I'm going to surprise Cade with a massage in the hotel spa. He's going to think I'm having a treatment too, but I'll be back in our room getting ready. When he's done in the spa, I've asked the staff to give him the outfit I've chosen for him and to direct him to the roof terrace when his treatment is over. Hopefully, he'll play along.

My phone vibrates on the vanity, and I snatch it up, seeing a message from Paisley.

Paisley: Too excited to sleep? Everything is ready and good to go. I'm so excited for you!

Me: Sorry. I didn't realize it was so early when I messaged you. I hope I didn't wake you up. Thanks for all your help, Paisley. I could never pull this off without your and Ash's help.

Paisley: No need to thank me. I've loved it.

I hear movement from the bedroom and my fingers fly over the screen as I reply to Paisley.

Me: Cade awake, got to go. Talk later.

I put my phone down just as the bathroom door opens and Cade walks in, his worried eyes finding mine.

ECHOES OF LOVE

"Hey, are you okay? I woke up and you weren't there. Have you gotten sick?"

I cross the room and wind my arms around his neck. "No, I'm good. I just couldn't sleep. I was just going to take a bath."

His eyes go past me to the almost full tub. "Mmmm. Is there room for two?"

I laugh. "Yeah, I think so. I actually want to talk to you, so the tub is as good a place as any."

He frowns. "Is everything okay?"

I nod and pull the t-shirt I'm wearing over my head, dropping it on the bathroom floor. His heated eyes watch me as I slide my panties down my legs and kick them off.

"Fuck," he mutters, as I walk backwards to the tub and climb in, sliding under the hot water.

"Are you coming?"

"Yes! Shit! I need to pee first." I laugh again as he uses the toilet before stripping out of his sleep shorts and climbing into the tub with me. "Scoot forward. I want to hold you."

I do as he asks and he winds his arms around me. I drop my head back on his chest. "What do you want to talk about?" he asks, his body tensing with the question.

I lace my fingers with his hand that rests on my swollen belly. "I wanted to say that you were right."

"Right about what?"

"The shelter."

"Soph—"

"Wait, let me finish." He squeezes my hand and I take a deep breath. "It's not somewhere to raise a family. I never wanted to take on the shelter, but when Mom died, I felt so guilty that I wasn't with her. I thought I could alleviate that guilt by carrying on something that meant so much to her."

"She loved you so much, baby."

"I know, and I loved her, but you were right. It's not safe, and I think deep down I knew that. I was just clinging on to the shelter, knowing it was somewhere she loved. I know it doesn't make any sense."

"It makes complete sense, Sophie. You grew up there, and all your childhood memories are in that house."

"Thank you for being patient with me while I worked through my feelings about the shelter."

"You don't need to thank me. Look, what do you think about moving in there when the work's done? It doesn't have to be a shelter anymore, but it can be a home. Our home. What do you say?"

I sit up and turn around, kneeling in front of him. "I would love that. Are you sure that's what you want?"

He smiles. "I want to be wherever you are, baby. If you lived in a box, I'd be right there next to you."

"I think we can do a little better than a box." I lean in and brush my lips with his. "Thank you. It would mean everything to me to bring up our child in my family home."

"Then that's what we'll do." He pulls me gently into his arms. "What do you want to do today?"

I smile and bite down on my bottom lip. "Actually, I have a spa treatment booked for us both straight after breakfast as a surprise."

"You do?"

I nod. "I figured we could both benefit from some relaxation time."

"You know I'm always happy to give you a massage. Any excuse to have my hands on you."

I laugh. "Is that a massage with a happy ending?"

"Sophie Greene! You little minx!"

"All this talk of happy endings has got me needy. Enough talking. Why don't you show me?"

"I have no problem with that," he whispers, his mouth going to my neck.

An hour after getting in the bath, and with multiple happy endings, we finally make it downstairs for breakfast. I'm too nervous to eat much, though, and push my eggs and bacon around my plate. Thankfully, Cade doesn't seem to notice, and before I know it, we're heading for the spa.

"Sophie Greene and Cade Brookes," I say to the pretty brunette behind the check-in desk at the entrance to the spa. Her name tag reads Chelsea.

"Ahh, yes. Come with me." She smiles knowingly. I'd emailed them earlier in the week to tell them of my plan, so she knows it's only Cade booked in. I follow her, playing along. "This is you, Cade, and Sophie, your room is a little farther along."

I go up on my tiptoes and kiss Cade on the cheek. "Have fun, and I'll see you in an hour or so."

"We're not in the same room? I thought it was a couples massage?"

"I'm afraid not, sir," Chelsea says. "Sophie has a *mom-to-be* massage scheduled. Special treatment because of her precious cargo."

"Oh. Okay. I'll see you later, then."

He looks a little disappointed I'm not coming in with him. I hope he thinks it's all worth it later. He disappears into the room and Chelsea closes the door behind him.

"Thank you so much for all you've done," I say quietly. "Do you have the outfit I sent over ready for him?"

She nods. "Yes. It's hanging in a suit bag on the back of the door. He'll be given it at the end of the session. I'm so excited we can help you with all of this. Will you stop by tomorrow and tell us how it went?"

"Of course. I just hope I can pull it off."

"You will. You've organized everything perfectly."

I smile and raise my hand in a wave before heading toward the elevators that will take me back to our room. As I pass through the foyer of the hotel, I stop at the check-in desk and ask for the dress bag that I know is waiting for me. Taking it from the woman, I smile and thank her, nerves erupting in my stomach. I hope Cade is going to like what I have planned. Now that it's only hours away, I'm beginning to doubt everything I've arranged.

CHAPTER THIRTY-SEVEN

Cade

Despite my initial reservations about a spa treatment, especially on my own, Sophie had been right. It was exactly what I needed to relax. The past few months have been some of the best of my life, but also the hardest, and I don't think I realized just how stressed I was. When the masseuse has finished, she covers me with a warm towel.

"Sophie wants you to put on the clothes in the suit bag on the back of the door and head to the terrace on the thirty-sixth floor."

I lift my head from the table and turn to look at her. "I'm sorry, what?"

She smiles. "The clothes." She points to the back of the door. "And the terrace on the thirty-sixth floor. I'll leave you to get dressed."

She leaves the room and closes the door behind her. I stare after her, wondering what the hell just happened. My eyes fall on the suit bag that hangs on the door, and I climb off the bed and reach for it. I open it and find a gray three-piece suit and a white dress shirt hanging inside. It's nice. Really nice, and I take it from the bag, slipping it on. There's a full-length mirror on the wall, and I take in my reflection. Sophie chose well for whatever she has planned, and I suddenly can't wait to see her.

Leaving the treatment room, I make my way through the spa and back past the reception desk.

"Have a great day, Mr. Brookes," a voice calls out, and I spin around to see the same woman who greeted Sophie and me when we arrived.

"Thank you. Has Sophie finished her treatment?"

"Yes, sir."

I nod and smile, feeling her watching me as I leave. I cross the foyer to the elevators, step into the waiting car, and press the button for the thirty-sixth floor. As the car travels upwards, I tap my foot, impatient to know what Sophie has planned.

The elevator doors open, and I follow the signs for the terrace. When I reach the double doors that lead outside, I pause for a second before opening them. My breath catches in my throat when I see Sophie standing on the balcony in a white dress, the Bellagio fountains behind her. She looks stunning, and I can't take my eyes off her.

"You found me," she says softly, walking toward me.

"Sophie, you look beautiful, baby. So beautiful." I reach for her hand and pull her against me. "Is this what I think it is? Are you wearing... a wedding dress?" My eyes drop to the lace dress that clings to her breasts and fans out over her stomach and hips. Her hair is curled in long waves down her back, and a diamond tiara holds her hair back from her face. She looks breathtaking.

She smiles. "I'd get down on one knee, but I'm not sure I'd be able to get up again." She reaches up and cups my face. "Cade Brookes, will you marry me?"

ECHOES OF LOVE

My heart explodes in my chest at her words, and suddenly, everything I've wanted since I was seventeen is happening. "Of course I'll marry you, baby." I pick her up and spin her around, my eyes fixed on hers. "Are we really doing this right now? Here?"

"Yes. Turn around." I hold her gaze for a few seconds before lowering her to the ground and reaching for her hand. Turning around, I gasp as my whole family stands watching us.

"What are you all doing here?"

"Do you really think I'd miss my son's wedding day?" my mom says, reaching for me and pulling me into a hug, her voice laced with emotion.

"Were you all in on this?" I ask, glancing over her shoulder at everyone. They all nod. "But how? Nash, you only dropped us off at the airport yesterday."

Sophie giggles from the side of me. "Nash and Paisley were on our flight."

"What?" I shake my head. "How?"

"We made sure to book seats at the back of the plane, knowing you were at the front. Everyone else flew in the day before us," Nash explains.

"I can't believe you organized all of this, Sophie."

"The fire put everything into perspective. I always knew you were it for me, Cade, but living without you for so long, and then almost losing you that night." She closes her eyes and takes a deep breath. "I don't want to waste any more time. The rest of our lives starts with you becoming my husband."

I smile and pull her into my arms. "A life with you is all I've ever wanted, Sophie. I still can't quite believe I'm finally getting everything I've ever dreamed of. First, a baby." I lean back and place my hand protectively over her rounded stomach. "And now you're going to be my wife." I drop my forehead to hers. "Thank you."

When I lift my head, silent tears are tracking down her face.

"Hey, no crying. This is a happy day." I gently swipe my thumbs under her eyes to dry her tears.

"I am happy. The happiest I've ever been."

"Me too, baby. Shall we get married?" She grins and nods.

Ten minutes later, everyone is in their seats, and I'm waiting at the top of the aisle with Seb, Nash, and Wyatt. They're all wearing the same gray three-piece suit as me, and I stare at the view of the iconic Bellagio fountains behind us. It's a stunning place to get married, and I don't think Sophie could have chosen anywhere better. It's perfect.

When the Bridal Chorus begins to play, I turn around and gaze at Sophie as she walks toward me on the arm of my dad. She hadn't arranged for anyone to walk her down the aisle, and while her father is still alive, she doesn't have a relationship with him. Ashlyn had suggested Dad accompany Sophie, and he jumped at the chance. My parents have always been like a second family to her, and I know how much Sophie loves him.

As they reach me, my dad shakes my hand and kisses Sophie on the cheek before turning and sitting down next to my mom, who is already crying.

"I know I've already told you, but you really do look beautiful, Sophie. I love you."

"I love you too."

I lean down and brush my lips with hers, cupping her face with my hand.

"Hey, don't you have to wait for this guy to tell you to kiss the bride?" Wyatt exclaims, gesturing to the officiant. I pull my lips from Sophie's as everyone laughs.

"Sorry. I couldn't resist," I tell him, winking at Sophie.

As we promise to love, honor, and cherish each other 'til death do us part, I know not even a lifetime of loving her would be long enough, but I'll take every second she's willing to give me. Six months ago, I never would have believed we'd be where we are today. Life definitely threw us a curveball when it came to loving each other, but what we've been through makes our love stronger than ever. I know for sure we'll never be apart again. I existed without her because I had no choice, but I wasn't really living. Being with her makes me a better man, and this time, I'm holding on tight and never letting go.

CHAPTER THIRTY-EIGHT

Seb

As the Bridal Chorus plays, I drop my eyes to the floor. I know everyone else will be watching Sophie as she walks down the aisle, but I just can't bring myself to join them. When she'd told me of her plans to surprise Cade with a wedding in Vegas and asked me to be one of Cade's best men, I knew standing here would be hard. I guess I never realized *how* hard. I want more than anything for it to be me she's walking toward, but I knew that wasn't ever going to happen.

We'd gotten close after she moved back to Hope Creek and spent hours talking whenever she came into Eden. She was so easy to talk to, and so beautiful she took my breath away. She never once gave me any indication that there was anything more than friendship between us, and I knew how devastated she was that she couldn't sort things out with Cade.

Despite knowing how amazing she was, my feelings for her

crept up on me. It was only when Paisley's husband fired gunshots into Eden and I sat behind the bar with Sophie pressed against my side that I realized what she meant to me. It took the possibility of losing her, even though she'd never been mine to lose. I never set out to fall for my brother's ex, and I wish more than anything that I didn't feel this way.

I knew there could never be a future for us. Even if she and Cade hadn't worked things out, I love my brother, and there's no way I would ever have gone after Sophie. Family means everything to me and it's because of that I'm standing here with a smile on my face.

Cade makes her happy and I want her to be happy more than anything, even if it means I'm miserable. I hate to admit that I've avoided her and Cade over the past couple of months. I selfishly didn't want their relationship thrust in my face, and I know Sophie's noticed I've been distant. I just hope she never figures out why. I can't lose her as a friend, and I know if she finds out how I feel about her, it will just make things awkward. She's a part of the family now and pregnant with my niece or nephew. As hard as it's going to be, I need to push my feelings aside and move on.

I just have no idea how to do that.

EPILOGUE

Sophie
Nine months later

As I stand in line for the Ferris wheel, I can hardly believe that Hunter is six months old already. Those six months have raced by, and I've loved every second. I feel like I'm finally doing the one thing I was always destined to do, and despite how sick I was at the beginning of the pregnancy, having him here now and in my arms makes every second of being unwell worth it. I definitely want to take my time and enjoy him while he's so young, but I know without a shadow of a doubt I want to give him a brother or a sister. I haven't spoken to Cade about it yet, but I figure we've had some big conversations on this Ferris wheel. This just might be the time for another one of those conversations. I know now that a few months of being unwell is worth it for a life-time of happiness. Having Hunter has shown me that. I just hope Cade thinks we can do it again.

ECHOES OF LOVE

There's another reason for coming here, though. Bringing Hunter to the end-of-summer fair in River Falls feels like we've come full circle. We fell in love here as kids, and years later, we reconnected here. It's only fitting that Hunter becomes a part of that circle. I hope that every year we're able to bring him, and that he comes to love the fair as much as we do.

"I've got the tickets," Cade says, appearing behind me and pulling me from my thoughts. He leans down and presses a kiss on my cheek before reaching out and taking Hunter from my arms. "I take it Mommy's explained how important this Ferris wheel is?" he asks him, and I chuckle as Hunter answers by blowing a raspberry. "I'll take that as a no."

"You know he has no idea what you're saying, right?" I tell him, linking my arm with his free one.

"Sure he does." He waves off my comment, turning his attention back to Hunter. "So, this ride is where I first told Mommy I loved her. We were just kids back then, but I knew. I'd known for a while, but I was waiting for the perfect moment to tell her. I plucked up the courage at the very top. She was so excited she nearly tipped us out of the car."

I roll my eyes. "Don't listen to him, Hunter. I did not nearly tip us out."

"She did," Cade whispers in his ear, tickling his side. He giggles, and my heart explodes in my chest. Hearing him laugh is the best sound in the world.

As Cade's been talking to him, we've reached the front of the line, and he hands the tickets over to the attendant. Taking my hand, he helps me into one of the cars before passing Hunter to me and climbing in himself. The car jolts as it begins to move around. We're quiet for the first rotation, and I bounce Hunter on my knee as Cade's hand rests on my thigh.

"Are you happy, baby?" he asks when we reach the top and look out over Lake Serene.

"Yes. Happier than I ever thought I could be."

When we sat in this very spot twelve months ago, we'd talked excitedly about riding the Ferris wheel with our baby on my knee. Even though we're here doing it, it's still hard to believe it's a reality. A reality I never thought I'd have.

"Can I ask you something?" I say quietly, glancing down at Hunter, who yawns and nestles into my side. Holding him close, I gently rock him to sleep.

"You can ask me anything, Sophie. You know that."

"How do you feel about a brother or sister for Hunter one day?"

I chance a look at him to see his eyes widen. "I thought you never wanted to go through a pregnancy again? It was so hard for you with Hunter."

"It was hard, but look at the outcome." I look down to see Hunter fast asleep in my arms. "I'm not saying I want to do it now, or even in the next year, but I need to know that it's a possibility. Now that you're working in family medicine, it gives you more time at home, and with your help, I think I can do it again."

He's silent for a long time, and my stomach drops. I know he loves Hunter with every fiber of his being, but I know he'll be worrying about me getting sick again. I can't lie, the first four months of my pregnancy were hard, and there were days I didn't want to carry on, but he was always there to hold me and get me through it. I know it's a lot to ask of him, but the end result is so incredible.

"Okay," he whispers, his face lighting up in a smile.

"Okay?" I repeat, wondering if I heard him right.

He nods. "If it's what you want, then I want us to try. I'd love to have another baby with you, Soph, but I also want you to know that if it doesn't happen, for whatever reason, then you and Hunter are enough. I've still got everything I've ever wanted with the two of you. Everything and more."

ECHOES OF LOVE

"You're really okay with this?"

"I'm going to hate seeing you so unwell if the HG comes back again, but we got through it once. We can do it again."

Tears fill my eyes, and his thumbs brush over my cheeks as he wipes away the tears that fall. "Thank you. You're incredible, you know that?"

"I think you're the incredible one." His eyes drop to a sleeping Hunter. "Now, kiss me while he sleeps. I know for sure next year when we come, he'll be climbing all over us, and there's no way I'll get to make out with you as we go around."

"So bossy," I mutter as my eyes drop to his lips. "I love you."

"I love you too, baby. Forever and always."

THE END

ACKNOWLEDGMENTS

Thank you to my beta readers, Anne Dawson, Layla Rathbone, Tracey Jukes and Tracy Wood. Your support as ever is unwavering.

As you can imagine I did a lot of research for this book. I've been fortunate in all three of my pregnancies to never suffer badly with morning sickness. It was only during my third pregnancy, where I carried a baby for a couple who couldn't, that I really became aware of Hyperemesis Gravidarum from other surrogates I'd befriended who had experienced it first hand. I have the upmost respect for these women who endured something so debilitating in order for someone else to know the joy of parenthood. You are amazing. Never forget that.

A big thank you to my editor, Karen Sanders. You are always amazing, but when I lost confidence with this book, you were there to pick me up and help me make this story as polished as it could be. Thank you x

ALSO BY LAURA FARR

Healing Hearts Series

Taking Chances (Healing Hearts book 1)

Defying Gravity (Healing Hearts book 2)

Whatever it Takes (Healing Hearts book 3)

The Long Way Home (Healing Hearts book 4)

Christmas at the Cabin (Healing Hearts short story)

Standalones

Pieces of Me

Crossing the Line

Sweet Montana Kisses

The Paris Pact

The Hope Creek Series

Loving Paisley (Hope Creek book 1)

SOCIAL MEDIA LINKS

Facebook Profile: https://www.facebook.com/laura.farr.547

Facebook Page: https://www.facebook.com/Laura-Farr-Author-191769224641474/

Instagram: https://www.instagram.com/laurafarr_author/

Twitter: @laurafarr4

TikTok: @laurafarrauthor

Printed in Great Britain
by Amazon